LIGHTBEARER

L.C. DAVIS

COPYRIGHT

Copyright © 2019 by L.C. Davis
All rights reserved.
No part of this book may be reproduced in any form or by any electronic or mechanical means, including information storage and retrieval systems, without written permission from the author, except for the use of brief quotations in a book review.

Content Warnings (Contains Spoilers)

This is an MPREG romance loaded with dark humor and steamy romance. Discusses potentially triggering themes of: abuse, terminal illness, death of a parent, and mental illness.

ALSO BY L.C. DAVIS

Wolf Conan & L.C. Davis Books
Undercover Alphas
Gray
Jayce
Lionel

L.C. Davis Books
The Mountain Shifters Series
His Unclaimed Omega
His Reluctant Omega
His Unexpected Omega
His Runaway Omega
His Second Chance Omega
Their Omega
His Reformed Omega
His Verum Omega
His Reclaimed Omega
Alpha, Beta, Omega
His Taken Omega
His Reclassified Omega
The Great Plains Shifters Series
A Cowboy for Caleb
Darren's Second Chance

A Mate for the Alphas

The Vampire's Omega Series

The Vampire's Omega

The Vampire's Wolf

The Vampire's Mates (Coming soon!)

With thanks to my beta readers, ARC team and Patreon Patrons.
Special thanks to Eli for your support as a Sigma Patron!

PROLOGUE

"ONCE UPON A TIME, a delivery boy met the devil.

"It's a love story. Kind of. At least as much of a love story as there can be between a human and a demon.

"Sorry. *Monarch*. He's funny about that.

"Anyway, it all started when my sister sold her soul to the devil--well, technically, it all started when *I* sold my soul to the devil, but the one wouldn't have happened without the other."

The angel who's been listening to me in silence while looking like he's dying inside runs a hand down his face. "Mr. Curtis, please, just stick with the facts. I asked how you came to be Apollyon's lightbearer."

"I was getting to that," I insist. "Geez, you guys are impatient."

"Continue," the angel says, his teeth clenched tightly.

I glance at the clock on the wall behind him. Seven-thirty.

Tick-tock.

The angel's hand covers the gun at his side, like he knows what I'm planning.

Come on, you sonofabitch.

"Like I said. It's a love story, and you know how all good love stories start." The blank look on his face tells me he doesn't have a damn clue. Guess the boys down south have all the fun. "With a meet cute," I add. "Love--or in this case, hate--at first sight?"

"The narrative format really isn't necessary," says the angel. "The facts will do."

I raise an eyebrow. "Look, buddy, if I'm gonna tell this story, I've gotta do it a la Sinatra--AKA, my way?"

More blank staring.

"Sinatra? Seriously? The Sultan of Swoon?" I groan. "Right. Okay. That's gonna make creating a mental soundscape for the emotional bits harder, but whatever, we'll figure it out."

"As you were saying, Mr. Curtis? How did you *meet* Apollyon?"

"Right." I clear my throat. "The setting's one of the most important parts of a love story, and of course, most of ours takes place in Hell. But it didn't start there."

"Of course it didn't," the angel says in a flat tone.

I'm starting to like him. Kind of. Too bad one of us has to die, and it isn't gonna be me.

ONE

*My Apartment
Providence, Rhode Island*

"CHEESE, YOU'RE AN ASSHOLE."

Cheese looked at me and blinked slowly, his green eyes glowing in a sea of striped orange fur. Total asshole move. I shooed him off the dish of store-bought cookies I'd arranged on a red platter for the homemade look and he leaped down onto the floor with a rattling meow.

"Damn it," I muttered, picking through the cookies until I found all the ones that looked stepped on. I popped one into my mouth and chucked the rest into the trash. No time to go back to the store. Sirena always freaked out when I was late.

We're twins, but she got all the stick-up-the-ass genes and I got all the anxiety and our mom's penchant for day drinking. Definitely the short end of the stick, but again, at least it's not up my ass.

I climbed into Karen, my little red beater and buckled the platter and wine bottle I shoved into a tall gift bag from my last birthday in next to me. Can't be too careful with all the potholes this time of year. The car coughed a little when I turned the key.

"No, baby, don't do this to me today," I groaned, dropping my forehead against the steering wheel. Another turn and she finally rumbled to life. "Boom!"

I peeled out of the lot, empty save for the creepy neighbor who lived upstairs and collectd exactly three head-sized parcels from the mailroom every Tuesday. Nice guy for someone who probably had a freezer full of heads.

Sirena lived in Providence, too, but on the nice side with all the vegan restaurants and parking garages. Her apartment even had a doorman with a hat and the whole shebang. Sure as hell beat a common room full of roach traps, but the building was poorly insulated, so sometimes I'd get a secondary high from my downstairs neighbors. Money can't buy *that*.

I pulled into the guest lot and grabbed the peace offerings I was hoping would make up for ruining last Thanksgiving. Hell, I ruined Christmas, too, according to our mother. I've always had a hard time keeping my mouth shut about "sensitive political topics" like who I fuck and whether people like me should have the right to exist. Sirena's always had an easier time pretending. Hell, she does it for a living.

I'd be lying if I said I wasn't the tiniest bit jealous of the fact that my twin was living her dream as a fast-rising indie film star while I was still living paycheck to paycheck shuttling drunks home from the club and taking the odd shift as a bouncer and-or stripper, but I couldn't have been prouder.

Sirena was always the type who worked hard and achieved whatever she set her mind to. Sure, our teachers always told us we were all capable, but she actually *did* it. In a way, she was everything I wanted to be when I grew up.

At thirty-two, it was looking less and less likely that was ever gonna happen, but when you drop out of highschool to pay for your mom's chemo, your plans for the future have a way of derailing.

Not that I'd ever really had a solid plan to begin with. My grades were shit and the only after-school activity I'd ever taken an interest in was picking fights with bullies twice my size. In some ways, taking a knee so my sister could pursue her dreams made it easier to justify the failure I probably would've turned out to be anyway.

According to my shrink, at any rate. She also thought my daddy issues were why my last five boyfriends had a leather kink, so I took everything she said with a grain of salt. In reality, I'm probably just a neurotic thirty-something with too much free time for introspection.

And you wanna know about Apollyon, not me. Since my sister is kind of the one who introduced us, we'll get back to her.

I knocked on the door and at first, she didn't answer. I figured she'd either gone up to the corner store or completely forgotten she'd invited me over for some super serious conversation we couldn't have over the phone.

Those never went well, especially considering all the topics on which she *was* willing to tear me a new asshole over the the phone. When she finally answered, relief and brotherly love overflowed within me and I blurted out, "Holy fuck, you look like shit."

Her matching hazel eyes narrowed as she leaned on the door. "Fuck you, too, Levi."

The bond between twins. Beautiful and everlasting.

"Seriously," I said, looking her up and down. "You look

like you got into a fight over the clearance DVDs on Black Friday and lost."

She was wearing sweats and I didn't even know she *owned* sweats. Hell, she'd sewn her own designer knockoffs in highschool just so she wouldn't look poor. Reality and Sirena have never been on good terms. Kind of like me and the local transit authority.

Her brown hair was piled up on top of her head in a messy bun--or maybe it was a cinnamon roll. Hard to tell. The only real similarities between us are the Roman nose we'd inherited from our deadbeat dad and our deep disdain for commitment--also, coincidentally, inherited from our father.

We're both kind of tall, too, I guess. She's fit because she works out, I'm fit because my habits haven't caught up with me yet. Compared to her, I usually look like someone who snuck into the family reunion for the free tacos.

"Just shut your mouth and get in here," she muttered, stepping back to let me in. She eyed the balloon-printed bag in my hand. "Is that the bag I put your birthday present in?"

"It's the gift that keeps on giving," I said, pulling the wine out of the bag with a flourish.

She rolled her eyes and shut the door. She locked it, which was unusual. I've been getting on her case about locking her door since forever, but given the three security doors I had to go through to get to this place, I guess it's not that big of a deal.

"What's going on with you?" I asked, just beginning to entertain the possibility that she hadn't invited me over to continue reaming me out for being the Gay Grinch.

"Nothing. Just a long day of auditions," she said, walking into her open kitchen to grab a couple of wine glasses.

"I take it the audition didn't go well?"

"I got the part," she said with a faint smile, sitting down at the counter on a high stool that looked like a repurposed milk crate even though it had probably cost a few hundred bucks.

I sat down across from her and popped the cork off the wine, filling a glass to the brim for each of us.

"Okay, so if work's not the problem, who's the asshole I need to punch?" I hesitated. "Or were you the asshole? Because I'm not opposed to giving the poor guy a conciliatory blowjob."

"It's not a guy," she laughed, gathering up her fallen strands of hair. She took a sip and wound up gulping down the wine like it was made of...well, wine.

"What is it, then? First I go three weeks without hearing from you, then you invite me over for some 'urgent' talk," I said. "You're starting to worry me, and it's not just because Messy Bitch is *my* role to play in the family."

She sighed, leaning on the counter. "We've always been honest with each other. Haven't we?"

The question took me off-guard. Like it wasn't already a given. "Yeah. Sometimes brutally so. It's kind of our thing."

"Well, there's something I haven't told you," she said, hugging herself. My eyes widened as I started to put the pieces together. The sweats, the nerves, the strange melancholy.

"Holy shit, are you pregnant?"

She blinked. "What? No."

"Are you sure? Because I already have the World's Best Uncle T-shirt," I told her, scratching the back of my head. "Actually, not really sure where it came from. I was just wearing it one night when I got back from the club, but it fits."

"I'm not pregnant, Levi," she muttered.

"Okay, then what is it? You know you can tell me everything." I pressed my fingertips together and gave her my best impression of our junior high guidance counselor. "This is a judgment free zone."

She snorted a laugh, which reassured me she wasn't entirely on another planet. "It's complicated. I don't really know how to tell you."

"I know you're the smart one, but I'm not *that* dumb," I said dryly. "Just go slow and try not to use words with more than five syllables."

She smiled. It was small, but not quite as rigid as before. "You know how I got that big break last year even though a bunch of big names were up for the role?"

"Yeah, sure. Gina Cloves is probably still crying her eyes out. My girl," I said, wiping an imaginary tear from the corner of my eye.

She laughed. Whatever it was, if the solution wasn't breaking a few skulls, I knew I probably couldn't do much, but I'd always been able to make her laugh. The day that changed, we were both in above our heads.

"The thing I haven't told you is that I didn't get the role by sheer luck."

"Of course you didn't," I said, pouring another glass. "You worked your ass off at RISD and five years of waitressing and pretending to be nice to assholes is practically boot camp for actors," I snorted. "You deserved that role, plain and simple."

Her smile was strained and it pulled at something in my chest. That invisible string that had always connected us, no matter how far apart we were.

Or maybe it was heartburn. Either way, it was acting up big time.

"As much as your confidence means to me, I didn't get the role on my own merits."

I listened carefully, trying to make sense of what she was telling me. The only possible answer was something I'd do, but not something she would do. "Are you saying you screwed the casting director or something?" I asked, cringing. "Because again, no judgment, but you said she was like seventy."

"I didn't screw anyone, Levi. Jesus," she sighed.

"Then what's wrong? Whatever it is, it can't be that bad. Blackmail? The mob?" I lowered my voice to a whisper. "Was it *treason*?"

"No, it wasn't treason," she scoffed. "But the mob's not far off."

"Shit." And here I was hoping that wasn't it. "Okay, here's what we're gonna do. We empty our bank accounts, you cut off your hair, I'll dress in drag and we'll go to Monaco to start over. We'll be llama farmers. Do they have llamas in Monaco? Never mind, we'll figure it out when we get there."

She raised an eyebrow. "Why is drag your solution to *everything*?"

"I look *amazing* in fishnets," I reminded her. "Seriously, whatever it is, we'll figure it out. You know if you told me you killed someone, I'd help you hide the body."

"I know," she said, reaching across the counter to take my hand. "You're the only person I trust. That's why I wanted you to come here tonight. There's no body, but I made a deal with someone I shouldn't have," she said, glancing away. There was a look in her eyes I hadn't seen there since the night our dad left. One I'd promised, come hell or high water, I was never gonna see in them again. Fear. Terror. Shame.

A fire burned in the pit of my stomach. I didn't know what she'd done or who she'd done it with, but if anyone thought they were gonna come for my sister and live to tell about it, they were in for a rude awakening and a boot up their ass.

Her voice lowered and something in it chilled me to the bone. "He's coming to collect. I don't know where or when, but it's soon."

"Soon?" I frowned. "How do you know? What, is this prick threatening you?"

"Not threatening. Like I said, it's complicated."

"Bullshit. Physics is complicated, making flan is complicated, those dreams I used to have about furries are complicated, but there's nothing *complicated* about some asshole scaring the shit out of you," I said firmly. "Give me a name and I'll make sure the creep never bothers you or anyone else again."

"It's not like that, Levi," she said softly. "He's not someone you can just intimidate, and I'm the one who came to him first. This is my responsibility."

"The hell it is. We've been in this together from the beginning and that's not gonna change now."

She squeezed my hand a little tighter. "I'm not telling you any of this so you can fix it like you always have. You can't. Not this time. No one can."

"You're scaring me, Sir." My throat grew tight.

She stood up and walked into the living room. She grabbed the edges of the frame housing the hideous abstract painting I'd been mocking for the last five years ever since she overpaid for it at a fancy art show that made the mistake of offering guests free martinis and pulled the painting off the wall. I felt like a kid bamboozled by a stage magician pulling a rabbit out of a hat when she entered a key code into the safe in the wall.

"Holy shit, what are you, James Bond?"

She glanced over her shoulder, smirking as she opened the door. She pulled out a small box and brought it over to the counter before grabbing a pen and paper from the kitchen drawer.

I watched curiously as she scribbled something on the paper. The numbers were barely legible, but I realized the ones on the top row had to be the safe combination. I asked anyway. "What is this?"

"It's the combination to the safe, plus the information for my bank account and every credit card I own," she explained, sliding the paper toward me.

"Why the fuck are you giving me that?" I pushed the paper back toward her. I was starting to panic. There weren't many reasons people you loved started giving you all their personal financial information, and none of them were good. All the talk of the unnamed weirdo already had me on edge.

"I want you to have it, in case anything happens," she said in a solemn tone I didn't like at all. "I don't trust mom, and I know you'll take care of her. My lawyer's already drawn up the papers to put everything into your name, so there shouldn't be any trouble."

"Lawyer?" I echoed. Shit was getting real in the worst possible way. "If you're this scared, we need to be going to the cops, not divvying up your assets."

"The cops can't do anything," she said quietly. "I'm not in danger."

"Right. Because it's perfectly normal for thirty-two-year-olds at the height of their careers to make wills and hand out passcodes."

"Actually, it's pretty standard for the upper class," she argued.

"Answers, Sirena. Now, or I'm calling Ben."

She groaned. "Don't drag him into this."

"You're not giving me any choice," I told her. I would've felt like shit for bringing up her ex-husband under any other circumstance, but she was scaring the shit out of me and I didn't know what else to do. Ben knew her better than anyone except me, and if she wouldn't tell me who was threatening her, maybe he knew. Either way, he had access to a registered gun and the police database. That was a start.

"I promise, my life isn't in danger."

"That makes me feel *so* much better."

Sirena sighed. "Look, there's a chance nothing is going to come of this, but there's also a chance I'm gonna be gone for a while. I just didn't want you thinking I up and left like dad."

Her words were a punch in the gut. Our dad had been threatening to leave for so long that it just became part of the nightly ritual. Screaming downstairs, cranking up the stereo so we could focus on our homework, hearing the front door slam and then creak open again around four in the morning when he came staggering back in from the bar. None of us thought he'd actually *do* it until one day, he left and never came back.

At least, I hadn't. Somehow, Sirena knew. It was strange, but for the first time, I felt like she must have that night and it was awful. A cold, empty feeling that someone you love is going to disappear and there's nothing you can do about it.

But God, I was gonna try.

"A name, Sirena. I need a name."

"He doesn't have one," she said quietly. "Not one you'll find in the phone book."

"When is he coming?" I demanded, with every intention of being behind the door waiting with a spiked baseball bat.

"Next week," she answered.

I took a deep breath. A week. I had a week to figure this out. Not great, but it could have been worse.

"I'm tired," she said, looking down at the box she'd taken from the safe. "I've got an early day tomorrow on set, but I wanted to give you this."

"How many times have we been over this? I don't want your third-grade macaroni art of Josh Groban, Sir. It's time to let it go."

She gave me the look she'd inherited from our mother and put the box in front of me. I opened it and found a watch just sitting in there. It wasn't a new watch or a particularly expensive looking one, but the gold plating seemed real enough. The hands weren't keeping time anymore, but a new battery would probably solve that.

"What is this?"

"It was Dad's," she said quietly, looking down at the box. "Grandpa's, really. He gave it to me shortly before he left and made me promise that I'd give it to you one day. When you turned out to be a better man than he was."

My chest tightened as I picked up the watch and let the band fall limp over my palm. After our dad left, our mother had cleared out all his things and dumped them off at the nearest charity shop. One day was all it took to make it like he'd never existed. He didn't have much more of a presence in our lives. To this day, I still wonder sometimes if he was just a figment of our imaginations.

"And you waited till now to give me this?" My voice

was hoarser than I wanted it to be. Made sounding like a smartass harder. "Should I be insulted?"

She smiled, but it didn't meet her eyes. "You were a better man than he was when you were a kid," she said softly. "Never seemed like the right time."

"You knew," I realized. "He told you he was leaving."

The sadness in her gaze kept me from feeling as angry as I probably should have. Then again, I could never stay mad at her for long. She was my other half. The better one, for sure. As much as I hated myself, I'd never been able to hate her. "I told you I was good at keeping secrets."

"Why?" It was the only question I could ask. The only thing I needed to know.

"You always bore all our burdens," she answered. "You were the one who took off his shoes and cleaned up his puke when he came home drunk. You were the one who took care of Mom when she got sick. You've always taken care of me. I wasn't going to put one more burden on you. Especially not with the Huntington's."

I touched my chest instinctively. My condition was something we rarely talked about. It was a fifty-fifty shot whether we'd inherit it from our father, and I was always a shoe-in for coin flips. Sirena acted like it was something she'd done to me. Like she'd somehow taken the healthy genes and saddled me with the sick ones.

Maybe she was afraid I'd leave, too. There were times when I thought about it. I figured I had another five, maybe ten years before the symptoms made independent living impossible, and there were times when I told myself that they'd both be better off without me. But then I remembered that look in her eyes the morning he didn't come down for breakfast and I knew even if I could probably do that to our mother, I could never do that to Sirena.

"I'm not going anywhere," I told her, standing in the doorway with the watch dangling from my hand. Putting it on felt weird. Like wearing a dead guy's clothes, even though we didn't know for sure that he was dead. Statistically, he all but had to be at what would have been fifty-three, but still. None of us had ever checked. Not knowing was better somehow.

"I know," she said, wrapping her arms around me. I held her and realized I didn't want to let go, but eventually, we both had to. I made her promise she wasn't going to do anything stupid and she swore she'd be there when I came over the next night to check on her after work.

Maybe I could get ahold of Ben before then. One way or another, we'd figure this out. I'd already been ghosted once and I wasn't going to lose her, too.

At one point, we'd been all each other had and while I knew I was just one part of her life now, she was still the only thing that kept me attached to planet Earth most days. The only thing I had worth fighting for.

If this nameless prick thought he was gonna take her from me, he had another thing coming.

TWO

I WAS halfway home when my "shit, something's wrong" radar started singing off the register. It wasn't something logical, but it's never been wrong. Not once.

Turning around in the middle of the road nearly got me creamed by a semi, but I ignored the horn blaring behind me and drifted into the right lane. Karen lurched in protest as I floored the gas, but it took half the time as usual to get back to Sirena's place.

A woman walking her Pomeranian gave me a look of concern as I blew past her up the stairwell, but by the time I made it to Sirena's door, I already knew it was too late. Whatever happened was over and there was nothing but a sinking pit where my heart should've been.

Time froze. It was one of those strangely intense moments where you know you're not dreaming, but you can't fully believe it's real life, either. Like there's a gap between your soul and your body and it's getting bigger with every second.

The door was open and I *knew* I'd locked it. The open

floor plan left few places to hide, but I already knew she was gone. I just fucking knew.

"Sirena?" I cried anyway, rushing to the spot she'd occupied in front of the counter so recently. The door to the safe was closed, and nothing seemed out of place. Nothing on the surface. As I walked through the empty apartment, it felt like the whole thing was going to end up being a high-definition photograph printed on a huge canvas that would be ripped away at any second, revealing some awful, unfathomable truth below.

Everything I touched felt solid enough. The door handle, as cold on my fingertips as I was inside. The floor, hard and unyielding. The window, sealed shut and locked eight stories up. No sign of forced entry. No sign of an intruder, but my gut never lied.

Not even when I wanted it to.

Her room was empty, save for the writing on the wall. And I mean the literal fucking writing. Eight letters, written in glowing red blood across the white wall behind the bed.

Apollyon.

A name I would never forget. One it felt like I knew on some deep, unsettling, instinctive level.

My right hand started to twitch again. I gripped my wrist with the left, trying to keep the spasming muscles in line.

I don't really remember calling the cops. They were just there, and as I gave my statement to a female sergeant I probably would have been trying to flirt with under any other circumstances, I felt like it was someone else doing the talking. Like some far more eloquent being had snatched my body and decided to take one for the team by detailing the events leading up to my sister's kidnapping.

I insisted that was what it was, but the individuals in

blue didn't seem convinced. I could tell from the way they were looking at me that they second guessed the whole psychic connection between twins thing that had led to me coming here, and I was sure they suspected me. I offered to go down to the station and give my prints and whatever else they needed to rule me out so they could get to the bastard who'd actually taken her.

At least the sergeant changed her tune when I got to the part about the mysterious threats Sirena had been receiving. It helped that she'd actually heard of the film she'd been working on the week prior. She wanted the names of her industry contacts, anyone who might have been jealous or up for a role she'd taken. I gave them what I could, but the truth was, I didn't know much more than what Sirena shared with me, and that wasn't much those days.

It was well after midnight by the time they told me to go home, and I insisted I wanted to stay in case someone came back. They told me the scene was off limits until the following afternoon at earliest, and after reasoning with myself that I wasn't any good to Sirena in a jail cell, I finally went home.

Sleep was a lost cause, and the terror-induced manic state I was in would ensure I didn't get any for a week at least. Like I could sleep knowing Sirena was out there with some creep.

The fact that she'd sworn he wasn't interested in physically harming her wasn't a comfort. Not by a long shot.

I called Ben and when he didn't answer, I left a voicemail. I'm not even sure what it said, I just know he showed up at my apartment somewhere around three in the morning looking scared as shit.

He still cared. He still loved her. One look in his eyes was enough to know that. The cops had asked about Ben, too, but whether it was because he was one of their own or because I'd vouched for him, they'd given up on that line of suspicion soon enough.

The prevailing theory became that Sirena had a stalker, and even though that didn't entirely line up with what she'd told me, I had to admit it was a possibility. She'd shared a few bizarre social media comments with mom and I over the years, and over the next few days, I became something of an amateur detective. None of her biggest fans on social used Apollyon as a pseudonym, but it sent me down the rabbit hole of research.

Apparently, Apollyon was the Greek name for Abaddon, King of the Demons, Lord of Destruction and all-around stand-up guy. All the lore I read about him pretty much painted him as the devil, so I started cyberstalking every edge lord with some variation of 666 in his username. None of it actually led anywhere, but hell, at least I was *doing* something.

Once the cops had cleared out, I'd settled in Sirena's apartment just in case the kidnapper made contact. Ben agreed it was a good idea, but I could tell he didn't have much more hope than the others did.

I knew what they were all thinking. She's in a ditch somewhere. Our mother was already acting like we needed to start prep for the funeral. Hell, I was thinking it too, but the same gut reaction that had led me to turn back that night--the one I *wished* had made me stay there--told me she was still alive.

We'd always been connected. I didn't know what it was like to live without her, I just knew it would be so earth shattering that I'd *know* if she was gone.

The police didn't put much stock into gut feelings, though. So I waited, when I wasn't casing the city. Being a delivery driver has its perks, including an intimate knowledge of the city's innards. I'd called in every favor and pressured every lead to no avail.

I was the last person who had seen Sirena, or at least the last one who was interested in her being found.

THREE

NOW, you might be asking yourself, "What does a muscular, fearless-seeming specimen such as yourself do when the most important person in his life goes missing for a solid week?"

I'll take your silence as a yes. See, in the action movies, when the hero's wife, daughter or some other close lady relation goes missing so the lazy writers can demonstrate his prowess at the expense of her agency, there's usually a montage. He makes some phone calls, busts some heads in a few shady bars, and finally returns home to discover a dramatic ultimatum written in blood on his mirror or some shit. His big break in the case of a lifetime.

In real life, there's just a lot of waiting. A lot of wondering if the weight on your chest is because your muscles are finally starting to atrophy like the doctors always told you they would, or because she's gone. Because she's gone and you could've fucking stopped it if your head wasn't so far up your ass you'd never need a colonoscopy.

Back then, I was still enough of a dumbass to think I was the hero in this scenario and she was the damsel in distress.

Like our thirty-two years of existence didn't make the very idea ridiculous.

Ben came over a lot. I was starting to remember why we'd gotten along all those years they were together. He gave our mom someone else to take shots at and he wasn't half-bad at pool. Wasn't half-bad at taking care of my sister, either.

We exchanged theories about Apollyon and what it meant. In the beginning, he thought I might be on the right track about some kind of weirdo username, but as the days went by, I could tell he was doubtful. And I couldn't really blame him. If his leads on the force weren't turning anything up, I could understand why he'd be lacking faith in my amateur detective skills.

Still, it gave me something to do and kept me from exploring the more bizarre theories. One night, while combing Sirena's bookshelves for something to take my mind off waiting for the kidnapper to call, I'd found a book.

A really weird fucking book.

For context, the other books on the shelves were all about stagecraft, self-marketing, and the kind of vaguely spiritual bestsellers gurus put out every year to keep the royalty checks rolling in. And then, here's this heavy black leather book with some shit that looks like emojis on the cover. But old-school emojis, like back in the day when we all used AIM and had our own personal Geocities pages.

The inside was in English, at least. Most of it. It wouldn't have surprised me if Sirena could read whatever pictorial language the other parts of the book were written in. She got way into her roles. Method acting, she called it. Once, she'd spent an entire semester learning to fence just so she could bring realism to her role in a high school play.

The parts of the book I *could* understand were the ones that scared me.

They were all rituals. And I don't mean the kind baseball players do to curry the favor of the homerun gods before a play. The kind that involved organs I was going to be optimistic enough to assume came from animals, lots of blood and various phases of the moon.

I read until I couldn't stomach the rest. I've never considered myself light of constitution. I enjoy a good slasher and nachos as much as the next nineties kid, but the possibility that this shit had anything to do with what had happened to Sirena made me shudder.

It also put the name on her wall in a different light.

Ben came over to check on me the night after I found the book and I'd spent most of the day deliberating over whether or not I was going to tell him. I knew what he'd say, but hell, if it was evidence the police had overlooked, it was worth letting him think I'd lost my shit.

When he showed up an hour later than he'd said, he looked beat. And I mean, fair enough. He's a crime scene analyst for the SVU and I can't think of many jobs that would have me turning in my humanity card faster than that, but still. He seemed more rundown than usual. His face was starting to show a few lines around the eyes, more from frowning than smiling. His hair looked greasy, like he hadn't showered in a couple of days, which made two of us.

Depression is one sexy mofo. In the med commercials, it's always attractive people gazing forlornly out a window while sipping herbal tea. They never show the time lapse of the days spent in bed, or the sniff tests to determine if your shirt is good enough or viable breeding ground for a colony of microorganisms you'd rather not flourish.

We had a deal going, Ben and me. He didn't ask how I

was doing and I didn't ask it back. Our little catch-up sessions had become the only human interaction in my life that didn't make me want to put my head through a wall.

"Any news?" I asked immediately.

He didn't seem to hold it against me. He was carrying a paper bag from the fast food joint up the street in his hand, and when the smell hit my nostrils, I realized I hadn't actually remembered to eat since... well, whenever the last time I'd taken my meds was.

Shit. Guess I hadn't taken those either.

"Yeah," he answered for the first time. "But first, when was the last time you ate?"

"This morning," I lied, because he wasn't about to believe me if I said I'd had lunch like a remotely responsible adult. The food should've been appetizing, but the thought of eating just made me feel sick.

Ben glanced at the open bottle of liquor on the counter. "And yet I see you had time for a nightcap."

"Are we really gonna start down that road? Because it goes both ways."

He gave me a look. "I'm not the one who takes a cocktail of meds that could put me into a coma if I have too much gin."

"You know, you're supposed to be out there *finding* Sirena, not adopting her personality."

He flipped me off and walked over to the table, taking out a couple of sandwiches from the bag. "Park your ass and I'll tell you what I found out."

"Blackmailing me with information about my missing sister? Really?"

He stood with his hands on the back of the chair and a "Do I look like I give a shit?" expression plastered on his face.

Realizing I wasn't gonna win this one, I sunk into the chair like a spoiled brat and unwrapped a burger. It was probably good, but it tasted like cardboard. Everything did. Still, I started to feel a little less like I was gonna pass out.

"Speaking of meds, how're you feeling?"

I glared at him. "What did you find out?"

"Answer the question, Levi."

"I feel fine," I snapped. I could tell he didn't believe me, but for once, it was the truth. "Really. Call it a prolonged adrenaline rush or whatever, but I've actually felt great, other than the unending terror and anxiety."

"Huh."

"What?"

"Nothing. That's great, I just...didn't think that was how it worked."

I knew what he was getting at. The doctors had told me that once I started showing symptoms, I had five to ten years before I'd rapidly go downhill, starting with my motor function, then progressing on to neurological and muscular deterioration. There might be periods of stasis, but once something became a problem, it was supposed to remain that way. Just the nature of the disease.

"Who knows? I'm not looking a gift horse in the mouth," I admitted. It was a little strange that I hadn't had so much as a hand twitch in the last few days, but it wasn't my focus.

"You should see a doctor," he insisted. "I hate to say it, but feeling good can be a symptom, depending on what's going on."

"What are you, my mother?"

He raised an eyebrow. "If I was your mother, I wouldn't give a shit."

"Touché. Ouch, but touché."

His lips quirked. "Just looking out for you."

"Yeah, well, we'd better find Sirena so it doesn't become a full-time job. Now, what the fuck were you gonna tell me or do I have to start playing charades?"

Ben grew sullen in an instant, but to be fair, he was always adjacent to it. Sirena and I both shared a type. Broody and easy to fuck with. "I don't know how to say this, and I've been debating with myself over whether I even should, but now that it's been two weeks... you know as well as I do the odds of finding her alive are slim."

"Bullshit."

"Levi, she's gone without a trace and if what she told you is the truth, she's with someone who could easily make her disappear," he said in the tone of a man who'd already given up.

Time seemed to stop. Up until now, Ben had been the only one clinging to the same shred of hope--or maybe it was delusion--that kept me believing she was still alive. That she could still come home.

A sane person probably would have realized, "Shit, this is it. If he's given up, there's really no hope."

But I'd never claimed to be that.

"Levi?" he asked worriedly. I could tell it wasn't the first time.

"You're wrong," I said in a flat tone that didn't seem to be coming out of my mouth. I'd been dissociating a lot lately. This was different.

"I have proof."

Another gut punch. Fuck, I couldn't even breathe. "What?"

"The writing on the wall," he muttered. "I had it analyzed. It's her blood, Levi."

It was never good when people went out of their way to

use your name. Maybe that was why the sound of my own name had always made my chest feel tight and cold.

"What? When?"

"Not long after she disappeared," he admitted.

"What the fuck? And you're telling me this now?"

"I knew what you'd think," he said quietly. "And I didn't have permission."

"Permission? Whose?"

"The police."

It took a second for his answer to sink in. "They still think I did it?"

"You and me are still the only suspects with a name," he sighed.

"And what do you think?"

"Come on, Levi..."

"I asked you a fucking question," I growled.

Ben stared at me for a moment. Felt like forever before he frowned and shook his head. "I know for as long as I've known you, I've been worried you'd off yourself, and Sirena was scared even longer than that. But her? No. I know you'd never do anything to hurt her."

My rage and tension slowly uncoiled as I sank back in my chair, but that just left more room for the grief. "Someone did this. Someone took her and he's still out there."

"I know."

"Wait here," I told him, jumping up from my chair. The quick movement startled him as much as it should've surprised me. Hell, I didn't know what was behind my miraculous remission or what the consequences of it would be, I just knew I was going to ride it for as long as it lasted.

When I came back holding the book, Ben was looking at me with fresh concern. To be fair, I probably didn't seem like the type who read a lot. I put the book down in front of him and sat back down.

"What is this?" he asked, opening the cover in search of a table of contents that wasn't there.

"You tell me. I found it on Sirena's shelf nestled between the Kamasutra and 'Yoga for Bitches.'"

He blinked. "Quite a TBR she's got going on there."

"Tell me about it. Any of that weird shit look familiar to you?"

"Can't say it does," Ben said, flipping through the pages. I could tell when he'd spotted the weird bits, because his eyes grew wide.

"It's witchcraft, or something like it," I said, too impatient not to put the pieces together for him. It was keeping me distracted from the impending meltdown when I finally let the weight of his newly revealed evidence sink in.

He gave me a dubious look. "It's probably research for a role, Ben. You know how she is."

Is. So he was still using present tense. Maybe he wasn't too far gone yet, or maybe we both were. "The book is full of all sorts of rituals, and one of them involves a summoning."

"A summoning of what?"

"I don't know," I admitted. "Even the parts that talk about it in English just repeat the same symbol on the cover. Look, I'll show you." I flipped to the back of the book, well aware from the look on his face that I had a few seconds before he was calling a shrink.

"Right here," I said, jabbing my finger into the page.

Ben took the book from me and frowned as he read along. "'Upon the hiding of the moon, thou shalt bathe in the Elixir of Purification and shed blood with a fitting instrument. His name must be written in thy tongue upon an eastern-facing wall while the following incantation is chanted."

He stopped there, not bothering to read the rest. I couldn't be sure if he was scared it would work or he just thought it was a waste of time. "You can't be serious."

"Are you kidding me? You read what that shit said!" I cried. "Write *his* name on the wall? You wanna take a guess about which way Sirena's wall faces? It would explain the blood."

And it was the only explanation that didn't dramatically reduce the possibility of her still being alive. I *had* to cling to it.

Ben's frown deepened. "Say you're right and Sirena is the one who wrote that. It doesn't mean anything other than that she was involved in some weird shit."

"Of course it does!"

"I can't run a demon's name through the police database," he said flatly.

"No, but you could show the book to the cops. Maybe they can find out where it comes from."

"If I show this to them, they're going to think she killed herself. You know that, right? The investigation will all but grind to a halt."

I stared at him, finally forced to admit that he was probably right. "So what?" I gritted out. "We're just supposed to give up?"

"No," Ben said quietly. "No, I'll take the book and see if I can pull some prints myself. And I'll try to track down where it comes from. Who knows? I'm sure Sirena didn't find out about this shit on her own."

I wasn't sure about that. She'd always been willing to go wherever a role took her, and that was a hell of a lot further than NYC or Boston. Still, from what little I knew about witches, they tended to band together in groups. Maybe he'd be able to find something I hadn't.

And in the meantime, I was going to do some more research of my own.

"I have to get going," Ben said, standing up from the table. "Do me a favor and go see a doctor."

I grunted a non committal acknowledgment. I *did* have an appointment in a couple of days that I was thinking of canceling, but if my out-there theory was worth testing, it would have to wait until the next new moon anyway.

FOUR

I STARED in disbelief at the doctor, replaying the words he'd just said because they didn't make any damn sense. "I'm sorry...what?"

"You appear to be in remission," he answered, looking down at the papers in front of him. His office was one of those corner setups with the big windows on both walls and a view of the permit parking lot below. You could even see the fabled Big Blue Bug statue of Providence. High class joint is what I'm trying to say.

"They said that wasn't possible," I reminded him.

"It is extremely unlikely, but I don't have any other explanation for the disappearance of your symptoms."

"So...what does that mean, exactly?"

The doctor pulled his glasses down like they do on TV and gave me a patient smile. "We'll run some more tests next month just to be sure it's not an anomaly, but what it means, Mr. Curtis, is that you should enjoy your life for as long as you can."

"Great," I said stiffly. I probably should've been overjoyed. No news was good news as far as my condition went, but remission? That shit was like hitting the lottery.

The whole way home, all I could do was think about how badly I wished I could tell Sirena. If the truth was a spinning neon sign, I still probably wouldn't have realized that her disappearance and my miraculous recovery were part and parcel.

I was used to a single errand, from going to the store to a doctor's appointment, taking all the energy I had for the day, but before I reached Sirena's building, I realized I might as well pick up a couple of things while I was out.

The occultic shopping list I had copied from Sirena's book was still burning a hole in my pocket. The ingredients weren't all that out there, save for the requirement of a liver. Again, I was *really* hoping beef liver would suffice. That was nasty enough for a guy who lived on takeout and pizza.

I hit the nearest market and grabbed a few things for lunch. The bread and lunch meat rarely made it into a full sandwich configuration, but it was the same difference. I got a few weird looks as I stood eyeing the various innards on display, or maybe I was just being paranoid.

I finally made a selection, tossed it in the basket along with some of the spices the infernal recipe called for, and whistled my way to the checkout line. Trying not to look like someone planning a dark magic ritual was harder than I imagined. The cashier kept giving me worried glances, but that could've just been the fact that I'd passed out the last time I was there.

She gave me my change and I headed home to make a sandwich and fridge the ingredients I was still trying to convince myself not to use.

Now all there was left to do was wait for the moon to disappear.

BY THE TIME the new moon rolled around, I had talked myself in and out of repeating the ritual I suspected of being the cause of Sirena's disappearance. When the day finally came, I did some prep work, because if it worked, I'd probably disappear, too. And if it didn't, I'd already vowed that not a living soul would ever get wind of it. Not even Ben.

I'd left everything Sirena had left to me in a place that would be easy to find, along with a note that explained the bare minimum of what he needed to know to get his police buddies off his back.

Investigating Sirena's cult. If you find this, I'm probably dead or sucking demon cock. Either way, don't bother looking for me.

P.S. I bequeath to you my evil cat. Don't ever give him catnip or you'll figure out why his name is Cheese.

P.P.S. This isn't a suicide note, but if anyone asks, tell them it was bears.

I signed my name with extra care and one of those cool swoops at the end. That should do it. Now it definitely wouldn't look like I'd offed myself.

Fully prepared to get sucked into an interdimensional portal or make a complete fool of myself and drink until I couldn't remember to be embarrassed, I set up everything the way the book had it laid out. I had to push aside Sirena's bed to make enough room on the floor to draw the chalk circle the way it was in the diagram.

Having never done ceremonial magic before, I felt a little out of my element, but putting together IKEA furniture seemed like decent preparation. Less blood involved in the actual magic, though.

The liver rested in a bowl in the center of the circle

with everything from black pepper to cardamom sprinkled on top. Not exactly the kind of dish you bring to a potluck, but who was I to question the tastes of the dark lord?

I knew I had to read the incantation, but considering that I didn't speak Latin and my attempts at Google Translate were dubious at best, it seemed risky. The book said I could speak it in my own language, but that also required a basic understanding of *what* I was saying. I felt ridiculous for thinking this was likely enough to work to even be afraid, but hell, there was something about putting it all together that made it feel real. Even the air in the room felt alive.

"Here goes nothin'," I muttered, lighting the candles. I cleared my throat and picked up the piece of paper with the rough translation of the incantation. "Oh, Dark One. Duke of Hell, Ruler of the Underworld... Keeper of the nine sanctums. Open the gates and walk freely between worlds."

Seemed like a dangerous invitation to a demon, but fuck, I'd tear the world apart if it meant bringing Sirena back. Even the chance of it.

Nothing happened, but the ritual instructions didn't exactly give a play-by-play, so I had to assume it was working. Now for the fun part.

I picked up a knife I'd bought fresh for the purpose, since none of the ones in the kitchen drawer looked sharp enough. I cut the inside of my palm, along the lifeline like the instructions said, and let the blood drip into a glass bowl.

Well...it was probably plastic, since it had only cost ninety-nine cents, but close enough.

I carefully carried the bowl over to the stool I'd set up next to the bed and cringed when some of it sloshed onto the floor. Then again, the place was already looking like a murder scene.

The idea of fingerpainting with my own blood made me sick, so I took a brush I'd bought for that purpose and started writing the same name on the wall that had obviously worked for Sirena. Assuming this wasn't just some elaborate cover-up of her kidnapping I was now perpetuating.

As I worked, I felt like I was running a gothic arts and crafts exhibit, but by the time I made the final stroke, I realized nothing was happening.

"Of course," I muttered, starting to step down from the stool.

The writing began to glow, faintly at first, but it was enough of a shock that I fell flat on my ass. The remainder of the blood spilled into my lap and all I could do was stare in disbelief as the blood turned to blinding white light that illuminated the entire room.

It occurred to me, as I watched the wall behind Sirena's bed split apart like an eye popping open, that I hadn't actually thought there was a chance it would work.

"Holy fucking shit," I breathed as the portal grew and stretched, a clawed red hand being birthed from the center of the blackness.

I'm not exactly sure what the proper reaction to realizing you've summoned the devil is supposed to be, but it's probably not, "Who's amounting to nothing now, Ma?"

But the smug fascination only lasted as long as it took for me to realize the demon wasn't coming *out*. It was reaching to drag me *in*.

FIVE

I SEE you looking at me. All judgy, like *you've* never summoned the Dark One under the new moon out of desperation.

As soon as that clawed hand grasped the front of my shirt, I knew I'd fucked up, but there wasn't much I could do once I wound up sucked into a vortex that seemed to bend time and space to meaninglessness.

(Take a minute if you wanna write that down, Gabriel, that one took me a while.)

[It's all being recorded, Mr. Curtis. And my name is Chemuel.]

Cool. Anyway, I end up falling through this hole that feels like it goes on forever. Total Twilight Zone shit. When it finally stopped, I landed hard enough to paralyze my left side for a minute, and by the time I peeled myself off the floor, I realized I was staring at a pair of giant black leather boots, complete with studs and everything. I followed them up to the muscular legs and dangerously cut torso above. His chest was bare, revealing bronzed reddish skin--or maybe it was just the ambient lighting. I realized the hand that had grabbed me was his. Both of his hands looked like they'd been dipped in dark blood, fading into his skin tone at the elbow joint. His absurdly broad shoulders were covered in a cloak lined with spiky black fur and the leathers he wore clung to those thick, hard thighs like latex.

And his face...

Hair as black as coal flowed in luscious waves around his sharp jawline, disappearing into the fur ruff around his shoulders. He had sharply pointed ears like an elf's, lined with gold rings, and a straight nose that perfectly balanced out his full lips and smoldering reddish-brown eyes. Two ram's horns decorated either side of his forehead, curling back over his head.

In short, he was like a boner generator on legs.

[Mr. Curtis, please. The *facts*.]

I'm doing my best. So I stood gawking at this nine-foot-tall manbeast, thinking I must be having one of *those* dreams, except my imagination ain't that good. He was a wall of sex and muscle and his bulging cock was unsettlingly close to eye level even when I stood up, so my brain turned to mush while other parts of me... hardened, if you catch my drift?

Again, I'm gonna take your silence as a yes.

I started babbling incoherently, something along the lines of, "Aw... uh... huah?"

He raised an eyebrow and in this super sexy Bond villain accent, he answered, "Come again, human?"

And here I was thinking, "Again and again and again," and he just kept staring, like *he* was the one in shock.

Better try again, I thought. Second time's always the charm.

"Hi, Devil Daddy," is what came out, and I smacked

myself in the face. "I mean...cock. Fuck! I mean fuck. Not you...me. Wait, that's not right either."

He kept staring and I didn't speak demon face, but I was pretty damn sure that look meant I had seconds to live if I didn't get my shit together.

"Apollyon," I said, choking out his presumed name with as much difficulty as I'd have choking down that monster cock of his. "You're Apollyon, right?"

"I am," he answered, his long, clawed nails wrapping around the ruby orb on top of his cane. Each one made a spine-tingling rap when it made contact. I hadn't even noticed the fucking thing, what with the dick in my face and all. "And you are?"

A second earlier, I'd known the answer to that question. At the moment, "the devil's rent boy" was starting to sound better than Levi.

"I'm.... uh... Levi."

Smooth as butter.

He raised a thick, sharply arched eyebrow. "Levi," he mused. "That name sounds familiar. Didn't one of my imps cure you of a terminal illness recently?"

His words were the first clue that maybe this wasn't just a freaky dream, which... pluses and minuses. On the one hand, shit, the ritual had actually worked! On the other...

Shit. It worked.

I swallowed the boulder-sized lump in my throat and tried to regain control of my tongue. It was a difficult task under the best of circumstances. "I'm sorry. Did you just say you *cured* me? With a limp?"

"An imp," he corrected impatiently. "A demonic servant."

"Right," I coughed. "But...why? How do you even know who I am?"

"It was part of a negotiation," he answered.

Negotiation? I should've pieced it together before, but I felt the truth hit me like a bullet train, right in the face. It left me flat as a pancake and I didn't know whether I should be furious, touched or some combination of both.

So that was the explanation behind the bizarre series of mysteries that had become my life. I wasn't "cured." There was nothing miraculous about my unexpected remission. Sirena had simply traded herself--maybe even her soul--in exchange for my health.

"Listen," I began, realizing that probably wasn't the best way to address a super powerful demon too little, too late. "I don't know what you've done with my sister, but I never wanted this. I never asked for it, so you can just take back whatever magical kale and yoga spell you used to poof me into wellness and give Sirena back."

"That isn't how this works," he answered flatly. The amusement in his gaze told me there was only one reason he was tolerating my insolence, and I had a feeling the second I stopped being so entertaining, he'd crush me like a bug against the wall.

Fuck. Now I knew how weird fetishes happened.

"Okay, so tell me how it does work."

"Sirena Curtis made a deal with full disclosure and consent," said Apollyon. "You really think you're the first little man to come through here trying to save a woman from her own choices?"

I cringed. Little? Ouch. I was a solid five-ten in boots. But I guess compared to the muscle skyscraper, I'd seem small. "At least tell me what she offered you."

Maybe I could match it. Sweeten the deal a little. I wasn't sure how much my soul was worth, but surely there was *something*.

"The agreement between a human and a demon is confidential."

"Sure, I get that. But what if it *wasn't*?"

He gave me a look I was sure I'd never get from a demon. "You do realize that I could banish you to the void, don't you?" He snapped his long, clawed fingers. "Just like that."

I gulped. "I do, and I appreciate your self-restraint with not banishing me and all. But you have to understand, Sirena isn't just my twin, she's my other half. My better half. The world wouldn't miss me for a split second, but she actually matters, and I'm not going back without her."

"Is that so?" His index finger started tapping the orb again as he settled back into a throne that seemed to be made of ivory. It was definitely bone of some kind, and I could be optimistic, couldn't I?

"Yep," I said, trying not to look like a glob of gelatin molded into the shape of a human being. "So the way I see it, we can do this one of two ways. The first, you let me take her place, whatever she offered you."

"And the second?" he asked boredly.

"The second way?" I croaked. I'd really been counting on him not asking. "Well... that would involve you refusing and me probably getting my insides turned into my outsides trying to stop you. But either way, I'm not leaving here without her."

Apollyon leaned back with his head on his fist, his dark eyes gleaming so much it looked like there was fire in them. It must have been a slow day in Hell, because I think he was actually enjoying our little repartee. Or maybe he just found my arrogance amusing.

Probably the latter, in retrospect.

"You are a most unusual human," he remarked.

I puffed my chest up a little, thinking he was referring to my bravery and willingness to sacrifice myself for someone I loved. "Oh, yeah?"

"For one thing, most who come before me are wearing pants."

I looked down at myself and realized for the first time that I'd gone into the underworld in little more than my underwear. A hoodie with spotted blue-and-gray boxers, to be exact.

(Again, I feel it's necessary to remind you I never actually thought the ritual would *work*.)

"Is that a yes or a no?"

"You say you wish to take your sister's place," he continued, ignoring my question. "And yet, you have no idea what our deal involves."

"It doesn't matter." And it didn't. Whatever Sirena had signed up for, the only thing that could possibly be worse than experiencing it was *her* experiencing it. It was the same as the day I'd gotten diagnosed. As much as it sucked, and as terrified as I was, there was still that thought in the back of my mind.

At least it's not her.

"How noble," he sneered, making it clear he was anything but impressed. "I see why she was willing to go to such lengths to preserve you."

"Really?"

"You're pathetic, but you have a certain charm." He studied me like a cat watching a mouse, and before I could come up with an adequately snappy retort, he added, "Alright. I'm in a generous mood, so I'll make an exception. I'll tell you the nature of our agreement, and you can decide for yourself if it's one you can handle."

I wanted to tell him the exposition wasn't necessary, but

terror had given me the filter that twelve-years of public education and parental guilt had failed to. "Great. Let's hear it."

He seemed vaguely irritated by my impatience, but he went on. "Sirena has contracted herself--quite willingly, I might add--to become my Lightbearer."

I blinked. "Sure. Right. A Lightbearer. And pretend I have no idea what that is, just for the hell of it."

Apollyon sighed. "*I* am the Duke of the Underworld. Are you with me so far?"

And I thought the chick at the deli was snarky about me asking for thinly sliced ham. "So far, so good," I said through gritted teeth.

"With that title comes great power and authority, but it is limited to *this* realm," he explained. "Let's just say I'm interested in expanding my real estate holdings into the surface world, and to do that, I need a mortal connection. An anchor, if you will."

I was lost, but afraid to admit it. "So you... uh... want a real estate agent?"

He flattened out the fist his chin was resting on and ran his claws down his perfect face with a look of utter exasperation. "Let me try to put this in terms even *you* can understand."

He raised his cane and held the long staff between both hands. Slowly, he began to pull the dark wood apart until the split halves of the cane became two identical replicas of each other. "This Hell," he said in a deliberate, mocking voice as he held the left cane up, and then the right. "This your world. In between is big space. Demon no cross. Need human vessel to transport energy."

My face burned with embarrassment and irritation, but I was mostly just pissed that his condescension was turning me on. Then again, maybe it was the tight leather pants. Or both.

The whims of my dick always had been an enigma.

"Okay, I get it," I snapped, even though that was only half true. "You want access to our world to unleash whatever demonic shenanigans you have planned, so you want to what, possess my sister? Like the Exorcist?"

Apollyon rolled his eyes. "I am a Monarch of Hell. A human body would never survive the incarnation of my power, the absurdity of the situation aside. Sirena will bear the seeds of my army, providing the anchor I need to manifest on earth."

As the pieces slowly came together in my mind, I went from ogling the guy to wanting to punch his sexy smoldering lights out. "You contracted my sister to be your infernal baby mamma?"

"In a manner of speaking, I suppose you're not far off," he mused.

"That's not fair," I spat. "You said I could take her place."

"I did no such thing. You assumed as much, as your kind always does," he scoffed. "But it is, nonetheless, an option."

I blinked. "Uh. As progressive as it is of you to not assume I don't have a womb--no rhyme intended--I don't."

"The seed is not a literal child," he droned, clearly running out of patience with my existence in his realm of dramatically lit stone and hellacious minimalism. "It's the energetic essence of my army. The unholy light that flows from my will."

"Oh. Sure. *Everyone* has one of those."

"The method of insemination, however, is quite similar to the impregnation of which you speak," he added, smirking. "For a cisgender human female, the process is relatively straightforward, but it can be done with a cisgender male. It's simply more...*invasive*."

That word took on a whole new ominous meaning, but I refused to let my mind drift to the possibilities. It wasn't the idea of fucking him that put me off. Hell, if the big guy was a carnival ride, I'd already have a stack of tickets bunched up in my fists. Still... as little as I knew about being a "Lightbearer," and as far from religious as I was, it sounded way too close to blasphemy for comfort.

But if it meant Sirena wasn't trapped down here with this freak, it wasn't even a question. "I'll do it."

The blank look on Apollyon's face told me he hadn't actually expected that answer. Probably the first time a human had ever surprised him, and given the circumstances, it was hard to be proud of it.

Pity, cuz it sure felt good to wipe that smug look off his pretty face.

"You're kidding."

"You said I had the option," I reminded him. "Are you going back on your word?"

"Of course not," he snapped, clearly insulted by the insinuation. Guess honor meant more to demons than I would have thought. "I'm just not sure you understand what you're agreeing to."

"I'd be your bitch," I said with a shrug. "I've had worse gigs."

He stared at me like I'd broken him. Could you break a demon? It felt like an accomplishment, even though I was pretty sure I should have been insulted by the look of horror in those red eyes.

"Are you even a witch?" he asked in disbelief.

"No. Is that a requirement?" I hesitated. "Wait, does that mean Sirena *is*?"

My theory that she'd fallen headlong into this mess was starting to grow thin.

"Confidentiality," he reminded me. More tapping. "And no, it is not a requirement, per se. I simply doubt that a regular, unpracticed mortal has the wherewithal for the position."

I chuckled, because really, how often does a guy like me get the chance? "Well, that's not gonna be a problem. I've been in *every* position you can think of."

More blank staring. "That's not the kind of position I'm talking about."

"Oh. Then... oh, you meant the job?"

"It's not a job," he snapped. "There are leagues of human witches who would sell their souls for the honor of being my Lightbearer, and you make it sound like an assignment."

"If all the witch bitches are so hangry for your dick, then why the fuck do you want my sister?" I cried.

He grimaced. "You are the most foul-mouthed creature I've ever encountered."

"Thanks. Again, why Sirena?"

He raised an eyebrow again. It was...unexpectedly cute. "Sirena is the one who came to *me*."

"All she did was follow the recipe in that stupid book," I protested. "She probably didn't even know what she was getting into."

"I find that unlikely, given that the 'stupid book' you refer to is one of a very limited number of copies, all heavily sought after and guarded through the generations of occult practitioners." He paused. "What era are you from?"

"Era?" I echoed. "Oh, you mean year. Uh, twenty-nineteen."

"Then in that case, my Codex would have cost upwards of six figures."

My eyes widened. "Holy shit."

If all she wanted was to heal me, she could've bought me a new fucking robot body for that amount. It wasn't inconceivable that Sirena might have that kind of cash tucked away. She worked a lot and my jaw had dropped the last time she'd told me how much her Youtube channel was earning, but *still*. That seemed like an absurd amount for someone who was usually as frugal as she was.

"As I said... your sister's summoning was anything but accidental."

"Whatever," I muttered. I'd deal with Sirena when I had the chance, assuming this asshole even let me see her again. "I'm still not letting you take her."

"Don't you think that's up to her?"

I clenched my jaw. "Look, I don't know if demons have family or whatever, but Sirena? She's my entire world, and there are people out there who need her. I'll do whatever you ask. Just please, let her go."

Apollyon watched me in a detached, studious way that made me feel like a maggot standing before a god. When he finally seemed about to pass his judgment, the stone wall parted, revealing a door tucked seamlessly within it.

Another horned demon rushed through, not quite as tall as Apollyon, but just as hunky. Stark white hair all the way down to his shoulders, big blue eyes that seemed to glow in the dim light, and muscles on full display in a slitted tunic that looked like a glorified loincloth. Apparently, Hell was a hotbed of horny supermodels. Shoulda figured.

"Sir!" the demon cried, casting a wary glance at me before he returned his focus to Apollyon. "The gates are under siege."

"Again?" the demon's rumbling voice echoed through the cavernous space I assumed was his office. Or maybe it was just a throne room. Either way, not very welcoming. He stood, lean muscles rippling as he rose once more to his full height.

"Under siege by what?" I asked.

Apollyon ignored me, whisking off toward the door his servant had come through. When I tried to follow him, he threw out his massive arm and blocked my path. "You stay here," he growled through clenched teeth. He waved his hand and something sent me flying back, even though he hadn't touched me.

"Hey!" I cried, rushing after him only to hit a wall where the door should've been.

Fucking demon magic.

SIX

I WAITED in the demon's chambers for all of ten minutes before I decided he was probably gone forever and started trying to find my way out. Turns out, the door wasn't even locked. Then again, I guess they're not worried about people trying to break *into* Hell.

The hallway outside was less otherworldly and terrifying than I would have pictured. Nicer than my dentist's office, actually. I crept along, convinced that sooner or later, *someone* would realize I didn't belong there.

It turned out, Hell's security system wasn't all that. The first time I passed someone, it was a seven-foot-tall guy with the abs of a titan and the head of a goat. Literally. I flattened myself against the wall and stared in horror. He just gave a snort that smelled like brimstone and kept walking.

"Holy shit," I breathed once I was pretty sure he was out of earshot, but who knew with those ears?

The next hall was even bigger than the last. There were high stone ceilings and the only lights came from torches posted on giant bronze sconces. Whoever designed this place had a Dracula fetish.

I found a door that looked promising and tried the knob. It opened up to a swirling void of hissing blackness that all but sucked me in before I managed to slam the door shut.

"Definitely not behind door number one," I croaked, staggering as far away from the door as possible on my Jello legs.

The next door had to have something behind it, but given the last experience, I wasn't eager to find out. I kept walking in hopes of finding friendlier pastures. Or, preferably, an exit sign.

Sure enough, the ceiling opened up to reveal a gray sky glowing faintly from some unseen lightsource. There wasn't a cloud or a star in the sky. In fact, the hazy texture seemed to hang so low I half-feared it wasn't a sky at all, but an illusion.

The fact that crisp if chilly air filled my lungs came as a relief, and the same scent of burnt something that permeated the rest of the castle grew lighter the closer I got to the arched doorways surrounding what I assumed was a lobby. There were chairs and couches, even a few bookshelves, like I'd stumbled into the common area of some subterranean dormitory.

I could hear the sound of water not too far off and decided the further I got from the castle, the better. The grounds outside were oddly beautiful. There were rolling green hills cast in a dreary hue thanks to the emo sky. Some kind of garden surrounded the property for as far as I could see, but none of the trees or flowers were familiar. Large, hanging vines drooped over a stone pathway carved with strange symbols and massive blooms in varying neon shades brushed against my arm as I continued down the path.

When I reached out to touch one of the invitingly succulent looking blooms, its petals clamped down on my hand and I felt the edge of something sharp like teeth against my fingertips before I managed to yank my hand out with a yelp.

"Levi?"

I'd know that incredulous, pissed off voice anywhere. I rushed down the path and found Sirena running toward me. She was dressed in some weird, Grecian gown in a shade of silver that didn't quite look real. Maybe it was just the lighting, but her eyes seemed to have a weird glow, too.

"Sirena!" I cried, enveloping her into an embrace tight enough that I heard her shoulder crack. I could only convince myself to ease up so much, terrified that she'd disappear if I didn't hold on. "Thank God."

Seemed like a risky thing to say in a place like this, but I'd never had a handle on my mouth.

"How the fuck did you get here?" she cried, pulling away to look at me. "Are you hurt?"

"No. As a matter of fact, thanks to your bullshit idea, I'm feeling right as rain," I said through gritted teeth.

Her guilty expression said it all. She wasn't even gonna bother to deny it.

"Selling your fucking soul, Sirena?"

"That's not what happened," she muttered, crossing her arms.

"Like the semantics make a difference! Selling your soul, offering to have the devil's kid. Same difference when you disappeared off the face of the planet."

"It's only for a limited time," she argued. "Apollyon said I could come back."

"Then why the fuck didn't you tell anyone?" I demanded. "How could you not tell me?"

"I tried," she answered. "It was just...too hard. I knew you'd try to stop me."

"No shit, I would! You had no right to do this."

"Bullshit. What was I supposed to do, just let you die?" she challenged. "I've seen how you've been slipping this past year, ever since your symptoms set in. It's like you've already given up."

Her words cut deep, mostly because they were true. Maybe I had sunk knee-deep into nihilism, but who the fuck wouldn't in my position? "There's a line between giving up and making deals with the fucking devil."

"Technically, he's just a Duke of Hell."

"Beside the point, Sirena!"

"Okay, okay," she hissed, looking down the path. "Keep it down or they'll hear you." She hesitated. "How did you get here, anyway?"

"Same way you did. I followed the ritual."

I wasn't sure if her look of disbelief should be insulting or not, but it hardly seemed like the time to dwell on it. "Where's Apollyon?"

"I don't know, some weirdo came and told him there was an emergency or something and he ran off."

"Then there might be time," she murmured, taking my hand to drag me down the path. "Hurry."

"Where are we going?" I demanded, even though I kept pace with her. Didn't seem like a good idea to linger and she knew this place a hell of a lot better than I did--pun totally intended.

"The portal," she answered. "If we're under attack again, the guards will all be at the gates."

I recalled what Apollyon's servant had said about being under siege. "Wait, what's the difference between the portal and the gates?"

"The gates lead into the other rings of Hell," she explained, quickening her pace. "The portal leads to earth."

"You're telling me you knew how to get home this entire time and you've just been playing Lady Macbeth?"

She stopped walking when I yanked my hand away and gave me a weary look. "I made an agreement with Apollyon of my own free will and I intend to keep it. Especially now that I know it worked."

"No," I growled, looking up at the thin sliver of light in the wall up ahead. The wall seemed to come out of nowhere, camouflaged in the thick hanging vines that stretched down from trees so high I couldn't even see the tops. Something told me that was the portal and I wasn't all that eager to dive in. "I'm not going back without you."

"I can't leave," she protested. "If I do, the deal will be cancelled."

"Who gives a shit? I'd rather spend the next nine years living my life than knowing my sister gave up hers."

"It's not just that," she said, shooting another glance down the path. I could hear people shouting and a sound not unlike lightning, but no telling where it was actually coming from.

"Then what?" I asked, wary of her strange demeanor. It wasn't like Sirena to keep secrets, let alone layered ones, but lately, I felt like I didn't even know who she was.

She looked away, like she was afraid to meet my eyes. I didn't know if it was because she was ashamed or because she was planning on lying, but either way.

"Sirena!"

"Your health isn't the only thing I bargained," she admitted, wincing. "I mean, that was why I looked into the ritual in the first place, but…"

"But what?" I demanded. It was clear she was in over her head, but there was nothing I could do if she wouldn't tell me how far.

When she finally met my eyes, I had my answer. It was shame. "It's just so hard," she said shakily. "You get typecast and there's only so many roles you can take. So far you can go without being out there by the big studios, and even then, it's a crapshoot..."

"Fuck," I groaned, pressing my hand to my temple to stave off a massive migraine. "Please, don't. Please don't tell me you pulled a cliche Hollywood move and bargained for fame."

"It's not like I'm the first person," she muttered defensively. "A year of my life in exchange for guaranteed success. I'm not getting any younger and these days, the devil's a lot friendlier than the other industry creeps you have to fuck to get ahead."

I stared at her, convinced she'd lost her mind. "Look around, Sirena. In case you haven't noticed, we're in Hell."

"I know that," she snapped. Her eyes grew wide as she looked behind me and I realized the shouting from before was getting closer. This time, there was more purpose to it. "Shit. They must've realized you left. You have to go, now," she cried, pushing me toward the glowing slit in the wall.

I dug my heels into the path and turned around. "I told you, I'm not leaving without you," I said, grasping her wrist. She tried to pull away, but the demons were within full view now. Judging from their armored uniforms, Apollyon had sent the big guns after me.

I knew I had seconds to spare, if that, and the look in her eyes told me she knew what I was planning. When one of the guards shouted, "Close the portal!," I realized they did, too.

"Levi, no!"

"I'm sorry," I muttered, pushing her into the glowing light. "See you in a year."

Assuming Apollyon didn't kill me first.

SEVEN

"THE LIGHTBEARER!" one of the guards cried as the others surrounded me. My face became so intimately acquainted with the dirt, it owed me dinner. I wasn't sure if demon knees were just knobbier than most, but damn if that sucker didn't dig into my lumbar like a knife.

If I survived this, I was pretty sure all of Sirena's efforts were going to be undermined by new and exciting ailments.

"By order of the Unholy Council, you are under arrest," the guard on top of me announced in a surprisingly lady-like voice.

"Of course I am," I groaned as she cuffed my arms behind my back. I must've been a bit too obvious in my attempt to look over my shoulder and figure out if I was at least being arrested by a hot succubus, because she cold clocked me and next thing I knew, I was bound up in a strange bed with chains from my shoulders to my ankles.

Given the fact that I had a semi-regular dream that started this way, I wasn't as terrified as I probably should've been. At least, not until Apollyon came in.

At first, he didn't say anything. Just took off his cloak

and hung it by the door like he was coming in after a long day of bargaining souls and profaning the natural order of the universe. Then, he looked at me, his face a mask of calm speculation.

"Well," he said, walking to sit in a chair that seemed to have been pulled up across from the bed for that very purpose. He folded his arms and stared at me. "You know your way around Hell's inner circle quite well."

"Delivery driver," I said sheepishly. "I'm good with directions."

"So it seems."

I gulped. "How was the uh, siege?"

"Contained," he answered in a tone that made me think his teeth were clenched together. His lips were so tight, I couldn't tell. He wound a strand of thick, dark hair around his finger with so much tension I was sure he was imagining it was my neck. "Unfortunately, all access to and from the underworld was sealed shortly after you returned my light-bearer to earth."

If he was expecting me to look ashamed, he had another thing coming. "So you can't get to Sirena?"

"You don't need to sound so triumphant. This won't go as well for you as you think."

"If she's back home and out of your reach, it's gone as well as I expected it to," I said, managing to sit up with some difficulty.

Apollyon's eyes narrowed. The change was slight, but menacing. "I'm not sure you quite understand the situation you've put us both in. Hell is under siege, which means that the portal won't be opening again."

"For how long?"

"In terms you would understand? A long fucking time."

Well, that was descriptive. "Guess we're stuck with each other, then. Heh."

His eyes grew even narrower. "Considering that you are currently the only living human within the Nine Circles of Hell, that would be the case."

"Why do I get the feeling you checked?"

"Exhaustively."

Ouch. "Look, I'm not any happier about this than you are, but I warned you. Sirena's off limits."

"Sirena is a grown witch perfectly capable of making her own decisions, and she was the only candidate worthy of bearing the seeds of my army," he said in a clipped tone. "What are you? Nothing."

"We're twins. Doesn't that count for something?"

"In fact, it's the only reason I haven't disposed of you entirely," he snapped. "Let's hope that her magical affinity is a matter of genetics rather than will."

"That's no way to talk to the mother of your future army."

His exasperated growl made me jolt before he rose from his chair to pace the room. "This is absolutely absurd. You'll need to be educated, and the magical training alone will take months."

"Uh, I'm pretty sure I don't need additional schooling to do the horizontal tango. Fucking a demon can't be that different."

I certainly had a few exes who could've used an exorcism.

"This is about more than just 'fucking,'" he warned. "The seed will require sustenance, and nurturing. An unsuited surrogate would result in a failed gestation and death, in your case."

His words brought a weight down on my shoulders and

I responded the way I always did to pressure. By being a smartass.

"So I'm guessing this is a little more involved than popping prenatal vitamins?"

Apollyon glowered at me, waving his hand. I cringed, expecting to be sliced apart by some psychic energy whirlwind. Instead, the chains around me fell away. "I'll be spending the evening arranging your crash course in infernal living. I suggest you take the opportunity to rest," he said, looking me up and down judgmentally. "You're not going to have much of a chance once we get started."

On that ominous note, he left me alone, simultaneously ensuring that I didn't get a wink of sleep that night.

EIGHT

TURNED OUT, by crash course, Apollyon meant it literally. I woke to someone banging on the door at the ass-crack of dawn--or at least, what I assumed was dawn. In Hell, did it really even matter?

When I opened the door to find a she-demon on the other side, wearing a skin-tight leather bodysuit, I was tempted to think I was still dreaming. When she barked, "Put these on," and shoved a stack of clothes into my arms, I realized I was definitely awake.

It became clear she had every intention of watching me change when she walked into the room, but the austere scowl on her face made the whole thing more menacing than erotic. I stripped down and unfurled the clothes she'd given me to realize it was a pair of black leather pants as tight as her own and a shirt that was more like a harness. Just two straps that ran across the chest and met in the middle with some huge metal hook.

"What the fuck is this?"

"Put it on," she ordered, her arms folded.

The look on her face and the bulge of her biceps kept

me from arguing. When I had too much difficulty figuring out the harness, she grabbed my arms and maneuvered me like a ragdoll until the thing fit securely over my chest.

"Ease up, Xena," I muttered, backing away. "I'm fragile."

She flung the door open and glowered.

"No, no, ladies first."

The way her eyes narrowed told me that wasn't the right thing to say. "Lightbearer or not, it's my job to teach you your place," she said with a malevolent sneer that made it clear she took more pleasure in her job than I would have initially assumed. "*Omega.*"

"Omega?" I echoed. "What the fuck is that supposed to mean?"

"You're a human male currently unowned by a demon. Bottom of the totem pole," she explained.

"Sirena was a lightbearer and I didn't see her wearing this getup."

"Sirena is a woman. Things work differently here."

"So they do," I muttered, following her down the hall. She led me to a room that looked way too much like a classroom for comfort and pushed me down into an empty chair toward the front of the room.

She pulled a massive book off the shelf and the glimpse I got of the title read, "Codes and Laws." Fun stuff.

"Read," she ordered, dropping the massive book in front of me.

I gulped. "Don't I at least get a name? You know, in case I need to call on teacher for a bathroom break."

She sneered, half her lip curled back. "Shera. You will refer to me as ma'am."

"Yes, ma'am," I sighed. "I don't suppose I could get a

snack for this study session? I'm kind of famished after all that interdimensional travel."

"Lightbearers are on a controlled diet. For the health of the seed."

"Of course," I muttered. When she left the room, I assumed that was that, but then she returned carrying a thermos and an apple.

"Seriously?"

"The shake has all your nutritional requirements."

"And the apple?"

"You know what they say. One a day..."

"Keeps the doctor away, yeah, yeah," I groaned.

She left me alone but I got the feeling I was still being watched. Then again, maybe this place was just driving me crazy. I took a bite of the apple, relieved it was *actually* an apple. Juicy, but not exactly substantial enough to take the bite out of two days' worth of hunger.

I eyed the thermos warily and when I opened it, it looked like any other vaguely purple health shake I'd ever made on New Year's day and never again. I sniffed and it smelled kind of like raspberries, but who the fuck knew what those weirdos put in it?

I slid the shake aside and cracked the giant book in front of me. Did Shera the Warrior Princess seriously expect me to read all of this shit? If so, she was dramatically overestimating my attention span. I had more than a few scars from being too impatient to read instruction manuals as it was.

The content was surprisingly mundane, given where I was. Just an overview of the structure of Hell, including the nine circles that I guess were more literal than figurative. To my amazement, there wasn't a "you are here" blip on the central map.

I zoned out somewhere between the intricate discussion

of the treatises that kept the Lords of each ring in their places and the propaganda about how one day the nine sanctums would rise and rule the earth.

Typical new guy orientation shit, really. I flipped to the index and started skimming for topics. Sure enough, there was an entire chapter on Apollyon, complete with a charcoal portrait of him standing gallantly with a blade the size of me over his left shoulder.

I had to admit, as flattering as the picture was, it didn't really do him justice. Guy was sex on legs. And what legs they were...

The one form of thirst reminded me of the other and I reluctantly took a sip from the thermos. It wasn't bad, and it didn't taste like people, so I took another sip, sure I'd come to regret it.

The chapter on Apollyon was just more of the same propaganda, but I did glean a few interesting bits. Evidently, he'd been the one to broker peace between the warring rings and unite the other Monarchs under the banner of conquest. He was a real infernal Alexander the Great.

The more I read, the more I couldn't help but wonder... What the fuck was Sirena even thinking getting involved with this guy? I was still irritated at the revelation that her deal had been as much about fame and material success as saving my life, but what the fuck was the point if the world was gonna get torched anyway?

I got bored of reading about how great my intended was, so I decided to look for the section on the Lightbearer. It was even longer, but one paragraph in particular caught my attention.

"The Indwelling of the light must be protected at all costs. Once a Lightbearer is chosen and bound, her soul

becomes inextricable from the demon lord's. For this reason, the Protocol must be followed carefully, to ensure the health of both the vessel and the light."

Well, if that wasn't just the creepiest little tidbit. For once in my life, I closed the book and decided I was done reading. Shera could fail me if she wanted to, but at that point, I was sure no amount of academic preparation could get me ready for the real thing.

NINE

"THIS IS PATHETIC."

I picked my head up off the table and realized I was laying in a puddle of drool. Of course, Mr. Sexy had to walk in looking perfect with a sheer black tank top that existed only as a window for his abs.

And apparently, his nipples were pierced. That was a new development.

"When Shera told me you'd fallen asleep on the job, I thought she meant it figuratively."

"In my defense, and I mean this in the most reverent possible way, your books are boring as shit."

Apollyon set his mouth into a flat line that somehow made him even more attractive and stared at me like he was trying to figure out what to do with me. I had a few suggestions I was sure he wouldn't appreciate, so I bit my bottom lip to keep my mouth shut.

"Tell me you're at least *somewhat* aware of the gravity of the situation you dove into headfirst."

"I wouldn't say headfirst," I argued. "More like assbackwards, but yeah, I get the picture."

"That's good, because when the portal sealed behind Sirena, it sealed for the foreseeable future," he said, crossing his arms. "For the time being, we're under siege, which means no one gets in or out."

"Like a slumber party?"

His eyes narrowed. "No, not like a slumber party. Like a siege. What is wrong with you?"

"Sorry, sorry," I groaned, standing from the desk. My spine was stiff, but in the usual way, not in the "I'm dying" way. Progress, to be sure. "Can we continue this lecture over dinner? That protein shake doesn't exactly stick with you."

"You're on a tightly controlled regimen," he informed me. "You will eat what's given to you."

"And if your army wants funnel cake? Cravings are the body's way of meeting your nutritional needs."

He blinked. "You're not even the lightbearer yet."

"And whose fault is that?"

Apollyon ran a hand down his face and I could all but hear him counting to ten in his head. "You are by far one of the most mentally taxing creatures I have come across in the seven realms, and that includes a troll who never stops speaking in riddles."

"You have trolls here? And I got stuck in the smartass demon realm?"

"Come," he barked, turning on his heels to stalk out of the room. I hated to admit it, but when his voice got all gruff and ragey like that, it sent shivers down my spine.

"So we're going to get food, right?"

"Shut up," he snapped.

I muttered nothing in particular under my breath, figuring that his imagination would be far more insulting than anything I managed to come up with. When we reached a vast room populated with robed figures standing around in a semicircle, I realized dinner was further away than I'd feared.

There was an altar-esque thing in the middle of the room and I put on the breaks immediately. "Is this a human sacrifice? Because I am *not* getting on that thing."

Apollyon rolled his eyes and turned back toward the others. "Brethren, the eve has come to induct the lightbearer."

The cloaked figures murmured in quiet discontent and I stayed behind Apollyon, even though my chances with him weren't much better. I'd seen enough weird ass looking demons to be fearful of what was waiting underneath those robes.

"What is induction, exactly?" I asked warily. "I know what the earthy definition is, but is it different in Hellspeak?"

He shot me a silencing glance over his shoulder and the figures drew closer, forming a tighter circle around the table.

Apollyon grabbed me by the wrist and pulled me around in front of him. He was a hell of a lot stronger than he looked, and he already looked like a guy who chewed glass to freshen his breath.

Apollyon's hands came to rest on my shoulders and I felt all weird and tingly inside, like some kind of heart boner. I froze as the hooded figures--nine in all--knelt down before us. Well, probably just before Apollyon, but I could pretend.

"What are they doing?"

"Hush," he muttered, his hands still firmly against my bare skin. Maybe this harness thing wasn't so bad. "Council of Fire, I present to you Levi Curtis, my chosen lightbearer."

He said "chosen" with a bitter clip, making it clear I

wasn't first string. Not that I gave a shit. As long as Sirena was in the world of the living, living *her* life, I'd won. The rest of this was just a cosmic acid trip.

"Turn," Apollyon ordered, his hands falling away. As soon as I turned around, he had a giant book spread out between his hands. I'd seen enough indie horror movies to know what that shit was, and the list of other names signed in blood confirmed it.

"You said I wasn't selling my soul."

He gave me a beleaguered look. "Just your servitude for this lifetime. Don't worry. No special treatment when you end up here for the long stay," he sneered.

I gulped. "What am I supposed to sign with?"

He raised his right hand with a flourish and a pen that seemed to be made of sharpened bone appeared out of nowhere. When I felt the rough texture, I realized it didn't just *look* like bone. I shivered and tried to pass it off as a shrug. Then, I realized his hand was still outstretched.

"Draw blood with the quill," he ordered calmly.

"*Yours?*"

He didn't respond, but his impatient expression was enough of an answer. I dug the sharpened tip of the quill into the meat of his palm and a few drops of blood sprang to the surface. I hesitated with the tip to the page and when I met Apollyon's eyes, there was unexpected gentleness in his gaze.

"You are aware of what you're agreeing to, yes?"

"Yeah." The word stuck in my throat, but I signed my name before I could change my mind. I don't know what I was expecting. A vortex opening up in the ceiling, maybe. Some magical whooshing sound. My signature dried with a flash of light that nearly sent me on my ass, but Apollyon took the pen from me and snapped the book shut.

"So it is written," he announced in a solemn tone.

"Hail the lightbearer," the robed figures chanted in unison. Creepy little fuckers, but I was already starting to get attached.

"Er, thanks," I said, deciding it was rude not to respond. Apollyon's weary gaze told me it wasn't necessary. "So, what now?"

"Now, we return to my quarters and sleep," he answered. "It's been a hell of a day."

"Heh."

"What?" he snapped.

"Nothing." Maybe I'd already gotten the slightest bit attached to him, too.

TEN

TURNED OUT, when Apollyon said we were going back to his quarters, he meant just that. To sleep. Who the fuck actually means what they say?

"What?" he asked, looking over at me as I sat on the other end of the bed.

"Nothing, I just thought...y'know."

He stared blankly. Guess he was gonna make me spell it out.

"I mean, I just got sworn in as your lightbearer, so I figured..."

"Yes?" he asked impatiently.

Damn, the guy was thick. In more ways than one, if the bulge in his leathers was any indication. "You know. Bowchicabowwow?"

He blinked slowly, like a cat who's just witnessed you eating cheese out of the bag at two a.m.. "Excuse me?"

I sighed. "You know, how sometimes when an underworld demon lord loves a lightbearer very much and they wanna make a little army of the infernal damned..."

His hand met his face and I knew at least he got my drift. "Can you ever just speak plainly?"

"Sure. I've kind of gotten myself psyched up for all this paranormal bullshit, so are you gonna fuck me or not? That plain enough?"

"Not," he answered, turning back toward the wall. "Tonight, at any rate."

"So what, I'm just in here to be your cuddle buddy?" I asked, not sure if I was relieved or offended. Maybe both.

"You're in here so I can keep an eye on you," he answered, even though both of his eyes were shut.

"What, like I'm a threat to the good citizens of Hell?"

"Your arrival just so happened to coincide with a perimeter breach, so yes, it is suspicious."

"What, you think I had anything to do with that?" Now, I was flattered.

"Of course not," he snorted, like it was the most ridiculous thing in the world.

I sighed, dropping my head back onto the pillow and staring up at the ceiling. I had to admit, the digs were nice, considering where we were. The bed was comfortable and the room had that draconian luxury vibe going on. Kind of felt like being Dracula's bride, without any of the fun bits.

I finally glanced over at Apollyon, studying the curve of the demon's muscular back. There were faint markings along his spine like stripes that I hadn't noticed before. His hair was soft and lush as ever, and it smelled faintly of some exotic spice I'd never encountered before. The room was chilled, but the heat coming off of him kept me warm, even though I didn't dare to move closer.

He didn't seem to be breathing, adding to his statuesque air of perfection, but I knew he was at least somewhat human if he could sleep and, ostensibly, fuck. "Hey, Apollyon," I whispered.

Nothing.

"You awake?" I tried again.

"Yes, I'm fucking awake," he snapped in a voice that could melt the polar ice caps. "What do you want?"

"Nothin'. Just checking," I answered, rolling on my side to face him.

He sighed dramatically and turned over to face me. "For a human who supposedly fears death, you test my patience boldly."

"The ritual's done," I reminded him. "And from what you told me, Hell's under a quarantine, so you can't just go get another lightbearer. I figure that gives me a buffer."

The empty look in his eyes told me I wasn't far from the truth. "What do you want?"

"Just an assurance," I answered. "I'm here. I'm yours, and I'll do whatever you ask of me. If you ask nicely, I'll even do it with a smile, but when all this is said and done, I don't want Sirena having anything to do with this. Or you."

He sat up on his elbow, and for the first time since we'd met, he wasn't looking at me like some bug who'd crawled into his room. "Sirena is already on earth. What more do you want?"

"I know her. She's already trying to find a way back," I muttered. "Sometimes she's too damn ambitious for her own good. I want her to forget. All the shit she asked you for, put it on my tab, but I don't want her to remember how she got it." I swallowed hard. "Or me."

Apollyon frowned in confusion. "What do you mean?"

Under any other circumstances, I might have taken some pride in the fact that I'd just stumped an ancient demon, but not these. "Ever since we were young, Sirena's had to worry about me. We're too close, and too different. All I can do is hold her back, especially now. If she remembers me, she'll never stop trying to put things right, and I may not know shit about Hell, but I know better than to think I'm just gonna be able to go back to my old life a year from now and pretend like nothing happened."

He raised an eyebrow. "You want me to make your twin forget you exist?"

"And our mom. And her ex. And anyone else who'd throw a wrench in them getting to live their lives without worrying about me."

"You already agreed to the terms of the deal I made with Sirena. I promised nothing more."

"I know," I muttered. "But I'm asking." I stared intently into his eyes and put my hand over his, pausing for dramatic effect. "As your baby mama."

Apollyon grimaced and yanked his hand away with a growl. "I should have known you weren't capable of being serious for a moment."

"Okay, okay, just trying to lighten the mood. I'm serious about everything else."

He sighed. "Far be it for me to question anything that goes through your mind, but what makes you think they'll be better off for forgetting you?"

"I don't have to think, I know," I answered with a shrug. "Our dad figured it out a long time ago, and as much as I hated the bastard for it, he's the only one that had the guts to go through with it."

Apollyon watched me for long enough that I was starting to wish I hadn't said anything. When he finally spoke, his voice was softer than I expected. "As you wish.

You will remain here and your family will not remember you until and unless you are able to return."

"Good," I said, lying back down. "Now, if you're done chatting, let's try and get some sleep. I'm wiped."

Apollyon heaved a growling sigh and my mouth twitched. Sometimes he made it too easy.

ELEVEN

WHEN I OPENED MY EYES, the bed was empty. Guess Apollyon was an early riser. I yawned and got up to change. There were magically more clothes in the dresser whenever I needed them, but that was by far the least unsettling aspect of being in Hell.

Just as I opened the door, it swung out and I found myself staring at an eight-foot-tall demon with bull horns on top of his head.

"Fuck!" I cried, staggering back into the room. "What the...?"

"Forgive me for startling you, sire," he said, bowing low.

The gallantry fit with his uniform, I guess. He was dressed like some sort of hellacious butler and his eyes glowed an unnatural golden shade. If we were in the real world, I would've assumed the horns were costume and the eyes were contacts, but I knew better than to hope for logic in this place.

"And you are...?"

"Maiz," he answered. "I serve Lord Apollyon and I've been assigned to you as his lightbearer."

I blink. "As what?"

"A servant."

"I get a butler?"

He tilted his head at the term. "If you wish to think of me as that."

"Er. What do the people you work for usually think of you as?"

"Servant. Assassin. Lover, if needed."

I blinked. "Um. Butler is good. We'll stick with butler. But I'm really not a high-maintenance kind of guy." I paused. "Unless you can make Belgian waffles, in which case, I wouldn't mind that."

"I can make anything you like. Shall I escort you to the formal dining room?"

"Uh. I don't suppose there's an *in*formal dining room?"

The blank look he gave me turned out to be the only answer I was gonna get.

"This way, sir," he said, walking down the hall. It was embarrassingly difficult to keep up with his long strides, but I managed, trying to steal glances of my surroundings when I could.

I told myself it was just my imagination, but it seemed like the hallways changed every time I saw them. Doors would be shifted, new turns I didn't remember from before.

I made a note to myself not to go exploring without a hellacious GPS.

Once Maiz led me into the grand hall with a huge stone table, I realized why it was called the formal dining room. He pulled out a chair for me which we were gonna have a talk about later, but I sat down, deciding to save that for when I had some caffeine in me.

"What can I get you, sir?"

I resisted the temptation to go all Kid President and order a buffet. "Waffles and coffee would be great, thanks."

"Of course." He reached down like he was setting a plate in front of me and then one fucking appeared. I'd like to say I watched in curious fascination but in reality, I screamed like a stuck pig and almost fell out of my chair.

Maiz looked at me in concern. "Are you alright, sir?"

"Fine," I choked. "I just...really like waffles."

He blinked and stepped back. "Can I get you anything else?"

"No, this is great, thanks." I hesitated. "You don't want to join me?"

"I don't eat that kind of food, sir."

"Oh."

In my head, I'm thinking, "Don't ask, Levi. Just. Don't. Ask."

And I mean, really, there's no good answer that could come from that question, is there? Not in Hell.

But I'm nothing if not a glutton for punishment--and cheese, but that's another matter entirely.

"What do you eat?"

He gave me this look like he pitied me for asking. Like he recognized it for the self-destructive compulsion it was. "Flesh, sir."

"Right."

If I took a deep breath and summoned all my cognitive dissonance, I could maybe convince myself he meant cows and still keep down my waffles.

Aw, who was I kidding? He could've eaten a human leg in front of me and I'd still eat the waffles, as long as they were slathered in syrup and butter.

"I'll leave you to your breakfast. Call if you need anything," he said with another bow.

"Thanks," I said, waiting until he left to scarf down the food like a wild dog.

Once I'd finished breakfast, I decided to take a stroll, since the gates were closed and all. Seemed like there was a lower risk of tumbling into the void.

The mansion was oddly sparse, considering it was teeming with demons. I tried not to think about how many dimensions might be on the other sides of those doors.

I heard footsteps behind me and froze. When I looked back, there was no one there, but I got that eerie sense of being watched, so I called, "Maiz?"

"Yes, sir?" His voice was coming from in front of me and when I spun around, he was standing right there.

"Fuck, Maiz, you're gonna give me a heart attack," I groaned.

"My apologies, sir. You called for me?"

"Yeah. Were you, uh, following me by any chance?"

He tilted his head again. Kind of adorable, really, for a giant bull man in a tuxedo. "I was not, sir. Why do you ask?"

"Nothing," I muttered, looking back down the hall. "Just my imagination."

TWELVE

"LEVI. COME."

After three weeks in this literal hell, I was starting to get used to being called like a dog. After the first couple of days, I'd rarely seen Apollyon and gotten used to the idea of being an infernal trophy wife. Not a bad gig, really. Not with a live-in chef and all the eye candy you could drool over.

When he did show up, he was usually distracted, moody and short on words, so it was basically like we'd jumped from the wedding to year ten, but all things considered...

I looked up from the desk I'd been reading at in an upgraded version of the room Shera had first taken me to. Turned out, the classroom morphed depending on your expectations, which had taken me awhile to figure out. Happened the hard way when I'd leaned back in my chair only to remember it was attached to the desk, and that realization made the whole thing disappear and sent me unceremoniously onto my ass.

I'd changed things around a bit. A few big leather couches, some more manageable book shelves, and a desk that made it easier to take notes. And a TV for trashy reality binges, of course.

Apollyon paused in the doorway, looking around the room. "What happened here?"

"Like it?" I asked. "I remodeled."

"Where did you get these things?"

"I made them. Duh."

He squinted in confusion. "You *made* them?"

"Yeah. This place is practically an interior design etch a sketch," I snorted, kicking my feet up on the table. I snapped my fingers and made a vending machine appear in the middle of the room. "Nifty, really."

The way Apollyon was staring at the machine I'd just poofed into existence made me wonder if he'd never actually been to earth. I set aside the book I'd been studying and walked over, pressing a button to vend a can. Next time, it'd be bottles, but not bad for a first try.

"Here," I said, offering him the drink. "Try for yourself."

He took the can and kept staring at me. "How long have you been doing this?"

"Drinking soda?" I grimaced. "My whole life, pretty much."

"Not that," he snapped. "Where did you learn manifestation?"

"Manifestation? The hell is that?"

"You changed things. You made something appear out of nothing," he said, drawing his words out like he was trying to be patient. "Where did you learn how to do that? Who taught you?"

"Oh, that." I blinked. "No one, I just...did it. It's the room."

Now, I wasn't so sure.

"There's nothing special about this room," he insisted,

studying me with a wariness that had me on edge. I doubted there was much in the universe that made an arch demon look that freaked, and whatever I'd done, I knew in that moment, it had changed the way he saw me.

If I'd known it was gonna be this much trouble, I would've made a machine that vended wine.

"Listen to me very carefully," he said in a low, deliberate tone, taking a step toward me. "If you are lying, I will find out."

"I'm not lying, dude." My voice stuck in my throat and I took a step back. Damn, he was tall. "Seriously, what's the big deal? I just rearranged some furniture."

"And have you done this before? In your world?"

"What? No, of course not."

"Let me explain something to you. What you just did is called transdimensional manifestation, and it is just as difficult on this plane as it is on yours."

It took a second for his words to sink in and once they did, I was still having trouble understanding his reaction. "So I'm what, a prodigy?"

"That's one way of looking at it," he said tersely. "The other would be security threat."

I gulped. "I think I'd prefer prodigy."

He grabbed my hand and turned toward the door, dragging me behind him. "Come," he growled.

Like he was giving me a choice. I struggled to keep up with him as he strode down the hall. He threw out his free hand and a crackling blue portal of pure electricity appeared before us. When Apollyon didn't alter his course in the slightest, I realized he planned to go through that thing and put on the brakes.

"Hell, no!"

He turned to glare and snatched me up in his arms

before I could protest. The indignity aside, it made my head spin and I let out a less than majestic scream as he carried me through the portal.

When I opened my eyes, the portal was gone and we were in a giant room made of dark gray stone walls that were cut and angled like bismuth. If I looked too hard or thought too much about the impossible angles on the seemingly flat surface, my head ached, so I turned to face the black crystal chandelier hanging down from the center of the room.

"Where are we?" I asked, my arms still draped around Apollyon's neck for balance. "You know, if you wanted to whisk me off somewhere romantic, all you had to do was say."

He glared and dropped me from his arms. I landed on my feet by some miracle, but didn't stay that way for long trying to catch my balance. "Hey," I muttered.

The sound of rocks shifting and sliding drew my attention to the other side of the room, and I saw Shera enter through a passage that had opened up in the strange wall. As it slid shut, her gaze landed on me and I pulled myself to my feet.

"What is it, sir?" she asked, striding into the room.

"His ability. Did you know about it?" Apollyon demanded, his voice harsh with accusation.

"Ability?" She frowned, looking sharply at me. "I'm afraid I don't know what you're talking about, unless it's his ability to put away an entire cake meant to serve eight people in less than an hour."

"Now that's just hurtful," I muttered, folding my arms. "Would you guys stop looking at me like I'm some space criminal for just moving a few pieces of furniture?"

Shera looked back at the demon lord. "Sir?"

"He manifested," Apollyon answered, as if that explained everything. Then again, from the way her face drained of color and her eyes widened, maybe it explained more than I understood.

"That's impossible," she said, clearly flustered. "I've been watching him this whole time, and so has Maiz. He's never shown any indication of being anything other than a mediocre human. Substandard, even."

"Again. Ouch," I said. "I thought we had a connection?"

They both ignored me and continued freaking out over nothing.

"He did it right before my eyes," said Apollyon. "I'm certain it wasn't the first time. Who else has seen him?"

"No one!" Shera cried. "He's been under close observation, never without supervision."

"Ever?" I croaked. "Like, even in the bathroom?"

Shera shot me a silencing glare and continued, "He must be a plant. It's the only explanation."

"That was my first thought, given the circumstances under which he came here," Apollyon said, studying me thoughtfully. "But if he was sent here to rend the gates, surely he wouldn't reveal himself in such a foolish way."

"Rend the what now?" I asked. "If I'm being accused of something, I'd at least like to know what."

"Silence," Shera snarled, her voice echoing through the cavernous space. It made me feel cold inside, like someone had just sucked all the warmth out of my core.

She turned back to Apollyon, growing somber. "The angels must be involved somehow. We'll have no choice but to report this to the forces that govern Hell."

"I know," he muttered. "But until I figure out what he is and who sent him, this stays between us. And he stays here."

"Hey. Excuse me? Who or what governs Hell?" I demanded. Insisting that no one sent me anywhere probably wasn't going to help, since that's exactly what an angel spy *would* say.

"You don't want to know," he answered, his eyes stone cold as they met mine. And here I'd thought he was intimidating before. I realized in that moment that I'd been getting the kid gloves version of Apollyon up to that point. Now, all bets were off and he was every bit the demon I'd feared he was.

THIRTEEN

THE MOMENT APOLLYON left me in that fucky gray room, I knew I was in for some shit. Especially when Shera paused in the passageway and gave me a look closer to pity than a succubus seemed capable of.

I'd been in trouble plenty of times in my life. Hell, I'd lived in the principal's office before I dropped out and every single one of those times, I'd done something to deserve it. Kinda ridiculous how much shit I didn't get caught for, really, so after a few hours in whatever purgatory Apollyon had left me in, I was starting to doubt my own innocence.

And then a day passed. And then a week. And then I lost track of time altogether. Since he insisted I was some kind of reality-manipulating traitor, I started out trying to force that passage to open, but realized pretty quickly that my abilities, if they really existed at all, were null and void in this place.

Guess that was why he'd brought me there to begin with.

At one point, the idea of dying young had been my biggest fear and the fact that it was inevitable meant nothing else really held that much of a sting. Nothing except for losing Sirena, but now that I was practically immortal and separated from her for good, I realized that the prospect of living indefinitely in this not-quite-anything space was something else to be scared shitless of.

For a while, the fear was all I had. And then, it became anger. And then, by the time I was huddled in a corner trying to keep my consciousness from splitting apart, it became something I didn't even have the words to describe.

When the passage finally opened, I'd been having such fucked up hallucinations that I barely noticed. Whether it was a six-headed monster on wheels or the devil himself, I really didn't give a shit. What was the worst it could do, kill me?

Apollyon's voice was just about the last thing I expected, and I loathed myself for enjoying the sound of it. I managed to raise my head just enough to get a glimpse of him sweeping into the room, wearing that cape like a royal prick.

His expression was impassive and as he loomed over me, I felt like a lab rat being studied. He nudged me slightly with his foot and I wanted to tell him to go to wherever the fuck was worse than Hell, but my voice was hoarse.

How I hadn't starved or thirsted to death by then, I didn't know, but it was just another mystery of this horrible fucking room.

"I see you're still clinging to sanity," he mused. "Very impressive."

"Fuck you," I croaked. It took everything I had, but the look on his face was totally worth it. When you were nothing more than a bug to a god, the best you could hope for was getting some nasty shit on the bottom of his shoe.

"Had to make sure you were in the mood to talk," he

sneered, snapping his fingers. The next instant, I found myself upright and tied to a chair in the middle of the room underneath a hanging light that hadn't been there before. Kind of cliche, but effective.

My head spun from the shift in position, but the sight of Apollyon standing in front of me in tight black leather jeans, his chest bare under the cape, would've had that effect anyway. He'd left me to rot in there for enough time that my mind couldn't even process it and I still responded to the sight of him like a horny idiot.

"We're going to try this again," he said, leaning down to face me like the inferior being he clearly saw me as. "Who sent you?"

"I told you. No one."

He frowned. Clearly, that wasn't the answer he wanted. "I'll admit, you have more mettle than I anticipated."

"It's not mettle, asshole. I can't confess to something I didn't do." I hesitated. "On second thought, sure. The Space Otters made me do it. The conspiracy goes all the way up to the big river bed in the sky."

Apollyon's eyes narrowed. "I'd assume the isolation had an effect on your intelligibility, but it's hard to gauge the difference."

After an eternity of silence, all this talking was giving me a migraine. "Would you just kill me already and get it over with?"

He chuckled. "Kill you? Now why would I go and waste a perfectly good Architect? Especially one who's already bound to me."

"Then what the hell do you want from me?"

"The truth," he answered. "I had hoped to spare your vessel the damage more intense forms of interrogation can cause, but you've left me no choice."

"So you're gonna torture me." I laughed, letting my head drop back against the chair. "That's just great. Whatever. Can't be worse than being in this place for the last what... six years? A hundred?"

"Three hours," he answered matter-of-factly.

I lifted my head and it throbbed. "Come again?"

"You've been in here three hours." He smirked. "And we're just getting started."

FOURTEEN

"THREE HOURS?" I echoed, convinced he was fucking with me.

"This is called an observation room, but that is perhaps not the best description. More like... a place beyond time."

"In English?" I pleaded.

"I meant what I said," Apollyon answered smugly. "We are outside the reaches of time, and to your mortal mind, the state is torturous and impossible to estimate."

"So you think driving me insane is going to make me give you the answer you want? No need. I'll give it to you now," I jeered. "It'll be bullshit then, just like it is now."

Apollyon reached into his pocket and pulled out a small switchblade. The knife popped out, just close enough to prick the side of my neck and draw a drop of blood, but barely enough to feel. My breath caught in my throat as I stared at him, frozen for a moment before the shock wore off.

"So you'd really torture an omega? That's not very archdemony of you."

"*I'm* not going to touch you," he said, swiping his finger

across the small puncture. He drew his fingertip into his mouth and sucked the blood off. "I'll leave that for the professionals."

I had no fucking idea what he was talking about, until I realized we weren't alone. At first, he was just a silhouette, but by the time I turned to see him, Maiz's full image came into view.

His hands were empty, but his eyes were full of sorrow that had me far more on edge than Apollyon's threats. I squirmed instinctively as he came toward us, stopping a few feet away from the other demon.

"Sir," he said, bowing.

"You've spent more time around him than I have," Apollyon said, looking down at me with only the faintest hint of interest. "I'm sure you can put your unique talents to use. Make sure he talks, and do it before the next moonrise. We're on a schedule."

I tried to swallow and my throat made an "unk" sound as Maiz came to stand before me. He raised his right hand and pulled off his white glove finger by finger. "Understood, sir."

One look in Maiz's eyes was enough to tell me that pleading for mercy wasn't gonna help. As pleasant as he'd been up to that point, Apollyon had given him his marching orders and in this fucked up world, his word was law.

"Wait!" I cried, suddenly desperate for Apollyon to stay. "Please. I told you the truth, what do you want fr--"

"Don't struggle." Maiz's voice cut me off short and I heard the stone sliding into place behind Apollyon. My pleas didn't seem to mean any more to him than anything else I did. "It'll only make this more difficult."

"I didn't do anything," I insisted, even though deep down, I knew this plea wasn't going to be any more effective than the last. "I'm no one. I'm just some schmuck from Rhode Island, I don't even know how to change a tire, let alone do whatever you guys think I'm capable of doing."

"Please, sir. Just hold still," Maiz said, his voice full of pity as he reached for me. I didn't know what he was planning on doing with a bare hand, but the prospect was terrifying enough to make me scream. The moment his palm made contact with my forehead, a shrill, mechanical shriek proved I had reason. The deafening pain was over as soon as it had begun, and when I opened my eyes, Maiz was gone. I wasn't in the strange gray room anymore, and I wasn't tied up, either.

The familiarity of my surroundings at once filled me with relief and confusion. I staggered out of the kitchen chair pulled up to the scuffed thrift store table I'd blown off my homework at for so many years. The mismatched floral curtains and the cabinet I'd carved my initials into when I was seven confirmed that I was back in my childhood home. Eight-hundred square feet of shag carpet, stale beer stains and disappointment like the years hadn't touched it at all.

"What the fuck," I whispered, looking around. This had to be a trick. No way this was real. Especially since there wasn't a hole by the front door from the last time I'd slammed it before moving out.

"Levi?" my mother's voice traveled down the narrow hall and I saw her carrying in a couple brown bags loaded with groceries. "There you are," she huffed, looking down at the table. It had been empty a moment ago, but now there were plates and glasses and silverware.

Four sets of them.

"I see you haven't gotten any better at setting the table," she remarked, setting the groceries on the counter.

"Sorry, ma," I blurted out. Force of habit. I stood there,

frozen as I watched her move around, opening the cabinets and bustling around the kitchen.

As I watched her, the weirdest sense of déjà vu came back. So much of my childhood was a blur. One day was as much like the next, with the odd milestone or class trip to make it stand out. There was something familiar about this one, though, and as the dread grew in my stomach, I realized why.

"Your father is going to expect dinner on the table when he gets back," she remarked. I found myself silently mouthing the words. The ones she'd said that last night, the ones she'd said so many times before, but the way she'd said it that time stuck in my head and replayed over and over and over. "He's got a long day tomorrow."

"He's not coming back," I wanted to tell her. To warn her somehow, like it would make any difference. But I didn't. I just stood there in silence, staring and stuck to the floor, and watched as she prepared dinner that was going to end up in the trash because one of us was gone and the other three wouldn't feel like eating for a good long time.

The strange feeling that I was being observed finally dragged me away from the awful rerun playing out in front of me. From the memory of picking up small plastic vodka bottles while my mom laid passed out on the couch and Sirena's muffled sobs were punctuating the Dolly record on the turntable.

There he was. Maiz, just standing there like he had been back in the room.

No. This *was* the room. We'd never actually left.

That had to be what this was. "Making me relive my worst childhood memories? Really?" I asked. "That's your game plan?"

"This isn't the worst," he answered calmly, looking over

at my mother. "Curious that a night like this is on the outer perimeter of your subconscious. You must really be hiding some things below."

My heart sank deep into my chest as I realized what he was getting at. "So this is your talent? A stroll down memory lane?" I snorted. "Hate to break it to ya, but no matter what traumatic memories of summer camp you pull outta the back of my closet, *I already lived through 'em.*"

"This part isn't my talent," Maiz answered casually. "Suppressed fears and the worst case scenarios you torture yourself with are always more cutting than reality. It just needs a bit of augmenting."

Before I could ask what he meant, the kitchen door opened and my father came walking in. He was wearing the same tan overcoat and boots he always wore to the site, or at least, the times he was working. He was staggering like he was drunk, which was really nothing new, but the sheen of something metal in his right hand made me realize it wasn't empty.

My chest went cold like my heart was pumping out solid ice as I watched his face contort while he aimed the gun at my sleeping mother.

"No!" I screamed, my voice still hoarse from before. I tried to lunge at him, but I couldn't move. Sirena's screams echoed through the halls and I dropped to my knees, trying desperately to cover my ears as the nightmare twisted and morphed and replayed itself a thousand different ways, each one more horrible than the last.

Begging and pleading did nothing to make the torment end. Screaming only seemed to make it worse. Sometimes Maiz was there, and others, I was entirely lost to the illusion he'd created of my own fears mixed with my worst and wildest nightmares.

One scene faded into the next, making my time in that gray stone room seem pleasant. By the time my mind and body finally gave out--if either truly existed in that place--I'd lost track of what was real and what was his over-the-top artistic spin on my deepest fears.

FIFTEEN

"HAS HE BROKEN YET?"

Apollyon's voice came from somewhere in the distance, beyond the weird, veiny light I realized was streaming through my eyelids. I groaned and tried to open my eyes, but it felt like peeling a stone cover off a well. It took more energy than I had to give.

I still didn't know where the fuck I was, only that I'd spent the last however long it was weaving in and out of one toxic memory after another.

"I believe so, sir. I called you as soon as he began to wake from the stasis, but there's never been a human who remained lucid after that long under my trance. Not even an Architect."

"Good," Apollyon said, his voice coming toward me. I opened my eyes just in time to see him looming over me and the sight of him made my stomach churn. He'd been part of enough of Maiz's twisted hallucinations to make me despise the sight of him all the more.

He reached for me and I flinched, but he only made slight contact, sweeping his fingers across my forehead. His touch was gentle and the look in his eyes almost pitying. It was a side I'd never seen of him, far more grotesque now that I knew what he was capable of.

Or at least, the dirty work he was capable of having other people do for him.

"Pity the angels got to him first," he mused. "He was hardly what I expected in a lightbearer, but he was amusing."

I gritted my teeth, trying to rally my strength to tell him where he could shove his condescension, but my body felt like complex machinery I had no idea how to use. All I could do was shudder and seethe, sickened by his touch and powerless to push his hand away.

"The barriers should be dissolved now, sir," Maiz said, his voice a bit more somber than usual. If I didn't know how good he was at it, I'd think he actually felt bad about turning my mind into both the battleground and army set against me.

Apollyon pressed the sharp tips of his clawed fingers against my forehead and I felt a surge of red hot energy piercing my skull. I was too stiff to scream, but it didn't hurt so much as it burned. My back arched and a groan escaped me, but nothing else seemed to happen.

Apollyon yanked his hand back and stared at me in dismay. I knew there wasn't a chance he was afraid he'd hurt me when that could be his only goal to start with. He turned to Maiz, his eyes narrowed furiously. "His consciousness is intact!"

"That's impossible, sir." Maiz rushed over to us and stared down at me, his eyes wide with sympathy and confusion. "Levi?"

This time, I managed to jerk away enough to feel like I'd

regained some control over my body, however minor. It seemed to shock them both.

"He's awake," Maiz said in a disbelieving tone, unblinking as he stared at me. "That's impossible."

"Obviously, you fucked up," Apollyon accused.

"No," Maiz insisted. "No, I used every ounce of power when I realized he wasn't breaking easily. There's no way his mind could remain intact."

"And yet, it is," Apollyon hissed. "I can't even get in the threshold."

Threshold? Why was he talking about my mind like a fucking house?

Wait. Was he trying to possess me?

I started struggling and realized I was strapped down to the bed. Of course I was. I kept straining and another groan made its way out of my throat along with the stilted words, "Let me go, you fucks."

The only five words in the English language you *really* need.

"Fix this," Apollyon snarled. "Break him or you're banished."

"I can't, sir!" the other demon protested. "I mean it when I say I used *everything*. If I do any more, it won't break his sanity, it'll just kill him."

Apollyon was silent for a long moment, looking furiously between me and Maiz. I could see the wheels turning and when he leaned in, I saw my chance. I spat in the fucker's face and the look of shock and disgust was so incredibly worth it.

He plucked a handkerchief from the pocket of his jacket and wiped his face, acting as if nothing had happened. "So it would," he said stiffly. "Change of plans, then. Have him returned to my quarters."

"Sir?"

"I won't repeat myself," Apollyon said, opening the door to the room.

When Maiz came near me again, I sputtered, "Don't you fucking touch me."

"I'm not going to hurt you," he murmured. "The time for that is over."

"Is that s-supposed to make me feel better?" I asked, stuttering from the chill that seemed to run through the deepest parts of me.

"No," Maiz said quietly. "Believe me or not, but I am sorry it had to happen. Sorrier still that it didn't work."

"The hell is that supposed to mean?"

"Insanity is the end of suffering," he murmured. "I'm afraid yours has just begun."

"I'm not whatever he thinks I am," I said, my voice so raspy it was hard to understand myself. "No one sent me here. I'm telling the truth."

"I know," Maiz answered. "Unfortunately, your understanding of the truth does not align with reality."

"What?"

"You are an Architect, Levi. Do you know what that means?"

"If that's what all this is about, I could've saved you a lot of trouble. I can't do a stick drawing of a house, let alone blueprints."

"It's just a name for someone who's capable of creative manifestation," he said, like that clarified anything. I must've looked as oblivious as I was, because he added, "Demons aren't capable of creation. We can only destroy and manipulate, not create something from nothing. That is a power only possessed by the angelic."

"Listed, I've been called just about every name in the book, but that sure as hell ain't one of 'em."

"You may not have any memory of your angelic masters, but I assure you, you didn't get that gift from nowhere."

"Masters?" I echoed. "Are you all out of your minds?"

Maiz tilted his head as if I'd just said something incredibly strange. "You're coherent."

"What?"

"It's strange," he murmured. "You shouldn't be capable of holding a conversation at all, and yet, there's nothing particularly notable about your biological makeup. Average intelligence, relatively standard neural makeup, manic-depression aside."

"Excuse me?"

"And yet," he continued, ignoring me, "You're quite lucid."

"Guess it's a flippin' miracle, then."

"Do yourself a favor. Make this as easy as possible. Whatever Apollyon says, do it, and don't talk back. That never goes well."

"I can't do the impossible! I can't confess to working for some damn angel when I didn't even know they existed until a few days ago."

"Then make something up," said Maiz. "Tell him you're one of Raphael's servants and plea for his protection. His ego is ripe for exploitation."

I frowned. Was my torturer really trying to offer me advice on copping a plea deal? "Even if I could keep that kind of lie straight, how is admitting I work for the enemy gonna make him friendlier?"

"He is not without mercy," Maiz said, lifting me into his arms. "Appeal to it."

I jolted and gave a horrified cry of, "Put me down!"

Damn, he was strong.

And evil. And I fucking hated him. But still. Impressive.

In the blink of an eye, we were back in Apollyon's room and I felt even more nauseous as Maiz put me down gently on the bed, like he hadn't just turned my mind into a hellish kaleidoscope.

"You should rest," he said, cupping my cheek in his gloved hand. I shuddered. "Poor thing. You're going to need it. "

SIXTEEN

AS SOON AS Maiz left the room, I tried to get out of bed and swung my legs over the edge. Once I put any weight on my feet, I dropped like a sack of potatoes. I barely caught myself before smacking my face into the floor, but I still ended up on my stomach, landing hard enough to jostle my already aching head.

I tried to push myself up just as the door opened and Apollyon came in. Fresh dread washed over me, but before I could drag myself upright, he lifted me off the floor and placed me back in bed.

Back to square one.

"You shouldn't be up," he remarked.

I stared at him in dismay. Was he kidding?

"How are you feeling?" he asked, looking me over as he drew the blanket over me. I was sure it was just another mind game, but I was freezing, so joke's on him.

"H-how do you th-th-think?"

He snapped his fingers and the fireplace across the room roared to life, filling the room with warmth that immediately seeped into my bones.

He studied me dispassionately, reaching out to stroke a strand of hair away from my face. The fact that it felt longer made me fear that this time, the torture had lasted as long as it felt like it had.

"There's no need for it to be this way," he said in a soothing, inviting voice. "You've seen the cruelty I'm capable of, but I can be quite generous, too."

"Yeah. You were a real charmer before," I said hoarsely.

His lips curved on the one side. "I was under the impression that you were just another mortal in the wrong place at the wrong time. But you're not, are you? You're so much more than that."

"Yeah, an Architect," I said bitterly. "Shitty deal, if you ask me."

"Perhaps, the way you've been managed," he mused. "But in the right hands? You could be quite useful."

"I'm flattered, but I'll pass. Matter of fact, why don't you keep your hands as far away from me as possible?"

His expression fell, but he returned his claws to his lap. "However this angel has secured your loyalty, I assure you, he sees you as nothing more than a pawn. If you give me the name of your master, I can shield you. Nothing will harm you here."

"You already have," I reminded him. "What happened to being your lightbearer, huh? We made a deal."

"Under false pretenses," he answered. "You offered me something that was not yours to give."

"What the hell is that supposed to mean?"

"Your soul belongs to an angel," he answered, like it should be obvious. "And yet, you pledged your body to me."

"Thought you said being a lightbearer wasn't selling my soul," I reminded him. "Not that I have a damn idea what you're talking about."

He frowned in impatience. I remembered Maiz's advice, and it was probably the wiser path, but I didn't have the energy or the desire to lie. Definitely not to keep it up. I'd already forgotten the name of the angel he told me to reference.

"You can pretend all you like, or perhaps he really has suppressed the truth so deeply that even Maiz couldn't unearth it," he reasoned. "Either way, your soul is not your own if you're capable of creation."

"And you know that how?" I didn't even know *how* to sell your soul. For all I knew, there was a category on eBay, but this guy seemed to think I was some kind of supernatural savant, so whatever.

"Because Architects can only be souls who possess divine energy," he said slowly, like his patience was strained more with every word. "Since you are obviously not an angel, you must be a bondservant."

"A what?"

"A mortal whose soul has been dedicated to the divine."

"Uh. The only time I've ever even set foot in a church was because they had a sign advertising peach cobbler out front," I said flatly. "You're really barkin' up the wrong tree here."

"Then perhaps the deal was made without your knowledge," he said, clearly irritated.

"Bullshit. My dad left when I was a kid and the only saint my mom prays to is Jose Cuervo. Neither of them sold my soul to an angel."

"And yet, here you are."

"Here I am," I muttered. "And I can't do the impossible, no matter how much of a temper tantrum you throw, so here we stand. What are you gonna do with me?"

"For now? Nothing," he answered. "You're going to remain here. And we're going to get the bottom of where you come from," he said, cupping my cheek in his hand. "One way or another."

SEVENTEEN

APOLLYON'S IDEA of the royal treatment turned out to be having the same guy who'd tortured me bring three gourmet meals a day to me in bed. I refused to look at Maiz or eat any of the shit he brought me--at least until I got desperate, which ended up being halfway between lunch and dinner.

And really, if I starved, wouldn't Apollyon just end up winning?

He came in toward the evening after doing whatever the hell he did all day. Probably finding other souls to torment. "How are we feeling?" he asked in a genteel voice I knew was full of shit.

"'We' are feeling like we just got mind-fucked for the last six weeks and then binged on M&Ms while waiting for a psychopath," I quipped.

He pretended like he hadn't heard what I'd said, or maybe he really did tune me out. He glanced distastefully at the empty wrappers by the bed. "I told Maiz to make sure you were eating decently."

"Trust me, chocolate is the first decent experience I've had since I came here."

Apollyon sighed. "You're recovering well, all things considered. Then again, I'd expect that from an angel's pet."

"I'm no one's pet," I spat. "Certainly not yours."

"We'll see about that. You know, it's strange," he murmured, looking at me thoughtfully. "The angels usually keep their bondservants close and guarded."

"I told you, I'm not a bondservant. I've never even seen a fucking angel."

"And I believe you."

"You do?" I asked doubtfully.

"It's the only explanation, really. You wouldn't be this powerful if you were a low-level angel's property, and you wouldn't be on your own if you belonged to a higher-up," he mused.

"So that means what, exactly?"

"You're lost," he answered. "Or stolen. Either way, I'm quite convinced that after everything we put you through, if you were actively connected to an archangel, he would have saved you."

"Great," I said through gritted teeth. "So I have a deadbeat dad *and* a deadbeat guardian angel. That's great."

"If it's any consolation, you were certainly wanted," said Apollyon. His tone was almost gentle, but I knew better than to think his intentions matched.

"So what happened?"

"I don't know. But I intend to find out." There was something menacing in those words, even if his eyes were smiling at me. He cupped my face in his palm again, his claws scraping harmlessly over my skin to make me shiver. "And when I do, you'll be the perfect bait."

"Bait?"

"The only way to catch an archangel is to have something he wants enough to be willing to come down from heaven," Apollyon explained patiently.

"If that's your plan, you're gonna be waiting for a long time."

"What makes you say that?"

"No one's gonna come after me," I snort. "Not the least of all because I'm not what you think I am."

"We'll see," he said noncommittally. "In the meantime, if you're capable of getting out of bed, I'll take you on a stroll."

"How quaint. If it's all the same, I'd rather stay here."

He gave me a look. "You can be bitter and petulant if you like, but you're stuck here for the foreseeable future. It's your choice if you want to spend it sulking in here."

I glared at him, but I threw the covers back and got up. I *was* going crazy staying in this room and who knew? Maybe I'd spot a way out, or at least catch the eye of a slightly less prickish demon.

Of course, my damn legs gave out on me. I gritted my teeth in irritation when Apollyon extended a hand to help me up. "Fuck off," I muttered, grabbing the edge of the bed instead.

His hands closed around my waist, lifting me back onto my feet with little effort. I loathed the instinct to lean on him. "It'll take a while for you to fully recover," he informed me. "But getting your blood flowing will help."

"How long?" I muttered.

"I don't know. You're the only person to survive without losing his mind."

"Great," I said wryly.

Apollyon offered me his cane and I reluctantly took it. Better than leaning on him. "Aren't I a little underdressed?"

He touched my shoulder and when I looked down, I was wearing a black tank top and dark leather jeans. "No nipple windows this time?"

He smirked. "That was for when you were the lightbearer."

"And what does that make me now?"

"A guest," he answered after a second's consideration.

"Am I still an omega?"

"Until the identity of the one who owns your soul is clear, yes," he answered, opening the door. "Come."

I reluctantly followed him out into the hall, relieved it was empty. Not that the demons I usually ran into had anything on the personalized horror show I'd been treated to.

Each step was slow and painful, but Apollyon was unexpectedly patient at keeping pace with me and the cane did help. Not that I appreciated his company. "Where are we going?" I finally asked.

"I thought we'd take a walk in the garden. You seemed to like it before."

I trusted him even less now that he was playing nice, but I kept my mouth shut and followed him outside. I wasn't going to complain about the fresh air. The moment it hit my skin, I sighed. The strange glow in the sky was brighter than before and I could see the faint glimmer of a moon behind the clouds, peeking out every now and again.

Hell was surprisingly beautiful at times. Just a shame it was run by a total asshole.

"Here," Apollyon said, leading me over to a bench beside a small pond. The water was so black I couldn't even see below the surface and it reflected like a mirror. Something about staring into it made me uneasy, so I tried to limit the amount of time I spent looking at it. "You should rest for a moment."

"You think fussing over me is going to make me forget what you did?" I asked, moving over as far as I could when he sat down on the bench with me.

"You know, it's a rare gift you possess," he said, ignoring my question. Of course. "The ability to breathe reality into existence... wars have been fought for less."

"I'd happily trade it to wake up back in my apartment, if you're in the mood to cut any other deals."

He smirked. "I'm afraid it doesn't work like that. I'm an infernal being."

"Right. Poor baby. You can't create life, you can only destroy it. Must be hard being you."

"Does that work for you?"

"What?"

"Using sarcasm as a shield," he answered. "I'd imagine it keeps people from seeing how vulnerable you really are, but humans tend to have a low tolerance for that kind of thing. I'm guessing you have more one-night stands than lovers?"

I clenched my jaw, trying to swallow down the rage he was capable of producing so effortlessly. "And you're the picture of healthy relationships? You've got a subterranean kingdom and you still have to put an ad in the occult classifieds to find someone willing to fuck you."

He sneered, but I could tell I'd hit a nerve. Tit for tat and all that. "There it is. The human ability to deflect is truly remarkable."

"Speaking of fucking," I said, intent on making this conversation as uncomfortable for him as it was for me. "What are you gonna do now that Hell's on lockdown and your lightbearer turned out to be a dud?"

"Your being an Architect complicates things," he conceded. "But for the moment, I have other concerns."

"Such as?"

"At first, making sure that you weren't being used to gather intelligence."

"What makes you think I'm not?"

"Your general ineptitude, for one," he remarked. "That much would have been clear from Maiz's exploration of your consciousness."

"Exploration?" I laughed. "Is that what we're calling it now?"

"Call it whatever you like. I'm quite certain no one is coming for you, but that just means we'll have to get your master's attention."

"Good luck with that," I muttered. I knew I shouldn't ask, but the morbid curiosity was getting to me. "How, exactly?"

Apollyon smirked. "Summoning an angel is a bit more complicated than summoning a demon, but it is possible. As for how, leave that to me."

"And if it doesn't work? If he doesn't come for me?"

He studied me thoughtfully, for long enough that I knew I wasn't going to like the answer and started to wish I hadn't asked the question. "That, my dear Levi, remains to be seen."

EIGHTEEN

I'D NEVER FALLEN asleep next to the same person so many times, especially never having touched them. As much as I hated to admit it, the only time I managed to fall asleep was when Apollyon was next to me. My dreams were still nightmares, though, and I woke up in a cold sweat feeling the frigid hands of my father's corpse wrapped around my neck.

Fuck, I didn't even know for sure that he *was* dead, but the impressions Maiz had left in my mind were more solid than memory.

Before I could stand, a hand wrapped around my arm and I found myself staring into Apollyon's knowing eyes. "Calm down," he murmured, seeming newly awake himself. "It was just a dream."

"Fuck you," I spat, jerking away from him. "Just a dream your minion planted in my head."

"There's nothing he created that wasn't already in the recesses of your subconscious. He just pulled it out."

"That's supposed to make it better?"

"No, but if you want me to, all you have to do is ask."

I stared at him, wondering if he was up to his usual cryptic shit or if the lack of decent sleep was just getting to me. "Meaning what?"

"I'm a demon," he said flatly. "Wishful thinking is among my favorite tools. I can turn those nightmares into dreams far sweeter than reality could ever offer you."

"In exchange for what?"

He shrugged. "In exchange for not being disturbed by your tossing and turning every five minutes."

I thought about it for a moment before I shook my head and turned over, pulling the blanket over my shoulder. "No, thanks."

"Excuse me?"

"I said no, thanks."

"I'm perfectly aware of what you said. What reason could you possibly have for turning that offer down?"

"Plenty," I muttered, staring at the wall. "Go fuck yourself, for one."

"Suit yourself," he huffed, lying back down.

I closed my eyes and tried to get back to sleep, but just as I started to drift off again, something rolled me onto my back and I found myself staring up at Apollyon, his long hair falling down around me.

"I changed my mind," he said in a growling voice. "You're going to answer the question."

I rolled my eyes. "For one thing, I don't want you anywhere near my head."

"And another?"

"I'm not interested in living in your demonic fantasy world anymore than I was in Maiz's nightmares," I answered.

"Why?" he pressed.

"Because it's not real," I said, shoving him off.

"What difference does that make?"

"Plenty."

He narrowed his eyes and I could tell sleep was gonna be a lost cause. He wasn't letting this go. "There are humans who've quite literally been willing to trade their souls to take the gift I just offered you, and you turned it down without a second thought."

"Guess I'm just principled like that."

"You think nothing of polluting your mind with alcohol," he remarked. "Why should this be any different?"

"So what, you peeked in while Maiz was traipsing through my head and now you think you know me?"

"Sirena told me, when she came to me about saving your life," he clarified.

"Of course she did," I muttered. "Anything else? She tell you about my crush on Steve Buscemi? The time I got a fear boner in the phlebotomist's office?"

Apollyon rolled his eyes. "This isn't..." He squinted. "*Steve Buscemi?*"

"He's an unconventional beauty. If he was a vampire, everyone would think he was hot."

"I don't even know how to respond to that."

"That's because it's the truth." I hesitated. "What were we talking about, again?"

"I have no idea," he muttered, running a hand through his hair. It was just plain unfair that even in the dead of night, it fell that perfectly.

Such a prick.

"Oh, right. Your offer," I sighed, rolling back over. "Unless you wanna blow me, I'm not interested in your idea of making me feel better, so hard pass."

"Alright."

I looked over my shoulder. "What?"

"If that's what you want."

I blinked. "Are you fucking with me?"

Apollyon smirked, lying on his side with his cheek propped on his fist and just enough of his bare torso visible under the sheet to fuel my overactive imagination. "I could be."

Usually, the retorts to his bullshit came easily, but as I stared at him, my mind was blank. "No," I finally blurted out. "I fucking hate you."

"Suit yourself," he shrugged, turning over.

I stared at his back for a second, telling myself to just roll over, shut up and go to sleep, but I'd be a damn liar if I said I hadn't wondered on more than one occasion what it would be like to have those lips wrapped around my cock. The fact that he was actually offering should've been a red flag, but I was getting slightly desperate.

Just not *that* desperate. I flopped back onto my side and shut my eyes, determined to tune him out for the rest of the night.

NINETEEN

"YOU WANT ME TO DO WHAT?" Shera asked in disbelief, staring at me like Apollyon had just asked her to teach a cat to fetch.

"Train him," said Apollyon. "It's clear he's only capable of using his abilities by happenstance, so I want you to give him a crash course."

"You want me to teach an architect how to *use* his power?" she asked, her hands planted on her hips. "In *here*?"

"If I wanted to discuss the idea, I would have said so," he answered in a calm voice that held the edge of a threat, his hand wrapped around the cane I no longer needed. I was steady enough on my feet now, but my mind was another matter. Then again, they seemed impressed that I remembered my own name and wasn't drawing creepy shit on the walls, so who knew?

"Yes, sir," Shera said, lowering her head. She cast a sideways glance at me, full of irritation and confusion, but if she thought I was any more into this than she was, she was dead wrong.

"I have matters to attend to in the inner sanctum," Apollyon announced, looking down at me. "I expect you to behave."

"Sure thing, daddy."

He grimaced and disappeared, leaving me with Xena the Warrior Demon. "I don't suppose there's any change we could just blow this off and go get ice cream?"

Her face was hard and blank as she stared at me, hands still firmly planted on her hips. "What are you capable of?"

"Uh. Moving chairs, mostly?"

She rolled her eyes. "And lifeforms?"

"You mean...*creating* life?" I asked slowly. "Cuz no, I...can't do that."

"If you're an Architect, you're perfectly capable of it. You're just an idiot."

"Tell me how you really feel," I muttered.

"Alright," she said, clearly never having heard of sarcasm. "I feel like my talents as an arch demon and mage of the deadly vices is going utterly to waste babysitting a smart-mouthed brat like you, but I swore an oath to enforce Apollyon's will when I left the Guard and I intend to keep it. First things first, I need to see what you're actually capable of manifesting." She looked around the courtyard and seemed displeased. "I'll have to take you to the dust bowl."

"What the hell is the dust bowl?"

"Come," she ordered, snapping her fingers. Without waiting for me to respond, she poofed us both to a seemingly endless expanse of desert made up of rolling hills of slate gray sand.

"At least now I know how it got the name dust bowl," I coughed.

"Even you should be able to conjure up something

useful in a distraction-free space," Shera said, folding her arms. "Try not to make something I'm going to have to put out of its misery."

"You were serious? About the creating life thing?"

She heaved a sigh. "Start with something simple, then."

"Like what?"

"Use your imagination."

I cringed. She really didn't want to say that, but the look on her face didn't leave room for argument. "Okay, fine," I muttered, staring at the blank space before me. It had been easy enough to use my "powers" when I'd assumed it was just a magic room, but I couldn't quite remember how I'd done it now that I knew I was the one in charge.

"Well?" Shera demanded, tapping her foot. Not sure how it made that knocking sound on sand, but I knew better than to ask questions.

"I'm trying, but I've got creator's block."

"What the hell is that?"

"I can't do it!" I cried. "I don't work well under pressure. Just ask my nurse practitioner."

She raised an eyebrow. "You've done it before. It comes easily for all Architects, it's in your DNA."

"Well, my DNA isn't talking right now!"

"We'll make this easy," she said through clenched teeth. "Just imagine a table in front of you. Given how much you like to eat, it should be a memorable object."

"Ouch," I muttered. At least I had somewhere to start, though. I stared harder and tried to imagine a table in front of me, but nothing happened. Eventually, a hazy outline of something began to take shape, but my eyes were so strained, it was hard to tell if it was there or not.

"Do you see that?" I asked hopefully, glancing up at Shera.

"No!" She groaned, smacking her palm against her forehead as a mangled glob of plastic with three misshapen legs sticking out like a cursed tripod materialized between us.

I stared down at my Frankenstein's monster and blinked. "I mean, it sort of looks like a table, if you squint real hard."

"Try again," she growled, waving her hand. My creation dissipated in a mist of hazy black smoke. Guess that was the destruction magic at work.

Over the next two hours, Shera coached and occasionally berated me through the various stages of infernal table-making. Eventually, I made a replica passable enough for her and she announced that we were moving on to more "advanced subjects."

It was hard to tell if she was pleased, or if her expectations were simply so low that anything less than disastrous was progress. Story of my life, grades K-through-ten.

"You're ready now," said Shera.

"For what?"

"Create something living."

I gulped. "There's a big difference between IKEA and homo erectus." I snorted. "Sorry. That word always makes me giggle."

She rolled her eyes. It had been almost an hour since the last time, so we were making progress. "It's not that difficult. Not for an Architect."

"You seem to be forgetting, I didn't know I was an Architect until Apollyon was kind enough to point it out."

"Regardless. You've come a surprisingly long way in a short time. Granted, it's base level crafting that any idiot with a hint of natural talent should be able to do in his sleep," she said, waving her hand.

"You give compliments like my grandma."

"*However,* you possess the necessary skill," she said pointedly. "The only difference between creating an inanimate object and a life force is life energy, which you already possess by virtue of being a mortal."

"Alright," I muttered. "I'll give it a shot, but what am I supposed to make? And if you say use your imagination again, it's gonna be a space pony."

"What the fuck is a space pony?"

"A pony who lives in space. Obviously."

"Just make a fucking dog," she muttered.

I blinked. "When you say that, you mean a regular dog, or --"

"A dog," she growled.

"Right. Got it. Dog." I gulped, trying not to dwell too much on the ethics of poofing a magical dog into existence. "You know, I'm really more of a cat person."

"Just do it!"

"Okay! Geez," I muttered, looking down at the table in front of me. I tried to visualize a cute, fluffy pomeranian, but then I started thinking about those giant black-and-white great danes in music videos and worrying I'd create some big-headed monster with a tiny puffy body that couldn't support itself.

I could feel Shera's patience waning, so I held up my hands and insisted, "I got this. I'm just... finalizing the design."

"It's not rocket science, Levi."

"You're right, it's just creating life. Easy peasy," I muttered.

"Honestly, I don't know what Apollyon is thinking," she huffed. "You were an improbable enough lightbearer, but this is ridiculous."

"What's *that* supposed to mean?"

"It means that whoever bonded your soul, I find it far more likely that you were discarded than lost."

I winced. "You know, if I weren't a card-carrying feminist, I'd be real damn tempted to call you the B-word right now."

Shera raised an eyebrow. "Bitch?"

"Worse," I said, putting a hand over my heart. "*Bad friend.*"

She opened her mouth to say something, but then her face went blank and her eyes went jet black. "Holy shit," she breathed.

"What? Too far?" I turned to look over my shoulder and let out a cry I'm not afraid to admit sounded like a hamster being castrated. I fell back on my ass as a hellish beast emerged from the black sand, shaking sheaths of dark grain off its deathly white coat.

The beast was easily seven feet tall at the shoulder, and it had two sets of piercing red eyes on its lupine head. Its body was lean and aquiline, the plush white fur bare all around its face, which was nothing more than a ghastly skull set with ruby eyes. The sight of it filled me with dread, but the sinister growl that rumbled through its bony jaws made my stomach churn.

"Shera?" I croaked.

I could barely see her out of the corner of my eye, but the fact that she was just as frozen as I was, looking up at the beast in unblinking fixation, dashed my hopes that this was just part of the training session. "Yeah?" she asked, her voice strained with concern.

"Hypothetically, if I were to piss myself right now, what are the chances that would stay between us?"

"Slim," she muttered.

"Just wondering."

The beast's awful, glowing eyes met mine and when it let out a roar that smelled like the depths of Hades, I screamed.

"Fuck," Shera growled, drawing the whip at her side. It looked like it was made of gold and I have to admit, if we hadn't been seconds away from getting gobbled up by a giant Hell dog, I probably would've enjoyed the front-row seat to one of my fondest adolescent fantasies.

Not a bad way to go, though.

TWENTY

AS SHERA'S whip sailed through the air, I started to have hope that I wasn't going to end up as kibble. When the beast caught the metal tip in its jaws and ripped the weapon out of her hand, all that hope turned to nausea.

"Fuck," I muttered, leaping to my feet as the monster approached us. "What the hell is that thing?"

"You made it!" Shera cried, grabbing me by the arm. "Run!"

When a super-powerful demon lady with a whip tells you to run, you don't dawdle. You fucking run until you can't feel your feet. Except, no one really outruns a hellhound. That's kind of what they're known for.

Of course, I didn't know for sure it was a hellhound then, I only guessed it was based on what I'd seen on TV and in movies. For all I knew, it was a guy in a costume, but I wasn't taking chances if it had Shera quaking in her stilettos.

I heard its footfalls fast approaching behind us, gaining ground. Shera was a good deal faster than I was, and by the time she realized the gap that had formed between us and turned around, I could tell from the look on her face that it was too late.

The beast landed on me and I went face-first into the sand. My head spun as the heavy creature pressed me down, and I felt its bony snout burrowing in my hair, sniffling and snorting like it was sizing up the flavor of its meal before taking the first bite.

I'd like to say I went to face my certain doom with dignity, but all I really remember is screaming a lot. And flailing. It took me a few seconds to realize I wasn't being mauled so much as drooled on. And licked.

When I finally managed to open my eyes, a serpentine black tongue swept out and dragged all the way up my face, leaving the scent of death and ass in its wake.

"Fuck!" I cried, breathless as I stared up at the beast now sitting on my chest. It stared back at me, all four eyes glowing as it panted with its bone jaws hanging open wide.

I managed to turn enough to see Shera, who was just staring at the thing with a blank look on her face.

"A little help here?" I pleaded, trying in vain to get the beast off my chest. Other than it being increasingly difficult to breathe, it didn't seem to have any immediate plans of eating me.

"It's not hurting you," she remarked.

"Sure. Just stand there and give it the chance to change its mind."

"This isn't possible," she muttered, all distant and spacey. Glad someone had the luxury of shock.

"Well, the impossible is crushing my lungs!"

"Tell it to get off."

"Thanks. That's so helpful."

"I'm serious," said Shera. "You made him. Tell him what to do."

There was no fucking way I'd thought that thing into existence, but if I wasted time arguing, I'd probably pass out and I didn't exactly trust Shera to help. "Off," I choked.

The beast cocked its head in a decidedly canine way I probably would've found cute if I wasn't utterly fucking terrified. "Off!" I repeated.

It jumped back, whining and when it leaned in to lick my cheek, I realized Shera was right. It *was* listening.

"Holy shit," I breathed, staring up at the creature as it wagged its bony tail and watched me like it was waiting for further instruction. "It's a dog."

"Not what I had in mind," Shera said flatly. "But I suppose that counts as a successful completion to your lesson."

"I seriously made this thing?" I asked, taking the hand she offered to get me to my feet. The hellhound pushed its hard nose into my side, almost hard enough to knock me over. "What is it?"

"I can't say for sure because it's been a few million years since anyone has seen one, but I think it's a hellhound."

"Whoa," I murmured, looking it over with new appreciation. Sure, it looked like a hellhound--or what I'd imagined a hellhound would look like--but knowing it actually was one...

"How did I make something I've never even seen before?"

"That's for Apollyon to figure out. I've done enough for one day," Shera announced. I noticed she was keeping a safe distance from the hound as he pushed into my hands, snorting like he was looking for treats.

Hopefully actual treats, and not my fingers.

"What do I feed him?" I asked, digging my fingers into the plush white fur surrounding his skull like a mane.

"That won't be necessary," she said, holding out her hand. The same hazy black energy I'd seen her use to vanish my other monstrous creations.

"No!" I cried, throwing out my arms as I put myself between her and the hellhound. "You can't kill it!"

She frowned at me. I knew that look, because it was the same one my mom had worn every time a stray had followed me home from school. "You can't keep that thing. Hellhounds were hunted to extinction for a reason. They're a menace."

"She's not!" I protested.

"It's a she now?"

"It has a feminine spirit," I informed her. "And her name is Janis."

"Janus?" Shera wrinkled her nose. "Like the Roman god?"

"No, Janis as in the goddess of rock," I clarified.

Shera gave an exasperated sigh. "You know what? Apollyon can deal with this. I'm off the clock."

She started walking back toward what I assumed was the palace and I patted Janis' neck. "Come on, girl. I won't let the mean demon lady poof you away."

Janis nudged me and started trotting along behind me, her bone tail dragging along in the sand, leaving a heavy line to mark our trail.

If I ever found a way back to earth, explaining her to my landlord was gonna be hella fun. "Hey, Shera, you think emotional support hellhounds are a thing?"

She gave me a withering look over her shoulder. "You'd better hope *that* thing doesn't eat you in your sleep."

Before I could respond, a scream pierced my ears. We were within sight of the palace, and apparently, someone had spotted Janis already. "Hellhound!" a guttural voice cried, followed by the sounds of chaos and people running from buildings.

I cringed, patting Janis' bony head. "Don't take it personally. They'll love you when they get to know you."

She licked my face and it was a struggle not to gag. How something without an actual mouth had breath like that was beyond me. Next on the to-do list was manifesting some extra-strength breath mints.

TWENTY-ONE

"WHAT THE FUCK IS THAT THING?" Apollyon cried as Shera opened the door to his study and Janis strolled in like she owned the place. I trailed after her, trying in vain to hold her back and keep her from sniffing all the old books that looked like they were going to fall apart if you looked at them too hard.

"It's Levi's new pet," Shera said in a wry tone, watching in satisfaction as I followed my newborn monster around, trying to keep her from eating shit. She'd already gulped down a crystal ball I hoped Apollyon wouldn't notice missing. I had to wrap my arms around her surprisingly muscular neck to pull her away from a giant grimoire he had on a lit display.

Someone took "Sink your teeth into a good book" a bit too literally.

"Where would he find a hellhound?" Apollyon demanded. At least he sounded more indignant than terrified, like the demons who'd fled the palace.

"He didn't. He made one," Shera said matter-of-factly,

folding her arms. "I tried to get rid of it, but he named it Janis."

"Janis?" Apollyon grimaced, looking over at us both while I was trying to inconspicuously remove a fragile scroll from Janis' jaws.

"Give me that," he snapped. The scroll materialized in his hand, dripping with slobber but otherwise unharmed. Apollyon scowled and placed it back on its shelf. He waved his hand and a steel muzzle appeared over Janis' snout. She whimpered and scooted back, pawing at the contraption in a vain attempt to get it off.

"You can't do that!" I cried, throwing my arms around her to keep her from causing more destruction. "She's sensitive."

"She's an abomination," Apollyon growled. "How did you even get the blueprints for a hellhound?"

"Blueprints?"

"We're not really at that stage of his lessons yet," Shera said, rubbing her temple.

Apollyon looked between us in confusion. "I told you to start him off small."

"He has two modes. Hopeless incompetence and mad genius. There is no inbetween."

"Aww. You think I'm a genius?"

Shera glowered at me and I shut my mouth. I felt like I was watching my parents argue over whether I got to keep the dog I'd just brought home.

"This shouldn't even be possible," Apollyon muttered.

"Welcome to my life for the past hour," said Shera. She waved dismissively, turning around toward the door. "It's in your hands now."

Janis sniffed in her direction and she gave the beast a wide berth on her way out of the room.

"She's just jealous," I reassured Janis, stroking her fur.

"Do you have anything to say for yourself?" Apollyon asked once we were alone.

"Um. Can I keep her?" I asked hopefully.

He shook his head, but it was more of an, "I can't believe I'm cursed with your presence," headshake than a, "No," headshake.

"Do you even know what a hellhound is, Levi?"

"Sure. It's a hound from Hell."

He rolled his eyes. "It's a creature of divine origin, believe it or not. Sent to earth to devour the souls of the fallen."

"Whoa," I murmured, looking at Janis in a new light. "That's metal, girl."

She wagged her tail.

"Janis isn't like that, though," I insisted. "She's not a threat to anyone, she's chill."

"Chill?" Apollyon asked doubtfully.

"Yeah. She totally obeys me. Watch," I said, turning to face the hellhound. "Alright, Janis. Sit."

She cocked her head and stared at me for a moment before sitting back on her haunches. I was pretty sure it was an accident, but I showered her with praise anyway. "Good girl! And she's only like, an hour old," I reminded Apollyon. "I'll have her trained in no time."

"You're going to *train* a hellhound?"

"Sure." I shrugged. "How hard could it be?"

"I suppose it wouldn't be the worst thing to have around," he muttered.

"So I can keep her?"

Apollyon hesitated. "For now," he said in a noncommittal tone. "But the muzzle stays on."

"But it looks uncomfortable."

He gave me a silencing look and I sighed. "Sorry, girl."

She whimpered as if she understood and leaned into me.

"I see you've grown comfortable with your abilities in a short time."

"I wouldn't say comfortable," I shrugged. "Guess I'm just a natural."

He smirked. "In that case, you won't have any trouble with the task I've been working on."

"Huh?"

"Finding your master," he clarified, taking a step toward me. "You see, every bondservant possesses blueprints passed down from its master. The fact that you were able to conjure a hellhound confirms my theory that you were contracted by an archangel."

"Then why don't I remember?"

"That remains to be seen," said Apollyon. "It's possible the agreement happened before your birth."

"Before my birth?" I cried. "How can you sell a fetus' soul?"

"The ancient texts are filled with children promised to gods before their birth," he said casually. "It's not uncommon."

"What about free will?"

He sneered. "That only matters to our kind. Not theirs."

"Oh," I muttered. "So...if I help you find this angel, I could get my soul back?"

"It's possible," he mused. "But complicated."

"Do I wanna know why?"

The gleam in his eyes told me no. "The blueprint for his summoning stone."

"What's that, a stone used for summoning?"

"No, you twit, it's --" He hesitated. "Actually, yes. That's exactly what it is."

"Told you I was paying attention."

He sighed. "With some practice, you should be capable of conjuring the summoning stone."

"And then what?"

"Then, we'll summon an angel and find out where you come from," he purred. "Won't that be fun?"

I gulped. "What're you gonna do with her?"

"Her?"

"It's rude to assume the archangel who bought my soul is a dude."

"All archangels are men, Levi."

"Well, that's sexist."

He rolled his eyes. "Take it up with the Grand Architect. In the meantime, try not to let 'Janis' eat any of the servants."

"Why in the meantime?" I asked. "I'm kind of on a roll. We might as well give it a shot now."

"Since the gates closed, the energy needed to materialize a celestial object on these planes won't rise until the black sun."

"Right. The black sun. Pretend I'm a total noob who doesn't know what that is."

"It's a celestial event, similar to an eclipse," he replied. "It happens to take place in one month's time." He gave Janis a judgmental lookover. "Better spend it training."

TWENTY-TWO

A MONTH of training wasn't actually that bad with Janis to keep me company. Eventually, I was able to conjure whatever Shera asked of me in the comfort of the palace rather than having to go into near sensory deprivation.

The latest homework assignment she'd left me with overnight had taken just about all my energy, but it was admittedly a fun challenge. Creating a machine with moving parts when I didn't even know how to work a DVD player wasn't easy, and it had required reading more than I probably had in the last ten years combined, but the structure in front of me looked close enough to the machine sketched on the pages. Hopefully it passed inspection.

Still wasn't sure what the fuck it did, though. The instructions were in antiquated English and as far as I could tell from the spinning propellers on top, it was some kind of...thing.

Looked a bit like a fancy litter robot, really. Now that I was thinking of it...

The door opened and Shera came into the room, casting a wary glance at Janis, who was sleeping peacefully on the rug across the room, bathing in the light streaming through the windows.

"Hey," I called, turning to greet her. "So, it took all night, but I finally did it. I think."

She blinked at me, then at the machine. "What is that?"

"What do you mean? It's the thing you asked me to make."

"You weren't supposed to actually do it."

"The fuck do you mean I wasn't supposed to do it?" I cried. Janis lifted her head curiously. "I stayed up all night reading that stupid book you gave me!"

Shera covered her mouth and snorted a laugh. "I was just fucking with you, Levi. That book was made by an eccentric creator on his way out."

"So what the fuck is it supposed to do?"

She shrugged. "I'd be surprised if the guy who drew it even knew." She walked over, inspecting my handiwork and spun one of the propellers. It popped off and hit the floor with an uninspiring *tink*. "A for effort, though."

My shoulders sagged as what little was left of my will eroded. "I can't believe I wasted all that time..."

"You didn't," she said, ruffling my hair with what I could only assume was meant to be affection. Aggression, sure, but there was definitely affection in there. "It's good practice, making something complex with moving parts. Even if it doesn't actually do anything."

I groaned. "We're gonna have to work on making your sarcasm a little easier to detect."

She gave me a triumphant smile. "Black sun rises tonight. You should probably get some rest before it's go time."

"Is this gonna be another wild goose chase, too?"

"We'll see," she answered, pausing. "You know, there's a bet going on."

"About what?"

"Who your angel will turn out to be," she answered, folding her arms. "My money's on Haniel, but it's ten-to-one against Raph."

"Glad to know the topic of who owns my soul is so amusing."

She laughed.

I knew better than to ask, but I did it anyway. "If Apollyon manages to summon this angel, what's he gonna do?"

"Negotiate," she answered.

"Negotiate? For what?"

She shrugged. "Prisoners. Stolen artifacts. The war between heaven and Hell's been going on for a long time, and if the fish we reel in with you is big enough, we could negotiate an end to the siege."

"So the gates would open up?" I asked hopefully. "Would it be possible to go back to earth?"

"Theoretically," said Shera. "But Apollyon's not just gonna let you go."

"He doesn't want me as his lightbearer anymore."

"You're an Architect," she said wryly. "That's a golden feather in any demon's cap. Conjuring the stone is only the beginning." She patted my shoulder on her way out the door. "Get some sleep. You're gonna need it."

"Sure," I muttered, lingering on her words long after she'd left. I'd already made my peace with being Apollyon's plaything, but while I didn't have any strong allegiances to heaven or the angel who'd obviously forgotten me, the idea of pulling one down from the sky made me uneasy. Good thing my soul was already accounted for, because that seemed like the kind of thing that got you damned.

"C'mon, girl," I called, patting my hip for Janis to follow me back to the bedroom. It was empty, of course. Apollyon had made himself scarce lately, and I wasn't complaining. I curled up in bed and Janis happily took his spot, snuggling into my side.

She was cuddly for a hellhound. Then again, I'd never met another, so maybe it was just a trait of the breed. Either way, her company made it a little easier to live with the fact that I was probably never going to see earth again. Or anyone on it.

TWENTY-THREE

"LEVI. WAKE UP. IT'S TIME."

Maiz's voice was the last way I wanted to wake up from an otherwise peaceful sleep, but at least it wasn't Apollyon. "What time is it?" I muttered.

"The black sun is rising," he said, like that answered it.

I got up, running a hand through my hair. It was longer than I usually liked, but I doubted Hell had a barber. Not one I'd trust anywhere near me with a razor, anyway.

"Where's Apollyon?"

"He's waiting. They all are."

Well, that was ominous. I got out of bed and realized Maiz had already laid out my clothes for me.

Not my clothes, on second thought. A black robe and sandals. I looked up at him doubtfully. "This?"

"It's protocol for rituals," he explained, bowing to me. "I'll wait for you outside."

I looked over at Janis, who was still snuggling blissfully into the blankets. "You're a shitty watchdog, you know that?"

She yawned innocently and I started getting dressed,

feeling even more ridiculous in the black robes than I did in my pajamas. I finally left the room, and Janis loped along at my side.

Maiz was unusually quiet, even for him. He turned around and started walking down the hall. Guess that meant I was supposed to follow him.

We went down the winding corridor Apollyon had led me through once and I realized we were headed to the same chamber filled with hooded, shadowy figures.

My blood ran cold as I saw them standing there, arranged in a circle around Apollyon, who stood behind a tall chair as ornate as a throne. The last time I'd been there, I was sworn in as Apollyon's lightbearer, but this time, it felt like I was selling my soul.

Shera was there, standing off to the side and Maiz joined her. Even she was wearing a flowing golden gown for the occasion and she cast a disapproving glance at Janis as she slipped into the room beside me, her bony tail wrapped protectively around my side.

As much as I appreciated the show of support, I wasn't sure bringing her in front of the hooded weirdos was such a good idea, but I didn't trust her alone, either. She got a hungry look in her eyes every time she saw a demon, even with the muzzle. I was feeding her raw meat, but something told me that wasn't her ideal diet.

"Have a seat, Levi." Apollyon's voice was patient and gentle, so I knew something was up.

I took a deep breath and walked over to sit down, feeling a bit like I was a Christmas turkey being invited to the platter. "I feel a little awkward sitting while everyone else is standing," I said with a nervous laugh.

"The beast smells of death and brimstone," one of the hooded figures remarked.

Janis growled and I immediately jumped to her defense. "You don't smell so great either, hotshot."

Its hood lifted enough to reveal the head of an ox and my snark dried up in my throat. "Sir," I croaked.

Apollyon cleared his throat, placing his hand on the back of my chair. "You're just going to do what you did before, Levi. Look at the air in front of you and materialize the stone."

"But I don't even know what it looks like," I protested.

"You didn't know what a hellhound looked like, and you manifested one."

It was a decent point, but it did nothing to ease my nerves.

"Just focus and let the energy flow through you," he coached. "Your subconscious blueprint will do the rest."

"Okay," I muttered, doing as he said and trying to relax, since that generally seemed to help. "It's just kind of hard with everyone watching."

"They're here to create a binding circle," said Apollyon. "Just pretend like they're not here."

"Right," I sighed, resuming focus. I held out my hands and tried to imagine what a summoning stone would look like, in spite of Apollyon's reassurances that my subconscious mind would do all the work. Unlike before, nothing came into view.

I ventured a glance at Shera and the look on her face was a strange combination of sympathy and nervousness. I knew it well enough, because I'd seen it on Sirena's face plenty of times. "God, please don't embarrass me. But I know you can't help it."

The more in my head I got, the less it seemed to be working. Every sound in the large room echoed loudly. I just kept staring at my hands, feeling like a complete loser while a bunch of demons looked on waiting for me to fail.

Or worse.

I swallowed hard. "I'm not sure this is--"

Pain in my chest cut me off, and Shera rolled her eyes as I clutched my heart. To be fair, I had a slight tendency to be dramatic. Just slightly. So she probably thought I was fucking around to get out of it, and again... fair. But my chest was getting tighter by the second and it felt like my heart was turning to stone.

When I started coughing up blood, it began to feel like a literal possibility. I slid out of the chair, grasping the arm desperately. I could hardly breathe and my vision was growing blurry. Janis ran over to me, whimpering and nudging me. I tried to reassure her with a pet, but moving proved to be impossible.

"Levi!" Apollyon bellowed, reaching for me.

With a monstrous snarl, Janis snapped at him and would've taken off his hand if she hadn't been muzzled.

"Let me try," Shera said, kneeling down beside me. Janis growled, but she let her through. "Levi?" Shera called. Her voice sounded far away as she looked down at me. I realized she was shaking me by the shoulders from the way the world jostled, but I couldn't feel anything other than the pain in my chest.

"He's not responsive," she said, looking back at Apollyon. "What do we do?"

"First of all, get that thing out of my way," he growled.

Shera reluctantly stood and grabbed Janis' muzzle by the side strap, pulling her away with a great deal of effort. Apollyon knelt in front of me and for the first time, I saw something other than irritation in his eyes. He was supporting me, I realized, which was good, because I didn't know how much longer I'd be capable of it.

I tried to speak, to warn him that it felt like a rock had taken place of my heart, but he somehow seemed to identify the problem without me being able to get out more than a gasp. His hand rested over my chest, impossibly warm, and his clawed finger cut through the fabric of my shirt.

I choked and sputtered, trying to take a breath, but he pierced my skin with his claw and I felt nothing. Nothing but an icy-hot blast of energy pouring into my heart. It felt like he was inside my soul, not just my body, and my spine arched in his embrace like he'd just used the shocky paddles of life to bring me back from the brink.

(They're called something else, but I don't remember what. Is that going on the record, Chimneyel?)

[Defibrillators, Mr. Curtis. Just stick with your best recollection. And it's *Chemuel*.]

Right, sorry. So anyway, Chimney, I was totally convinced I was a goner and then Apollyon heart-fingers me out of the blue. His eyes flashed this weird white-green color, and at first, I thought it was a hallucination, but he gave me this, "Oh, shit, no way" look and breathed, "Lucifer."

And then they all gasped.

Okay, so a few of them gasped. One was more of a cough, but there was a general air of, "Oh, no, he didn't," in the room and the look on Shera's face would've been priceless, if I hadn't been in agonizing pain. Apollyon pulled his unnecessarily long finger out of my heart and I started coughing blood up all over his nice white pirate shirt. I swear, he's the only guy who can pull off a shirt like that. I just look like someone's uncle got lost in Epcot, y'know?

I looked down at my chest and realized the hole was

closing before my eyes, and then back at Apollyon, but he was still staring at me like he'd seen a ghost, even though his eyes were back to normal.

Normal for him, anyway.

"What the fuck?" I choked. My chest was still aching like a son of a bitch, but at least I could feel my heart beating. A little bit too well if the drumming in my skull was any indication.

"Did you just say Lucifer?" Shera asked, her voice strained with something I'd never heard in it before. Fear.

"Yes," Apollyon said listlessly, staring at me. Or maybe through me.

"Where's the stone?" one of the hooded figures hissed. His voice was far too serpentine for him to be anything close to human.

"It's inside of him," Apollyon answered, unblinking. Then, he uttered the three last words I ever thought I'd hear him say. "I was wrong."

TWENTY-FOUR

"WHAT DO you mean you were wrong?" Shera demanded.

"It wasn't an archangel," Apollyon answered, looking up at her. "Not anymore."

Her face went white with terror. "Are you sure?"

"I saw it when I touched his heart. The blueprint... there's only one being who possesses that kind of power."

"But he didn't conjure the stone," she protested.

"No," Apollyon muttered. "He *is* the stone." When he saw her blank expression, he clarified, "It's inside him. I stopped the transformation, but his heart was in the process of becoming the stone."

Her voice went raspy as she asked, "You mean --?"

"The philosopher's stone," he answered, lifting me into his arms. I groaned in pain at the sudden movement, but I was way too dizzy to risk trying to get down. Janis had gotten loose from Shera and she was whining and licking my hand through her muzzle as it dangled down at my side.

"I don't understand," said Shera. "That would've killed him."

"It wasn't supposed to happen while he was alive," Apollyon said, whisking me out of the room. Shera followed, but to my relief, the cloaked crew stayed behind.

"What?" I managed to choke out. "What do you mean it wasn't supposed to happen while I'm *alive?*"

"He's not just an Architect," Apollyon said without slowing his pace, his boots tapping loudly on the stone as he carried me down a dark hallway I'd never been down before. "He's a Vessel."

"Lucifer's?" Shera's voice was shrill with terror. "How did he end up here?"

"My assumption is that Levi was a sacrifice," he muttered. "Since he was until recently afflicted with a terminal condition, the transformation would have taken place naturally upon his death."

"Excuse me? Someone wanna tell me what the fuck a Vessel is since apparently I am one now?" I pleaded. It was getting hard to keep up.

"It's a human possessed by an angel," Shera answered. "Or a demon."

I swallowed hard. "And I'm Lucifer's new costume? *That's* my fucking destiny?"

"It would seem so," Apollyon answered, placing me down on a stone table in the center of a darkly lit room. I tried to sit up but he pushed me down, his hand on my aching chest. "Don't move," he ordered.

I ignored his command, but as soon as I started struggling, I realized vines wrapping around the table were stretching across me. "Fuck!" I cried, squirming and trying to get away. The vines just wrapped tighter around my arms and chest, making it harder to breathe the more I strained.

"Calm down," Apollyon growled. "I just saved your life."

"Says the guy tying me to a stone altar!"

"If I wanted to sacrifice you, I've had ample opportunity."

He had a point, but still. How was I supposed to relax?"

"How did you stop it?" Shera asked. I decided to shut up and let her ask the questions since Apollyon was far more willing to give her the answers.

"The transformation reversed as soon as I interrupted the energy flow," he answered, pacing like he hadn't quite figured out what to do yet.

"Do you think Lucifer knows?" Shera asked, lowering her voice.

He shook his head. "I don't know. The stone had only begun to form, but it might have been enough."

"Enough to what?" I chimed in. "What happens if Lucifer finds out about me?"

"He already knows about you," Apollyon snapped. "You're his Vessel. He's just been waiting for you to die. If he finds out you're *here* in a demon's custody, he'll be extremely eager to meet you."

"Really?"

"No!" he snapped. "He wants to wear your corpse like a well-tailored suit, you fool. What do you think is going to happen?"

"So you're saying he doesn't want to be friends?"

Shera and Apollyon both glared at me.

"If Lucifer finds out we were trying to summon him, he'll have our heads," Shera warned. "We should turn him over now. Say it was an accident."

"Hey!" I cried.

Apollyon studied me thoughtfully, but I couldn't be surprised he was actually hearing her out. What did come as a surprise was the fact that he seemed to be hesitating.

"No," he murmured, pushing the hair away from my face so he could look intently into my eyes. Not in a romantic way, more in a, "Wonder how these would look hanging from my lamp chain" way that made me shudder. "No, we can use this."

"To what?" Shera demanded. "Get our ring wiped off the surface of Hell?"

"If Lucifer is hiding the stone in plain sight, he's not going to want that advertised," Apollyon sneered. "That puts us all in jeopardy."

Shera's eyes widened. "Please, no. Please tell me you're not thinking about blackmailing the *Prince of Hell*."

"We've been waiting for a chance, centuries. A big move," he said in a conspiratorial whisper. "If this isn't it, what is?"

"We're talking about Levi!" she cried. "Guy can barely put his pants on without zipping up his dick and you want to use him as bait to blackmail *Lucifer*."

"Ouch," I muttered. "Still here, and that happened *one time*. You said you weren't gonna tell anyone!"

They both went back to ignoring me and talking about me like I wasn't the elephant chained to the stone table in the room.

"Not blackmail him," Apollyon said, stepping closer. "Usurp him."

Shera's eyes widened and she lowered her voice to a harsh whisper. "Have you lost your mind?"

"You said it yourself, he's getting old. Complacent," Apollyon insisted. "If someone with a united army were to strike first --"

"We don't have an army!" Shera cried. "Half of us were wiped out in the last ambush and in order to resurrect their souls and mount any attempt at a reasonable resistance against Lucifer, you'd need a lightbearer and right now, you're batting zip for two."

"Uh, I'm still willing to fulfill my contractual obligations if it means my heart not turning to stone and the devil trying on my body," I interjected. "Just putting it out there."

Apollyon glanced over at me and sighed. "Technically speaking, it is still possible."

"How?" asked Shera. "His soul belongs to Lucifer!"

"His soul was *promised* to Lucifer," Apollyon corrected. "If the agreement is remotely conventional, it was contingent upon Levi's physical death. If he becomes my lightbearer, he'll be immortal. The grounds of his contract would be shaky at best."

"Yeah. Shaky," I said excitedly. "Good train of thought we're going down, let's stay on it."

"He's not ready," Shera protested. "He's untrained."

"I can train," I argued. "I made Janis, didn't I? How much harder could a demon army be?"

"He is quite adaptable," Apollyon conceded. I think that's the closest to a compliment I'd ever received from him. "We have some time before the gates are weakened. Lucifer will be expecting us to be mounting a defense against Heaven, not a mutiny."

"For good reason. It's *insane*."

Apollyon sighed, putting a hand on her shoulder. I felt a twinge of jealousy, but for the life of me, I couldn't figure out which one of the two it was over. "It's now or never, Shera. You've been a faithful soldier, but I won't ask you to follow me into this. The decision is yours."

She grit her teeth, her nostrils flared as she held his gaze with a defiant one of her own. "I'm not abandoning my post," she snapped, looking over at me. "I can't believe the fate of this realm depends on an underachieving delivery driver."

"You think I'm *under*achieving?" I cooed. "Someone's softening up."

She rolled her eyes. "I suppose I'll get the training room ready, then."

"What's the training room?" I asked. The vines gradually loosened around me, allowing me to sit up and stretch my arms. "Simulated combat? Target practice? Ooh, is it like Battle Royale where everything's filmed?"

"It's like a sex dungeon mixed with a laboratory," Shera answered matter-of-factly.

I blinked. "What? What the hell is that for?"

"If a male demon fucked you right now, you'd die," she said flatly. "That's to say nothing of the energetic insemination process it takes to become a lightbearer."

I looked at Apollyon, desperate for any hint that she was joking. "Please tell me she's joking."

His face went blank. "I told you that mating was an...involved process. Having a change of heart?" he asked wryly.

"No," I said quickly. "No change of heart, just.." I sighed. "If this works, I get to keep my soul, right? And the guy who bought it goes down?"

"Among other things, yes," said Apollyon.

"Okay, fine," I muttered. "But you have to buy me dinner first. A *nice* dinner at one of those places where they don't put the prices on the menu. I want mystery price surf'n'turf out of this."

Apollyon rolled his eyes and turned back to Shera. "Yes, please do prepare the room, and make sure that I remain undisturbed for the next..." He hesitated, looking back at me. "Better make it all month. I don't have high hopes for this one."

TWENTY-FIVE

"YOU WERE SERIOUS ABOUT THAT?" Apollyon asked, staring at me in the incredulous manner to which I'd become so accustomed.

"Of course I was serious. You're talking about a twenty-four-seven fuckfest for the next month, co-starring me and your freaky demon dick," I informed him. "I don't think I'm out of line expecting at least a *little* foreplay in the romance department."

He sighed, raking a hand through his hair. "Technically, since I've been feeding you since you came here, I've bought you dinner on plenty of occasions."

"It doesn't count," I said, folding my arms. "And it had better be somewhere fancy, with napkins that aren't disposable."

"That's your definition of 'fancy?'" he scoffed.

"Surprise me, hotshot, but you're not gettin' any of this until I get dinner," I said, purposely doing the Vanna White gesture up and down my body.

He raised an eyebrow in confusion. "Any of what?"

"You know." I repeated the gesture. And he just kept staring blankly. "Oh, come on!"

He wore a ghost of a smile on his face, proving that he was just being a prick, as usual. "Fine. If you want dinner, we'll have dinner." He cast a judgmental glance over my outfit. "You've been provided with clothing. I suggest you choose something less...sad."

I looked down at the jeans and sweatshirt I'd worn on my way into Hell and frowned. "What? I've washed these."

"Be ready to go in an hour," he ordered before turning and walking down the hall.

I was just surprised he'd actually agreed to it, but there was no way I was gonna just jump into this lightbearer bullshit as complete strangers. Sure, I'd come damn close to letting him blow me the other night, but I didn't need to act as desperate as I was.

I found myself back in his bedroom, sorting through the clothes hanging in my side of the closet. In some ways, it already felt like we were a couple. Or maybe I was just his pet. The latter was probably closer to the truth, despite what I wanted to believe.

"May I help you, sir?"

I froze when I heard Maiz's voice and turned around to find him in the doorway, smiling faintly. I knew what had happened technically wasn't his fault. It was Apollyon's, but somehow, it was easier to get over that. Maybe because he'd never pretended like he was my friend or treated me with anything other than disdain.

"I think I can get dressed on my own, thanks."

"Forgive me, but I couldn't help but overhear your plans with Lord Apollyon."

"What about it?" I wasn't used to being a dick to people,

but most people hadn't literally tortured me, so. I felt like I had a little moral wiggle-room there.

"I just thought you might be interested in knowing his...preference for certain items of clothing over others."

I raised an eyebrow. "Go on..."

Maiz motioned for me to follow him down the hall and into another room. It was filled with heavy wooden furniture, some of it covered in white sheets. Maiz pulled the sheet off a huge armoire and opened the painted doors to reveal a host of items hanging up inside, most of them seemingly made of leather.

"What the hell is this, Apollyon's closet?"

"No," Maiz chuckled, sorting through the rack. "This is the storage room for his consorts' wardrobes."

"Consorts?" I echoed, sounding far too jealous for my liking. "He has...consorts?"

"Has, at varying points," Maiz corrected, giving me a knowing look. "He has not taken one for some time."

"Huh. Guess being evil doesn't leave much time for romance," I shrugged, trying to be a bit more nonchalant. Definitely not relieved. Why the hell should I have been relieved, anyway?

"He's always been partial to this one," Maiz murmured, holding an item up to my chest. When I looked down, I realized it was less of a shirt and more of a see-through black mesh top with a criss-cross leather back. The tight leather pants were ripped to shreds, but it was obviously a fashion choice, considering the chains hanging off it.

"Seriously?"

Maiz smirked. "It would certainly take him by surprise."

"Huh," I said, pretending to think it over even though my decision was already made. "Well, what the hell?"

"I can leave if you like, but you may find it easier to put this on with some help."

I grunted. "Whatever. You've seen worse."

His eyes met mine and I was surprised at the sympathy in them. "For what it's worth, I'm sorry about what happened. This may not mean anything to you, but I took no joy in your pain."

He said it so sincerely I actually believed he meant it. "Yeah, well...just following orders, I guess."

"That's not really an excuse," he sighed.

"Isn't he your god?"

"It's not like that," said Maiz. "Some demons rule their realms like despots, but not Apollyon. We serve him because he's honorable."

"Honorable?" I scoffed.

"It may appear differently from a human perspective, but I assure you, when it comes to the other gods and devils out there, you could have fallen into far worse hands."

"That's not exactly comforting."

He gave me a sympathetic smile and held out the half-leather shirt. I peeled mine over my head and slipped into the top easily enough. When it came to the pants, sticking my feet through the foot holes and not the strips torn in the calves and thighs was more of a challenge. I stumbled a little and Maiz caught me, to my embarrassment.

"Here," he said, helping to connect a chain from one shoulder to the opposite hip.

"He's really into this shit?" I asked doubtfully, looking down at all the metal. Maiz fastened a leather cuff to my wrist that connected to the collar around my neck and I felt like I was dressed for training school rather than dinner.

"Demons love shiny things," he said with a glimmer in his eyes. There was enough arousal present in his gaze to both unsettle and reassure me that this was actually going to work on Apollyon.

Not that I was even sure why I wanted him to want me in the first place. I knew what my therapist would say, but all her advice was geared toward helping me come to terms with my mortality and live a relatively normal life in the process. I was pretty sure the limits of her talents were breached when we went interdimensional.

"Comfortable?" Maiz asked.

"Not really, but I doubt that's a possibility in this."

He chuckled, reaching out to muss my hair up. "There. Perfect."

"I doubt that, too."

"You know, he may talk a big game, but deep down, he's still a man," said Maiz.

"As opposed to what, a bunch of possums in a trenchcoat?"

He laughed, shaking his head. "I see why he's so charmed by you."

"He's what now?"

"He doesn't show it, but I've known him long enough to tell." He tenderly brushed a strand of the hair he'd messed up behind my ear and stepped away. "Enjoy yourself, Levi. There are benefits to being a demon's chosen."

"Sure," I muttered, following him out of the room. "I'll believe it when I see it."

TWENTY-SIX

I'D BEEN WAITING in the room for a damn hour when someone knocked on the door. About time, but it wasn't like Apollyon to knock before coming into his own room. I walked over and opened it up to find a demon I didn't recognize on the other side of the door. I knew it was a demon because one, who else would it be in Hell and two, despite his relatively human appearance, he still had two pointy horns sticking up from either side of his head, like a deer's antlers.

"Levi Curtis," he said, bowing to me. "Apollyon is waiting. I'm to escort you to him."

"Escort me?" I frowned, realizing for the first time that the hall behind him wasn't the one I'd stepped out into so many times. I followed him through the door and looked around in dismay. The ceilings were lower, glowing with some kind of backlight behind the glass tiles, and there was pulsing music coming from further down the hall.

"What the fuck is this?"

"Interdimensional transportation," he answered casually.

"Interdimensional?" I croaked. "Where are we?"

"Hell's inner circle, known otherwise as Hades."

"Of course," I muttered. He started walking and I followed him to a room with a ceiling made of stars. There were darkly lit tables everywhere, sparsely populated with posh looking diners who seemed more interested in their drinks than the food in front of them.

Most of them were demons, but a few looked human, including one dark-haired woman in a flowing red gown. She glanced at me, her blue lips parting in a smirk. When her eyes met mine, they flashed a jarring white and I quickly looked away.

"This way," my demonic escort said, motioning for me to follow him up a set of floating stairs. It took a second to convince myself to take that first step and I gripped the railing, refusing to look down until I'd reached the top. Even then, I regretted it.

I wasn't surprised that Apollyon had reserved the biggest private room the restaurant had to offer, just surprised he'd done it on my account. Sure enough, when we came up the stairs and turned a corner, he was waiting at a table in a dark red suit, sipping a glass of something I hoped was wine. His hair fell perfectly over his dark horns, and he looked even more devilishly handsome than usual.

Guess it was fitting.

When his eyes met mine, his casual demeanor faded. The slip lasted for just a fraction of a moment as he looked me up and down, but it was enough to know Maiz hadn't led me astray on the outfit.

He definitely knew how to get on my goodside. Nothing I cherished more than fucking with Apollyon.

"Thank you, Ambrose," Apollyon said, dismissing the antlered demon.

Ambrose bowed and took his leave. For a moment, the only sounds were the muffled music coming from downstairs and the trickle of a black water fountain sitting against the frosted glass wall that separated our room from whatever lay beyond it.

"I see Maiz helped you get dressed," Apollyon said flatly, setting his glass down.

I walked over to sit in the booth across from him. "You don't approve?"

His only response was a snort. "Is this 'fancy' enough for your liking?"

"It's not Benihana, but it's close," I said, looking around. "Where are we? I thought we couldn't leave your realm."

"Technically, Hades is an annex," he answered. "It's within my control."

"Impressive. I take it our little minions will be getting into demon Harvard with all those connections."

He rolled his eyes. "You're taking this all a bit too literally."

"I have to find humor in it somehow."

"How does that coping strategy work for you?"

"Well," I said, helping myself to a glass of what was either wine or human blood. Guess I'd find out soon. "I'm a thirty-three-year-old whose closest relationship is with his cat, and my net worth is a stack of Maxim magazines and a linty button, so I'd say it's fair-to-middling at best. Then again, we're both sitting at the same table, so do with that what you will."

"Fair enough," he scoffed, pausing. "Maxim? Really?"

"It's classy."

"I doubt that."

"So what do you do to fill the void?" I asked, swirling my

glass around. It was definitely wine, to my relief. Probably the kind you were supposed to sniff and ponder deeply before you drank it, but I'd never been able to tell the difference between the shit in the bottle and the shit from a box. "I'd expect a big Prince of the Underworld to have a few harems at least."

"Duke," he corrected. "Lucifer is the Prince."

"Same difference."

Apollyon sighed. "Believe it or not, companionship is not high on my priority list."

"Right. Fighting an unholy war and all that."

"You disapprove?"

"Of the war?" I shrugged. "Not really. Just seems like a waste."

"How do you figure?"

"I mean, you guys have immortality and despite the reputation, the neighborhood's not bad," I remarked. "You'd think you'd find something better to do than the same old power struggles and bullshit up top, but I guess humans get it from somewhere."

"If you think that about hell, I have bad news about heaven."

"Not like I was going there anyway."

He chuckled. "You'd be surprised. Present occupation aside, you've lived what most angels would consider a moral life."

I blinked. "Sorry, have you met me?"

"I got the rundown from Maiz," he admitted. "All in all, you've lived a fairly selfless life. Especially considering the lot you were given."

"So is that why Lucifer snatched up my sparkly soul before I was born? I'm just too pure?"

He snorted. "No, but your guess as to why he chose you

is as good as mine. His whims have always been beyond my understanding."

"Why would he want to possess a human, anyway?"

"For the same reason I need a lightbearer," he answered. "Even he is limited in how long he can manifest a physical presence on the surface."

I grimaced. "So what, when I died, I was supposed to come back as a meat puppet?"

"More or less."

"And this Philosopher's Stone thing… is that gonna happen again?" I asked, rubbing my chest. I could still feel his claw sticking into it.

"If Lucifer gets his hands on you, yes."

I gulped. "And when we finally go up to the surface?"

"You will be protected," he answered. "Once the indwelling has taken effect, you will be mine. Irrevocably."

Those words should've pissed me off, or creeped me out. Anything other than filling me with an inexplicable warm, tingly feeling. I took another sip, realizing the drink in front of me had yet to do shit to take the edge off my nerves. "Because you can't be owned by an angel and a demon?"

"Because I don't like to share," he answered without missing a beat.

My heart did, though. I stared at him for a second before I caught myself and looked down at my glass. "You know, for such a nice place, this is some watered down shit."

"It's not alcohol," he answered.

I blinked. "Then what the hell is it?"

"Blood flavored with currant."

"Blood?" I choked. "You let me drink *human* blood?"

"Who said anything about it being human?" he asked, folding his hands.

"I'm glad you're so amused," I muttered.

"You'll have to get used to it when you're my lightbearer," he said, taking another sip. "The only way a mortal vessel can sustain that much demonic energy is a steady diet of blood."

"You could've mentioned that earlier."

"Would it have changed your mind?"

"No," I admitted.

"Then what's the point?"

I grunted, not willing to acknowledge he was right. I looked down and realized a plate was sitting in front of me that hadn't been there a second ago. "How did you--?"

His eyes glimmered in amusement. "You know, it should be old by now, but it's not."

"What?" I asked in confusion.

"Your perpetual amazement. It's like watching a kitten discover the world around it."

"One, fuck you. Two, it's less amazement than it is dismay."

"Either way. It's charming."

I blinked at him, wondering if he'd actually meant to give me a compliment, even if it was a patronizing one. He said it so casually, too, and acted like it was nothing.

"You did say you wanted romance," he remarked out of the blue. "I can't imagine discussing Lucifer is very conducive to that."

"Don't kinkshame me."

That actually got a chuckle out of him. "Go ahead, eat. And before you ask, no, it's not anything you'd object to. Not unless you're vegan."

"I'm whatever the opposite of vegan is," I admitted, taking a bite of what mercifully turned out to be steak. It wasn't bad, either. Definitely not the kind of cuisine I thought they'd serve in Hell. "So, what are you planning on doing with this army we're gonna raise? Mass destruction? Armageddon?"

"Averting it, actually." He must've seen the disbelief on my face, because he added, "I'm interested in preserving the status quo, not rebellion. That's Lucifer's game."

"And yours is what?"

"Mediocrity," he answered. "It's surprisingly underrated."

"The angels must love you."

"Hardly," he chuckled. "There are as many among their ranks pushing for the end as there are in Lucifer's army."

"What makes you different?"

"Do you really want to talk about that right now?" he asked, raising an eyebrow. Whenever he said anything in that tone, it made me second guess myself. "Surely there are more entertaining things we could be doing."

"Such as?" It was hard to sound cocky when all I could think about was that invitation I'd turned down not so long ago.

Somehow, his eyes literally smoldered. Like there was fire in them. Fuck, there probably was. "I could tell you," he purred, rapping his nails on the table, one by one. "But showing you would be so much more fun."

TWENTY-SEVEN

APOLLYON SLAMMED me up against the other side of that frosty glass wall and I saw just enough of the room hidden behind it to get a glimpse of a bed fit for a king and a tinted window overlooking a glimmering city below. Not that my focus was on the architecture at the moment.

"Is that a doomsday device in your pocket, or are you just happy to see me?" I asked as he pressed himself up against me, his claws digging into my arms.

"Shut up," he muttered, kissing me hard enough to make me lose my bearings. I was also pretty sure we were gonna break the wall, but fuck, it was worth it. For someone so salty, he tasted surprisingly sweet. I finally took the opportunity to dig my hands into those glorious waves and he did the same, tugging my head back to bare my throat.

I'd expected him to be rough, but not the hurricane of lust and fiery caresses that swept over me. When his teeth grazed my neck, I let out a moan I was sure they could hear downstairs, my legs parting as his thigh slipped between them. What he was doing to my neck alone was fucking mind-blowing and I found myself grinding against his thigh and groping at his shirt like a lovesick virgin.

"Fuck," I gasped as he grabbed my ass. He stopped sucking on my neck long enough to look up at me, his eyes flashing in challenge.

"Too much?"

I was too breathless to answer, so I pulled him back in for another kiss and pushed myself against him, like that was going to do anything but add to my frustration.

He chuckled under his breath and grabbed the front of my shirt, yanking me back just far enough to push me back onto the bed. I dropped easily, my head spinning as he came down on top of me and continued where we'd left off.

"Been a while, hasn't it?" he taunted, palming my stiff cock through the tight leather.

"Since I fucked a demon? Yeah."

"You're in for a treat," he purred, his lips brushing against the side of my neck. He leaned in and whispered in a sultry voice, "But I'm afraid you're not going to be doing the fucking."

I shivered with need. "Guess the outfit really does get you worked up, huh?"

He smirked, tearing the shirt open without hesitation. "I don't enjoy being caught off-guard."

"I'm sure I can find another one."

When he bent his head and started kissing down my chest, I lost the taste for smalltalk. Not that our banter wasn't adequate foreplay. I moaned as his tongue darted across my nipple. I'd never been all that sensitive there, but my body seemed to respond differently where he was concerned. Everything was heightened and I was too afraid to ask if it was a demon thing, in fear of realizing it was just my infatuation.

"So uh, how's this work exactly?" I asked once I realized he planned on going all the way downtown. "I'm guessing protection is counterproductive?"

Apollyon looked up, slightly irritated by the interruption. Then again, he existed in a state between contentment and annoyance at all times, so it was hard to tell. "I'm not impregnating you tonight. I told you, you'll need training for that."

I winced. "Could you *not* call it that?"

"I'm going to be filling you with energy that you will gestate to term. Impregnation is the term that fits best."

"Okay, but there's a reason we say 'sucking dick' and not 'repeatedly inserting cock into your mouth.'"

He rolled his eyes. "You're welcome to come up with an alternative term."

I thought about it for a second before deciding. "Enlightening."

"Enlightening?" He raised an eyebrow.

"You know. Lightbearer. *En*lightening."

"I fail to see how that's more appealing than impregnation."

"Just shut up and repeatedly insert my cock into your mouth, asshole."

He tugged my leathers down past my hips and gave me a withering look that seemed to have the opposite effect of what he'd intended. "Good to know you can't even keep your mouth shut during sex."

"I'm good at multitasking," I said, my voice petering out into a pathetic moan as he wrapped his mouth around my cock. "Fuck..."

Okay, so sucking dick turned out to be an insufficiently artful term for the things that man was capable of with his tongue.

His long, pointed black tongue. How the fuck had I not noticed that before? And judging from the hard, metal bud pressing against the underside of my crown as he sucked, it was pierced.

"What the fuck is with your tongue?" I gasped, breathless.

He looked up impatiently once more and it flicked past his full lips. "You like?"

I gulped. Like was an understatement. Was there a word for erotic horror? All I could think about was that thing snaking around my cock, and my fear that he could read minds gained new ground when he proceeded to give me a pointed demonstration of that very mental image.

"Son of a--" I choked back another moan, afraid his ego was going to swell through the roof if I let on just what the sight and sensation of his tongue winding around my cock was doing to me. He finally grew bored with taunting and deepthroated me again.

I had plans of outlasting my record, just to disprove whatever preconceived notions he had about the virility of a human lover, but by the time I came, shame was the last thing on my mind.

He raised his head, that pointed tongue gliding along his fingertips as he licked off the streams of cum on them and his eyes glowed with malevolence.

"Don't worry, pet," he said in a sinfully husky voice as he slithered up between my legs, his muscular body pressing down on mine like a letter's seal, marking every part of me as his own. "There's more where that came from."

"You said you're not fucking me tonight," I reminded him.

"You lack imagination," he purred. "Roll over."

I swallowed hard, both aroused and humiliated by the thought of what he was going to do at that angle. I rolled over anyway and when his tongue ran up my spine, I couldn't help but shiver again.

"Not a bad view," he mused, running his hands down my sides.

"Would you stop talking?" I mumbled, burying my face in a pillow.

"Prefer me to put my mouth to use elsewhere?" he taunted. Before I could come up with a suitable quip, I felt his claws scraping down the small of my back and moaned. Everything in my core tightened up at the sensation, just close enough to pain to drive me wild. I didn't know how he planned to "prepare" me, because there was no fucking way he was getting those claws up my ass. He spread me open easily enough, though, and while I'd never been wild about rimming, I decided maybe the technique was more the issue than the act itself.

"Fuck," I muttered, gripping the pillow a little tighter. My face was burning, but damn, that tongue...

By the time he'd worked the tip in, the awkwardness of having a demon eating me out had worn off into need. I was already hard again, and the deeper he pushed into me, the harder I became. Then he pressed into my spot and I didn't just see stars, I saw fucking galaxies.

"You lasted longer that time," he taunted as I collapsed, panting and still too high on pleasure for the shame to set in, even though I'd come again without him touching my dick. "Best of three, or does the human need a break?"

"I'd tell you to go to hell if we weren't already there," I growled into the pillow. "Just give me a minute."

"As you wish, pet," he said smugly, settling in beside me.

To my surprise, his hand came to rest gently on my back for no reason other than the contact. It was...nice.

"I'm not your pet," I grumbled. For the first time, I just wasn't sure I minded, but I wasn't going to let him get comfortable. Shoving his tongue up my ass was one thing, but emotional vulnerability was something I didn't do, no matter how irresistible the guy happened to be.

I rolled over, realizing he was still completely dressed. "Do I at least get to see what I'm gonna be working with?"

"Working with?" he chuckled.

"You've definitely surrounded your dick with an air of mystery." Not that those pants left all that much to the imagination. "Can't blame a guy for being curious."

"I think I'll make you wait just a bit longer," he said smugly. "But I'll give you a hint. It's barbed."

"Barbed?" I choked. "You're kidding, right?"

"You should get some rest, Levi," he said with a smile that made sleep the last thing on my mind. "You're going to need it."

TWENTY-EIGHT

WHEN I WOKE UP, Apollyon was gone, but I was getting used to it. What I wasn't used to was waking up in a bed I hadn't fallen asleep in. When exactly had he transported us back to his room in the palace?

Janis was still sleeping soundly in her bed across the room, so he must've been gone for a while. The moment my feet hit the floor, the door opened and Maiz walked in, carrying a tray of food.

"Ever heard of knocking?"

He gave me a knowing look. "I'm afraid you're going to have to let go of the idea of privacy from here on out."

"And why is that?"

"Because I've been assigned to prepare you for training."

I gulped. It was one thing to have Apollyon talk about it and another to be this close to finding out what the hell he meant. "And that involves what, exactly?"

"To begin with, I'm to make sure you have a decent meal. Don't want you passing out," he said, setting the tray down on the bed.

"Cuz that's not ominous," I muttered, taking a bite of toast. I'd say one thing for him, he was a decent cook.

"Would you prefer someone else?" he offered.

"No," I sighed. "You've already seen me at my worst. Might as well not humiliate myself in front of someone new."

He gave me a patient smile and stood aside, making it clear he intended to wait there until I was done. I still wasn't used to eating in front of someone, but I reminded myself that Maiz and all the other demons didn't see me as someone as much as Apollyon's pet. It wasn't exactly a comfort, but it helped to keep things in perspective.

Why Sirena had ever agreed to any of this was beyond me. She barely tolerated taking direction from people who were paid to give it.

I finished eating as quickly as I could and Maiz held out a robe. "What's that?" I asked warily.

"It's time for your bath."

"Seriously? I'm not a dog."

"Apollyon's orders."

"Right," I muttered, reluctantly slipping the robe on over the pajama pants I'd put on at some point in the night. I followed him into the bathroom adjacent to the bedroom, relieved that it was at least somewhat private. Until I realized he planned on following me in.

"Whoa. We part ways here. I think I can handle showering on my own."

"There is a grooming regimen," he said, picking up a basket by the clawfoot tub.

"Of course there is," I muttered.

"Most lightbearers find this to be a pleasurable experience," he said, taking a step closer. "Tending to your needs is my soul purpose for the next month. Anything you wish is my command."

I raised an eyebrow. "*Anything*, you say?"

"Within reason."

"And if I wanted to take a bubble bath while watching trash TV and sipping vodka?"

He chuckled. "I'm afraid alcohol is off the menu for the time being, but as for the rest..." He snapped his fingers and a flatscreen TV appeared mounted on the wall above the tub. The faucet turned on and started filling the tub with thick, foamy bubbles that smelled like vanilla.

"Anything else?" Maiz asked, clearly amused.

"No," I muttered, my face growing warm as he slipped the robe off my shoulders. His fingers danced down my torso and tugged on the waistband of my pajamas, but his expression remained as blank as ever.

"Shall I dim the lights, sir?" he asked in a sultry voice.

I swallowed the knot in my throat and tugged the pants off before he could get to it. "Nope. I'm good," I said stiffly, stepping into the tub. The water was the exact right temperature and as I relaxed underneath the bubbles, I had to admit, it was kind of nice. Definitely a far cry from my cramped shower back home.

The TV turned on and I wasn't sure if my favorite guilty pleasure just happened to be on or if Maiz had pulled that from my mind, too. I decided it was better not to ask and sank back, resting my head against the edge of the tub. To my surprise, there was a cocktail glass waiting for me on a tray right next to the bath.

"I thought you said I couldn't drink?"

"This is a non-alcoholic beverage," he assured me. "Part of the required regimen."

I studied the red-tinted mixture with unease. "Let me guess. Blood?"

"You won't taste it," he assured me.

"Doubt that," I grunted, reluctantly taking a sip. He was right. It didn't taste like blood, or at least not what I imagined blood would taste like. The fact that it tasted like crisp, sparkling cider probably should have been more unsettling than if it had been disgusting, but I decided to just chug it while I had the stomach.

"Very good," Maiz said, like he was praising a dog. He took the glass and it disappeared from his hand. Definitely the ultimate butler. Too bad you'd probably have to sell your soul to hire him.

"So, how often do you play watchman to Apollyon's pets?" I asked once I realized he had no intention of leaving me anytime soon.

"You're the first lightbearer, but I've tended to many of his omegas in the past."

"Let me guess. You warm them up for him?"

He chuckled. "I'm not permitted to touch his things. Certainly not you." The way his gaze flickered over my naked torso told me it wasn't for lack of want.

"Not a lot of action here in Hell, is there?"

"You'd be surprised," he remarked.

"Then why does everyone look at me like I'm a piece of meat in a butcher shop window?" I wasn't bad looking, but I sure as hell wasn't worthy of the cartoon eye popping stares I'd been receiving from demons from day one in this place.

"You're a rare breed," he admitted. "Demons prefer mortals to our own kind, and nearly all the souls here were damned."

"So what, relative morality is a kink for you guys?"

"Why do you think so many rituals call for virgins?" he asked wryly.

"Well, I'm sure as fuck not that."

"Humans take things so literally. A virgin soul is one that's untainted, not untouched physically."

"Progressive of you, I guess."

Maiz walked over and knelt beside the tub. He reached for something in that basket of his and when he pulled out a bottle of shimmering white liquid, I did a double-take. "The hell is that?"

"Just shampoo. Close your eyes," he warned, squirting a bit into his palm.

"There'd better not be any blood in that," I muttered as he worked the lather into my hair. "Or any other human byproduct, for that matter."

"Just herbs and soap," he promised. I had to admit, it did smell good. I usually just used body wash. His fingers were magic, too, and by the time he was done, I didn't have an ounce of tension left in my body.

"Damn, that feels good."

"I told you this would be a pleasurable experience."

Maiz finished rinsing my hair and as soon as I stepped out of the bathtub, he had the clean robe waiting for me.

"What now?" I asked.

"If you're ready, I'll take you downstairs to the training room."

"Already?"

"I'll give you a massage first, to help you relax and settle in," he assured me. "This is about making you as comfortable as possible. No one is going to rush you into anything you're not prepared for."

"Never imagined demons were so big on consent."

"We're all proponents of free will here," he said, taking my hand. "Come along."

"What about Janis?" I asked, glancing over at the lazy hellhound. She raised her head and yawned before placing it back down to keep sleeping.

"I'll assign a servant to keep an eye on her," he promised.

"Be good, girl," I said, patting her head before I followed Maiz out of the room. I felt uncomfortable wandering through the halls in a bathrobe, but no one gave me a second glance. Guess they'd all gotten used to the resident human.

Maiz led me downstairs and came to a stop in front of a door guarded by two giant demons, one with the head of a ram and the other who was covered in green scales from head to toe.

"Lightbearer," the green one said with a flicker of his serpentine tongue. He opened the door and they both bowed, stepping aside.

I wasn't sure how I felt about being so formally welcomed into a sex dungeon, but at least the place was classy. Looked more like the waiting room of a fancy office than anything.

"Apollyon will be taking care of you down here," Maiz said, walking to a room at the very end of the hallway. He opened the door to a large room with four red walls, lit with huge torches that reminded me of what I'd originally thought Hell would be like. The thick rug covering most of the stone floor gave it a more comfortable ambiance, but the metal furniture strategically positioned around the room left no room to doubt what this place really was.

One fixture in particular caught my attention. A massive bench upholstered in black leather set under a black wooden frame and the various chains and cuffs hanging off of it made it look like the sex toy equivalent of a multipurpose gym.

"What the fuck is that?"

Maiz gave me a knowing smile, putting a hand on my back as he walked me into the room. "That's not something you need to worry about now," he said, leading me over to a comparatively harmless looking massage table. "Take your robe off and get comfortable."

Easier said than done when I was expected to get buck naked in front of a demon I wasn't even going to fuck, but I laid down on the table, deciding face-down was the slightly less awkward position.

The lights lowered and I jolted as Maiz's hands settled on my shoulders, unnaturally warm. I realized it was the oil he'd coated his hands with as he began working it into my skin.

"You're very tense."

"Gee, I wonder why."

"I'm not surprised Apollyon wanted a month to prepare you," he mused, digging his palms into my shoulder blades. It hurt at first, but a moan soon escaped me as I began to relax. Fucker knew what he was doing. The oil smelled like cinnamon, and between it and the shampoo, I'd never been so fragrant in my life.

"Just keep your hands above the waist, bud."

"As you wish," he said, smoothing his palms down my biceps. As he rubbed, working out tension in places I didn't even know I had, I felt myself relaxing deeper than I ever had.

All the humiliating facets of being a lightbearer aside, this was something I could get used to.

The sound of the door opening and closing softly

reminded me that the real game was just beginning. Maiz took his hands off me and I heard someone else's footsteps come into the room.

"Lord Apollyon," Maiz said in a tone of respect. "He's ready for you."

"Thank you, Maiz. That will be all." There was something different about Apollyon's voice. It was huskier than usual. Commanding. Whatever it was made my spine tingle, but I told myself it was just the aftereffects of the massage.

I sat up to get a better look, but nothing could've prepared me for the sight in front of me. "Damn," I blurted out before I could stop myself.

Apollyon was standing there with his muscular torso fully exposed, save for the skintight black leather painted over his broad chest and arms, accentuating the muscle beneath. His shoulders were saddled with horned plates of armor that peeked through his dark, flowing hair and my gaze traveled down the sculpted path of his abdomen to the low slung leather pants that left even less to the imagination than usual.

Given the size of that bulge, he was working with an impossibly huge thirteen inches unerect. Suddenly, I wasn't so sure a massage was gonna cut it.

"Enjoying yourself?" he asked, wandering over to me with that infuriatingly casual gait.

"Sure. I've been getting the full spa treatment," I said, trying to sound confident despite the fact that I was staring down a living god in leather. "Gotta say, you've got a high bar to meet after that massage."

"I'm sure I can find a way to raise it," he said without missing a beat, trailing a clawed finger along my jaw.

I gulped audibly, falling into the trap of meeting his

eyes. "I have to admit, I'm a little disappointed that you're still wearing pants."

Apollyon leaned in, his smiling lips brushing against my cheek. "Patience, my pet. We're just getting started."

I shivered involuntarily. If just a single touch was capable of doing this to me, what the hell had I gotten myself into? Intimidating as the prospect of spending a month in training with Apollyon was, I was too curious to back out and, if I was being honest with myself, my heart was already too far gone to turn back.

TWENTY-NINE

"COME," Apollyon said, holding out his hand. I took it and let him help me off the table, but when I saw that he was leading me toward that massive bench, I put on the brakes.

"What is that thing?"

"It serves many purposes," he answered.

"And tonight?"

He smirked. "Primarily, an exam table."

"If you wanted to play doctor, all you had to do was ask."

"I need to ascertain that you're in condition to do this in the first place."

I snorted, covering my mouth a little too late.

"What?"

"*Assertain.*"

"What are you, a frat boy?"

"Aw, you think I went to college." I tapped his nose. "That's cute."

"Just get up on the bench."

"Fine," I muttered, doing my best to climb up without making a fool of myself. "Bossy much?"

When he pulled out two stirrup attachments from the edge of the bench, I gulped. "So the full workup, huh?"

"Would you prefer I had someone else do this?"

"No," I muttered. "I'd rather limit the number of people who've had close encounters with my asshole, thank you very much."

"Feet up."

"You know, this isn't very romantic. Kinky, but not romantic," I remarked as I followed his instructions.

"Last night was about romance. Tonight is about determining whether you're suitable to bear my energy," he said, draping a sheet over my lap.

I blinked. "The hell is that supposed to do?"

"It's to make you more comfortable."

"Seriously? I'm sitting spread eagle in front of you so you can size me up to be your hellspawn incubator and a towel over my dick is supposed to make me comfortable?"

"Would you prefer I remove it?"

"No," I muttered, dropping my head back on the table. "Only because it's soft. What is this, Egyptian cotton?"

"I'll have to ask for you," he said dryly, putting a hand on the outside of my thigh.

No, cock. Not now. Sit your ass down.

"Are you alright?" Apollyon asked, frowning.

"Fine," I croaked. "Just get on with it, yeah?"

His hand ran up the inside of my thigh and I resisted the urge to shiver. It was entirely unfair that he could play me like an instrument without even trying.

"Just relax," he said gently, cupping my balls in his palm. I tensed up because his claws were never far off, but his touch was tender enough that I had to stifle a moan in my throat.

"Good," he murmured, in response to what, I didn't

know. Maybe the fact that my dick was at full mast, but at least he was professional enough not to comment on it.

Was professional the right word if he planned to fuck me after the exam? Gentlemanly didn't seem to fit either.

"I'm just going to put a finger inside you now," he warned, pulling something off the shelf above the rack.

I grimaced. "I really don't need the play by play. Just do what you gotta do."

"Suit yourself," he said, pulling on a pair of stretchy black gloves and squirting something into his hand that I hoped was lubricant. When his fingers pressed between my cheeks and probed my entrance, the gel heated up everywhere that it touched and this time, I wasn't successful at holding back a moan.

"You know, you're free to enjoy yourself," he said in a knowing tone. "Just because I need to do this for your safety doesn't mean you can't find it pleasurable."

"I'll keep that in mind. Won't your claws fuck things up?"

"The gloves are durable," he answered. He added more of the lubricant to his fingertips and began to work one in. The thick but flexible material of the glove did enough to dull the sharpness while still keeping me on edge and my spine went stiff as I tried not to breathe too much.

"You're doing good," he coached. "Just a bit further."

"Fuck," I cried, my spine arching despite my best efforts to hold still. He'd barely grazed my spot, but it only took a drop of that lube to drive me wild.

"Good boy," he chuckled, pressing in gently. I was already hard, but my dick felt like a searing rod underneath the sheet, hot and tense with need. "My, you're tight."

I took a deep breath, trying to see through the stars as he

slowly pulled his finger out and left me writhing. I didn't even care about the stirrups anymore, or the fact that I was spread open for him as he moved casually around the room, gathering more tools on the tray in front of him. I didn't even care what came next, as long as it came with more of him inside of me.

Apollyon picked up what looked like a black silicone finger crooked invitingly and I could guess from that sharp angle what it was meant for. It didn't look half as intimidating as some of the stuff I'd used in the past, but then I saw the pump handle hanging off it from a tube.

"What's that?"

"It's inflatable," he explained. "In order for the insemination to be effective, you'll have to take my knot and that's going to require some extensive preparation. First, I need to know what your natural limits are."

"Oh," I said, realizing my mouth was dry. "So that uh, inflates inside of me?"

"That's the idea. May I continue?"

I nodded and laid back down, trying not to think about the aching spot inside of me that had me desperate enough to actually be looking forward to the experimentation. Apollyon was surprisingly gentle as he worked the thoroughly lubricated probe inside of me. Once it was locked in at the flared base, I felt the curved nub pressing against my prostate and arched my back again.

"Fuck," I breathed. "That feels good."

"Try to hold still," he said, pressing down on my hips as he took the pump in his palm and gave it a firm squeeze. At first, the difference wasn't really enough to feel, but as it inflated gradually, the pressure on my spot became maddening.

"Oh, fuck," I moaned, writhing as my heels dug into the

stirrups. The sheet slipped off, leaving my stiff cock bare to the world.

"You like that, hm?" His eyes were dark with curiosity as he watched me squirm under the effects of his experimentation. It made what should've been humiliating all the more arousing and if I wasn't so breathless, I probably would've begged him to touch me.

Yeah, I wanted to actually get to the deed itself, but if he was to be believed, I was nowhere near ready to take his cock and there was no way I was gonna hold out that long, anyway.

"You're eager today," he chuckled, releasing his hold on the pump. It dropped and the slight weight of it tugging on the firmly stuck plug inside of me was even more maddening.

Apollyon pulled something else off his tray and I groaned when I saw that it was a thick black cockring. "Can't have you come just yet, or we'll have to do it all over again."

Was that supposed to be a threat? If so, he really underestimated my willingness to "suffer" for the sake of science.

I whimpered in need as his fingers brushed against my cock and he slipped the tight silicone ring all the way down to the base. When he stretched it over my balls, my hips surged off the padded bench and I clenched my teeth together so hard they shook.

"There," he purred, giving my balls an apologetic roll in his palm that made even more heat surge into my core. "I'll make it worth the wait."

The tone of his voice would've probably pushed me over the edge if it wasn't for that ring, but what was I supposed to say to that?

"Think you can take more?"

It took me a second to realize what he was asking. "Y--yeah," I said, breathless. If the only stimulation I was getting was from him pumping that damn thing inside of me, I could take it as far as it went.

At least, I had every intention of doing so until it started to hurt like a motherfucker. "Ow, fuck," I finally gasped. "There, that's my limit."

He stopped pumping immediately and stepped back. "Is it tolerable like that?"

"Yeah," I winced. "Man..."

"Just need to take a measurement," he told me, picking up what looked like a pair of bladeless scissors. The device clicked as he cranked it open and I tensed up, feeling the cold metal touch the sensitive skin around my stretched hole. "Eight-and-a-half inches around," he announced. "I've certainly got my work cut out for me."

"I don't know whether I should be offended or flattered."

His eyes glimmered in amusement. "Do you find that tolerable, pet?"

"Yeah... why?"

"Because I'll need you to hold it in for at least an hour."

"An hour?" I echoed.

"Ideally. As long as you can, in any case. That's more than enough for our first session."

"You weren't fucking kidding about training, were you?"

"Not at all," he said, stroking my thigh. "But I think I know a way to pass the time that you'll find enjoyable."

I swallowed hard. I bet he did.

When he bent his head, my cock twitched in anticipation. He was as gentle and skillful as the night before, and trying to hold back my moans for the sake of dignity proved just as futile as it had then.

As his head bobbed between my wide spread legs, I dug my hand into his hair and he did nothing to stop me. Guess not having a gag reflex was another benefit of being a demon.

"Y'know, if you ever get tired of this demon lord gig, you could make a mint doing this," I said breathlessly.

His only response was to suck harder, then wrap his silken tongue around my crown again. The pointed tip danced on the edge of my slit and teased its way in. Guess he'd noticed that had been my favorite the night before.

My hips bucked and I was powerless to stop them as he kept sucking, bringing me closer and closer to a threshold that damn ring wouldn't let me cross. When he finally released my tortured cock, the look he was giving me could've melted diamond. "Would you like me to remove the ring?"

"God, yes," I breathed.

He did it so gently it had to be to fuck with me, but once my cock was free, he sealed it in his grip and I shuddered from head to toe. The toy was still filling me, stretching me open wider than I'd thought possible, and it was all I could do to think straight. When Apollyon started stroking me, I bucked into his hand with shameless desperation.

It didn't even matter if I was an experiment. A prop. A plaything. As long as he kept playing with me, as long as he kept pushing the right buttons, as long as he didn't fucking stop.

I came in his hand with a moan and cum splashed onto my chest and stomach, but that inflated toy still pressing against my prostate left no room for relief.

"Damn it," I growled through my teeth. "Has it been an hour yet?"

"Not quite, but good enough for your first time," he said, giving my thigh another stroke. "Just relax and I'll take it out."

He turned a dial and the fake knot began to slowly go down inside of me. It never returned to its original state, and when Apollyon positioned his fingers on either side of the toy, I realized pulling it out wasn't going to be an easy affair.

"Brace yourself," he warned me.

I took a deep breath that faltered when his fingers spread me open even wider, but it only lasted a moment before he managed to pull the toy out. I groaned as my aching hole tried to return to normal, but Apollon's fingers reappeared at my entrance, massaging gently.

"There," he said in a surprisingly pleasant tone. "You did good today."

"That's it?" I asked doubtfully. "I thought I was finally gonna get to see your dick."

He chuckled. "You're really that curious, are you?"

"Uh, duh. And at this point, if it doesn't have a vibrate function and light up, I'm gonna be pretty disappointed."

"I'm afraid my cock doesn't vibrate, but my tail does."

"Tail?" I echoed. "You have a tail?"

It was always hard to tell if he was joking. When something pushed aside his cloak without him moving his hand, I yelped. Turned out, yeah, he had a tail. A snaky red thing with a sharp, textured tip on the end. And judging from the fact that it playfully flicked across my thigh, it had a mind of its own.

"Fuck."

"Prehensile," he said knowingly. When the thing started vibrating against me, sending shivers up my leg, I realized he wasn't kidding about that, either. "That enough of a show for one night?"

"Yeah," I choked.

And it was enough to fuel for my imagination for a damn eternity, too.

THIRTY

FOR THE FIRST time since I'd been released from Maiz's prison, Apollyon didn't take me back to his bed. Instead, he revealed a separate bedroom attached to the training room. It wasn't quite as large, but it was comfortable and far more lavish.

"Guess I'm getting the royal treatment, huh?" I asked, sitting back on the mattress. I winced because my ass was still sore as hell from all that stretching, but hopefully he didn't notice.

"You'll be staying here for the duration of our training," he explained. "Can I get you anything?"

"You're not coming to bed?"

"I have some matters to attend to upstairs," he answered. "The realm doesn't run itself."

"Sure," I sighed. "When will I see you again?"

"In the morning." He patted my head like I was a damn dog. "Get some rest."

I flipped him off while his back was turned and sank back into the plush pillows, unable to keep the smile off my face. This whole experience was nothing like I'd expected, but I decided it wasn't a bad thing.

Not by a long shot.

When I finally fell asleep, I slept without dreaming. Probably something to do with being in Hell's basement, I'd guess.

I woke up in what I assumed was the morning feeling...not bad, actually. I smelled food coming from somewhere in the basement lair and crept down a hallway I had been too tired to explore the night before.

When I found Apollyon at a fancy ass stove, holding a frying pan, I was sure I was still dreaming. "Please tell me that's not eggs in a basket."

He turned around, frowning in confusion. "What? It's bacon."

"Nothing, just a movie," I sighed. "You're making me breakfast now?"

He smirked. "I have to take care of my pet. You're on a strict diet."

"What kind of strict diet involves bacon?"

He snorted. "Have a seat. And before you say anything about the spiky purple fruit in front of you, no, it's not a sex toy and yes, you have to eat all of it."

I stared down at the oblong gourd that looked like some kind of fetish mace and pursed my lips tightly to resist the temptation to prove him right. "What's it called?" I asked once I finally trusted myself not to crack up.

He gave me a skeptical look. "I'm not sure I should tell you."

"Please." My voice was strained, trying to hold back the laughter. "Tell me."

He sighed, turning off the stove and dropping the eggs onto my plate. "Bonga Melon."

I laughed so hard I almost tore something. When I finally collected myself, Apollyon was glowering at me. "Come on. Even you have to admit, that sounds ridiculous. Everything here is ridiculous."

"That's hardly the case," he said, clearly offended as he sat across from me. There was no plate in front of him, so I guess he'd already eaten. That or he didn't need to, but the thought creeped me out for some reason, so I tried not to dwell on it too much.

"I just saw a guy with the head of a chameleon. You're telling me this place isn't absurd?"

"You live in a city whose most prominent landmark is a giant blue bug."

"You don't get to talk shit about him, you're not a Rhody."

He rolled his eyes. "Just eat."

It wasn't something anyone usually had to tell me, but I was surprised by how decent the food was. Then again, it was just eggs and some weird ass fruit. "What's this supposed to do, anyway? Aphrodisiac?"

"No, it's supposed to make you bleed less."

I choked on the pineapple-y chunk of Bonga Melon halfway down my throat. "What?"

"I warned you the actual mating act was dangerous."

"Yeah, but how much blood are we talking here?"

"Well, the head of my cock is bladed when fully erect, and it has to penetrate your abdominal wall in order for the insemination to take effect."

I was starting to feel dizzy and not just because my morning coffee was extra strong. "Bladed and knotted? Anything else you wanna tell me? Does it spin and light up, too?"

"Not usually." His flat affect had me going for a minute, but the gleam in his eyes was a dead giveaway.

"Glad this is so amusing to you."

"I thought you were a bit cavalier about volunteering," he remarked. "Has it finally sunk in?"

"It's starting to," I grumbled.

"Not too late to change your mind."

"I'm not gonna pussy out, sorry to disappoint you."

"Oh, I'm not disappointed," he said, propping his chin on his fist as he watched me. There was something about the amusement in his gaze that felt more intimate than anything we'd done in that room. "Quite the opposite."

For once, I didn't have a comeback, so I just took another sip of my coffee. "Think I'm developing a tolerance," I muttered. "This shit isn't working."

"Oh, it's not caffeinated," he informed me.

"Excuse me?"

"You're not allowed to have caffeine. Part of protocol."

"So your protocol is fine with you stabbing me with your knife cock, but caffeine is off the table?"

"It's for your benefit," he assured me, smirking.

"So when are we getting started?"

"That won't be for a while yet. You're nowhere near ready."

"If it's gonna hurt anyway, why does it matter if I'm ready'?"

He shrugged. "I don't want to hurt you."

I blinked. "That's...sweet."

"I'm a demon, not a devil," he said flatly. "Believe it or not, torturing you was not an easy matter."

"That's a surprise, considering you're not even the one who got your hands dirty."

"I thought you were sent here," he admitted. "I'm still not convinced you weren't."

"So what changed?"

"I've at least come to accept that you're entirely ignorant about your true purpose."

"Gee, thanks."

"No offense, but there's no way you've ever come face to face with Lucifer."

"How do you know?"

"Because you're not utterly mad, for one thing. He has that effect on humans."

I shuddered. "Looking forward to meeting him."

"With any luck, you never will."

I took another sip of lies, AKA decaf coffee, and sighed. "Here's hopin'."

THIRTY-ONE

"ARE YOU SURE YOU'RE READY?" Apollyon asked, looking down at me as we both stood in front of the door leading into the training room.

"How many times you gonna ask me that?" I challenged. Sure, I was nervous as hell and had been ever since he'd told me tonight was the night. We'd been training for the last three weeks, and while I'd sampled just about every flavor of erotic delight the demon had to offer, we'd yet to actually do the deed.

"As long as you're certain," he said, stepping back for me to walk into the room. The configuration that greeted me was a bit different from what I was used to. For one thing, there was a bed in the center of the room rather than the cold exam table that had served as the location of most sessions.

"What's this?"

"I didn't want our first time to be so... clinical."

"Surprisingly thoughtful."

He smirked as I walked past him and went to sit on the edge of the bed.

"What, no candlelight?"

He snapped his fingers and the candles I hadn't even noticed stationed around the room began to flicker. "Better?"

"You have style, I'll give you that."

He chuckled, walking toward me. As he moved, his armor began to shift, peeling away from his chest so that only the tight black pants that barely concealed the bulge of his cock and his gloves remained.

"I'm glad you think so. You're very easy to impress."

"So I've been told. Then again, I lost my virginity in the back of a truck, so..."

He raised an eyebrow. "Country boy?"

"Woman," I corrected. "My mom's best friend, summer I turned eighteen."

"Of course," he snorted.

"What's that supposed to mean?"

"Nothing at all," he said innocently.

"You jealous?"

"Oh, yes. I'm burning up with envy."

"Mhm," I grinned.

He rolled his eyes, but I was surprised he was even bothering to deny it. Maybe there was something to the idea, after all. "Y'know, if I didn't know better, I'd think you had a thing for me."

"I'm planning on fucking you and making you my lightbearer, is that not enough proof?"

"Nah, I'm not talking about that. I mean actual feelings."

"I'm a demon," he reminded me.

"A demon with feelings for a lowly human."

He sighed. "I suppose you've grown on me."

"You *like* me," I taunted. "That's why you're going to all this trouble." I waved around the room.

"What, candles?"

"You can deny it if you want, but it's pretty damn obvious. You've totally got the hots for me."

"And?"

Well, wasn't prepared for that. He must've realized he had me caught off-guard, because he took the opportunity to pin me to the bed and my head spun.

I was also hard as a rock in an instant, especially with the feeling of his body pressing down on mine. "Are you done?"

"Just getting started," I purred, arching up against him.

His eyes filled with lust, leaving no doubt that my assumption was spot on. I wasn't sure how I felt about the fact that Apollyon had developed feelings for me. Hell, I wasn't sure how I felt in general, but it made the prospect of what we were about to do a bit more thrilling.

It was still intimidating as hell, but when his lips claimed mine, I allowed myself to relax and give in to the moment. I slipped my fingers into his hair as he pulled my shirt off and ran his long claws down my bare chest.

"You know, there's something I should warn you about before we do this," he said in a husky voice.

"Something worse than the bladed dick thing?"

He chuckled. "After we mate, we'll be bonded. Permanently."

"I thought you said I'd be free to leave after a year."

"You will," he answered. "The obligation is on my end. Your soul and mine will be connected. The difference to a mortal is negligible, but to a demon..."

"Is that the real reason you waited so long? You weren't

sure you wanted to be stuck with me?"

I must've failed to sound as casual as I was, because his gaze softened. "It had nothing to do with you."

"Then what? Not ready for the demands of parenting a hellacious army?" I challenged.

"Claiming you means going up against Lucifer," he answered. "It's an act of sedition, punishable by eternal death if I fail."

"Eternal death?" I echoed. "Is that like the extended edition of a DVD?"

"Director's cut."

I winced. "Yikes."

His hands tightened around my wrist and the pressure went straight to my cock. "I wanted to be sure, but there is no doubt in my mind that this is the path I wish to take. I want you to be equally certain."

I take a deep breath. "Not like I'm running the same risk, but...yeah. I'm sure I wanna do this."

"You want to be mine?" he pressed, his gaze sweeping over me. "In every way?"

God, yeah, I thought. I shrugged, because I've never learned how not to be an asshole.

His lips claimed mine again and the moan he elicited was far more genuine. My hands traveled down his sleek body, lingering at the paper thin leather slung so low on his hips. To my surprise, he let me unbutton them and took over sliding them the rest of the way off.

My breath hitched in my throat as Apollyon stood before me, fully undressed. I'd had plenty of time to let my imagination run wild about his cock, but it hadn't done him justice. Not by a long shot.

His skin turned from golden bronze to the deep red of his half-erect dick, which was a good twelve inches at least, weighted down by the sheer girth of it. The damn thing had ridges and a sharply curved head that resembled a spade. And then there was the knot. Hoisted high above his heavy balls was a solid knot more than the circumference of my fist, and while I couldn't see the blade he'd warned me about, there were metal studs lining the entire left side of his shaft.

All I could think was, "Holy shit, that must've hurt."

And then I realized I'd said it out loud. He was just watching me in amusement, a hand resting on his hip as I inspected the goods. "All the better to tempt you with, my dear."

I swallowed hard. A fairy tale fetish was the last thing I needed. "Can I touch it?"

He raised an eyebrow, reaffirming my suspicion that wasn't a very sexy thing to say. "If you like."

I ran my hand along the studded piercings and swallowed again, since my mouth was watering. The thought of those things inside me, rubbing against my most sensitive spots, was maddening. And then the tip... His cock twitched and stiffened as my finger traced around the pointed crown and teased the tip. His slit was already leaking precum I longed to taste, but I was wary of getting cut if I took him into my mouth.

"Doesn't look that sharp."

"Not yet," he said cryptically, gently guiding me onto my back. "You're going to need to hold perfectly still. Can you do that?"

My throat tightened up too much to speak, so I nodded as he spread my legs open. My erect cock slapped against my stomach, ready to go just from the sight of him.

And damn, what a sight it was. I wasn't sure how something so inhuman could be so irresistible, but fuck, I wanted him more than I ever had. I took a deep breath and focused on breathing without moving unnecessarily, the way he'd showed me. He went in with his fingers first, spreading the warming lubricant I knew so well around my tightly clenched hole.

"Y'know, if you sold that shit at stores, you'd have enough money to buy Earth."

He chuckled. "Money has never been a problem," he informed me, slipping his clawed finger even deeper inside of me. I knew now that he was capable of fingering me without causing damage if I held especially still, but he was putting a lot of faith in my ability to reign in my horniness.

Once he deemed that I was stretched enough, he positioned his cock at my entrance and I gasped involuntarily at the alien sensation. "You alright?" he asked, his voice husky with lust and concern.

"Just feels weird," I admitted. "I'm good."

His hands settled on my hips and I felt the pressure of him pushing in gently. His angled tip made it easier than the toys he'd used at first, until it widened and I realized that as narrow as it looked compared to his knot and shaft, it was still damn thick.

"Still so tight," he muttered in a tone of disbelief. I could tell from the way his eyes glazed that it was far from a problem for him. His right hand covered my knee, pushing my legs open a bit further as he kept applying increasing pressure to my hole. When the tension broke and his crown slipped in, I tensed up, waiting for the pain that didn't come. There was stiffness, my muscles aching from taking something almost as wide as the last toy he'd used, but it didn't actually hurt.

"I trained you well," he mused, stroking the outside of my thigh. "Tell me if it hurts. I need you to communicate."

It was hard to focus on anything other than the bizarrely pleasurable sensation of his alien cock inside of me, even if it was only part of the way. "Yeah, communicate. I got it."

He snorted, easing in a bit more until I felt the first ridge stretch me open. I knew from the glimpse I'd gotten that it was only going to get wider from there, so I started putting more focus on my breathing and tried not to let myself tense up too much.

Apollyon seemed to understand the problem I was having, because he kept stroking me and his voice gentled. "You're doing good, Levi. Just a little more."

My name in that sultry voice would've been enough to make me come, if not for the dull ache beginning to spread throughout my lower body. It wasn't just my entrance, it was every muscle that seemed to tense up in apprehension of what was to come. No matter how much I wanted it, he'd warned me it wasn't going to be easy.

It occurred to me that if he wasn't being gentle, he could easily impale me with the damn thing. It should've been a turnoff, but it wasn't. Shamefully, the opposite.

My own cock was leaking precum as Apollyon wrapped his clawed hand around it and started stroking. "It'll be easier for you to take me if you come," he advised.

"Are you halfway yet?"

He gave me a sympathetic look. "I'm afraid not."

"Geez," I breathed, feeling myself stiffen in his palm. It was almost impossible to resist the urge to buck into his touch, but the second I moved even slightly, his eyes glowed in warning.

"Hold still, you'll hurt yourself."

"Sorry, it's just..." I trailed off, moaning as his cock brushed against my prostate. "Fuck, that's good."

"Easy," he warned.

"What, am I not supposed to enjoy this?"

He blinked, making me think it definitely wasn't common. "I just know how you get when you're turned on."

"I'll be good if you just fuck me already."

He looked at me like I was insane, but he was the one who needed a checkup if he hadn't figured that out already. He pinned my hands down, which was counterproductive if he was trying not to get me more worked up, and his gaze softened in a new way. I was used to pity from him, even sympathy on occasion, but this was something different. Something I didn't have a word for.

"The mouth on you," he muttered, shaking his head.

"Didn't hear you complaining about my mouth last night."

He eased into me a bit further and I winced as my body was pushed beyond its previous limits. "Fuck."

"Now that's about halfway," he purred. "You sure you can handle the whole thing?"

"Shut up and fuck me," I growled, kissing him again. He returned it, his tongue slipping into my mouth to dance with mine. He tasted so good it made me dizzy and for a second, I forgot about the pain as he pushed ever deeper inside of me.

"It'll be easier if I go in all at once," he told me, gazing down. "But it'll hurt like a son of a bitch."

I took another deep breath and nodded. "Yeah. Just do it."

Apollyon put his hands on my shoulders, his grip gentle but firm. "I'll have to hold you down to make sure you don't hurt yourself."

"You know, if you're trying to turn me on, I'm already at maximum."

He rolled his eyes, but his grip on my shoulders tightened, and so did my core, disproving that whole maximum theory. "One," he said in a voice like sex, "Two..."

By the time he said, "Three," I was seeing stars. If there was a point where pain and pleasure became the same thing, I'd just found it. For a moment, I couldn't even scream. The sound just died out in my throat, too much to process as he filled me to the knot.

How the damn thing was going to get inside of me, I had no idea, because I already felt stretched to the point of splitting open. The strangled gasp that finally escaped me as the pain became real sounded far more desperate than I'd expected and Apollyon gathered me into his arms.

"It's alright," he coaxed, stroking my hair with tenderness that contrasted sharply to the pain. "I'm in."

"I fucking hope so." The words all came out in a single rush of breath, but now that my head had stopped spinning, I felt the unexpected surge of pleasure deep inside of me. As far as his toys had pushed me to my limits of tolerance, none of them had ever felt as good as it did to have him all the way inside of me. Good, excruciating, it all kind of blended together.

"God, you feel..." His voice tapered off as he touched my cheek, his claws grazing my flushed skin. His eyes were aglow with desire. The entire time he'd been training me, the lust had only peeked through in bits and pieces. He was always in control, always perfectly detached. Now, something had shifted. He was the one inside of me, buried knot-deep, but I had power over him I was pretty sure no one ever had. That look in his eyes made it so fucking clear.

"You've never done this," I realized. "Not with a human."

He didn't answer, but his knowing gaze told me enough.

"I didn't know it would be like this."

His tone was quiet, like he was muttering a confession. I stared at him in fascination. "Like what?" I asked, breathless as he began to thrust slowly, gently, even though every slight movement was torturous. It was blissful, too. It was everything, good and wicked and entirely forbidden.

His fingers slipped through mine and he squeezed tight. "I don't know if there's a word for it," he breathed.

And that answer was more flattering than anything he could have come up with. I kissed him to stifle my own moans, because I couldn't hold back anymore. From the pleasure or the pain, it was all so unbearable, but I wanted more. I needed it. The idea of stopping, that was what I couldn't handle.

Every time he pulled out of me just slightly and drove back in, his knot pressed against my battered hole and I moaned from the delicious sting of it. His crown was notched such that he was never in any danger of slipping all the way out, no matter how far he pulled back. How he was going to pull out once all was said and done was a far more concerning issue, but I refused to dwell on it.

There were far more pressing matters, like the deviously enticing sensation of him edging even deeper into me, his long tongue buried in my throat. He was deeper inside of me than anyone had ever been, but it wasn't enough. I dug my fingers into his hair and moaned, surging my hips into him for more even though my aching body was screaming at me in protest.

"Levi," he warned, breathless.

"Just do it," I moaned, biting his bottom lip. It wasn't going to get any easier, and I wasn't sure it was possible for me to want it anymore than I did, even knowing the pain that would come with it.

He looked down at me, his gaze softening in understanding. I took a deep breath as he held me firmly and thrust into me one more time, harder than all the others. I felt the sharpness like ice deep inside of me, but it didn't hurt. Not in a way my brain was capable of processing, at least. Not even when his knot filled me.

He'd pierced me. I felt him deep inside, in my very core, pulsating and throbbing and burning icy hot. I stared up at him and he stared back at me, neither one of us breathing.

The pleasure came first. The dizzying perfection of his knot pushing against my prostate. Then, the pain, but the light in his blood red eyes lessened it somehow. He was beautiful, like the flames of Hell itself, and even though I knew I was at risk of being consumed and burned away entirely, I couldn't look away.

Heat spread throughout me and the pain was eclipsed by the burn of his seed filling me. It heated everything it touched and soon, I felt his energy taking over everything until I was sure there was nothing left. And I squirmed and moaned desperately for him to make me disappear. To swallow me whole, to tear me to pieces, whatever the consequences of the indefinable *more* I so ruthlessly craved happened to be.

A snarl tore from his throat, animalistic and intense. His long fangs dripped with lust as he gazed down at what he'd claimed so thoroughly, his cock piercing me through and knotting me to keep his ethereal seed from escaping.

It felt like I'd swallowed the sun, burning through me, but when he came, I came, and I forgot how to feel anything but the ecstasy that went hand in hand with the agony.

For a moment, I was sure he was about to tear into my throat, the look of hunger was so intense in his eyes. I would've allowed it, too. Enjoyed it. That's just how sick I'd become, and as the all-encompassing fire within me began to die down, I remained committed to this new form of unwellness. This fixation that would be the death of my soul, if I somehow survived the cost of the physical pleasure.

He kissed me and I kissed him back, even though I felt like my lower half was incapable of movement with his cock all but running me through. Maybe it was for the best. I had the urge to squirm in the aftershocks of orgasm, and I'd probably end up doing the damage he'd tried so hard to mitigate.

"It's alright," he whispered, seemingly taking my dismay for fear. "It's done. The energy will heal you, but I have to stay in until my knot goes down or --"

I kissed him again, because I needed to. Because the warning didn't matter. I didn't want him to leave me, and not just because it felt like he'd hollow me out if he pulled out now. I wanted him like this, inside of me, part of me, all of me, for just a little bit longer.

Or forever.

The difference seemed minor in a place like hell, and for the first time, as I laid there beneath him, his arms wrapped around me and his tongue down my throat, it started to feel like heaven. My version, at least.

"You took that well," he finally panted, coming up for breath.

"I don't think I could handle this every night, but fuck..." I moaned.

He gave me a strange look. "It wouldn't be like this if we had sex again. I wouldn't need to knot you."

"Oh."

He cocked his head. "Why do you sound disappointed?"

"I don't," I lied. "I'm just... it's nice. Kind of. Excruciating, but nice in its own way."

He shook his head. "I don't know what to make of you."

I laughed, letting my head drop back against the pillow as I caught my breath. "How much longer is it gonna take before this thing goes down?"

"Another twenty minutes, maybe more." He hesitated. "Are you in that much pain?"

"Just wondering if we had time for round two," I admitted.

He made no attempt to hide his disbelief, and if I didn't know better, I'd think I scared *him*. "You are a very strange human. Has anyone ever told you that?"

"Often," I answered, leaning up so my lips could brush his. "But coming from you, it sounds like a compliment."

His lips turned slightly, not quite a smile, but enough to soften the still ravenous look on his face. Even that was hot. I really was fucked up, but for the moment, I didn't care. "It was," he confessed. "You're full of surprises."

"Full of demon cum right now, but semantics."

He rolled his eyes and lowered his head, running his long tongue along my throat. "Just hold still and try not to hurt yourself. I'll give you all the pleasure you can handle."

One of the best things about demons, as I learned that night, is that they're surprisingly true to their word.

THIRTY-TWO

IN THE DAYS THAT FOLLOWED, I learned the magical healing process wasn't all that different from the boring old mundane one, even if it was somewhat faster. I stayed on bed rest by Apollyon's orders and demonic doctors came in and out to perform humiliating exams that were a hell of a lot worse than anything I'd pictured happening.

According to them, the insemination had been a success, but only time would tell if it lasted. The one-week mark was the most tentative, and I wasn't to so much as blink without assistance to maximize the chances of the energy growing within me.

For his part, Apollyon had been dutiful in keeping me entertained, both with media and seduction. Eventually, duty called and he had to go back to doing whatever the fuck he did all day, which left me with Maiz as my constant companion.

At least I was back upstairs in my own room.

Well. Apollyon's room. It was hard to tell when I'd started seeing it as my own, but he made it clear he didn't feel the same way whenever I left my socks on the floor.

Anal retentive bastard for a demon, but damn, he was pretty.

That night marked a full month since the insemination and I was sure I'd read and watched everything in Hell's archives by that point. If I didn't get out of the damn bed for longer than it took for Maiz to sponge me down, I was going to lose my fucking mind.

Or what was left of it.

"How much longer is this gonna go on for?" I demanded.

Maiz sighed, looking up from the book he was reading in a chair across from the bed. Janis lounged at his feet, traitor that she was.

Then again, I had long since given up my grudge in favor of having someone to talk to.

"Until the physicians give the go ahead for you to be up and about," he answered. "You know this."

"Yeah, but if I'm stuck in bed, you're stuck listening to me whine about it."

He rolled his eyes. I'd once imagined the stalwart butler didn't have a limit to his patience, but I was kind of proud to have proven otherwise. If I couldn't torture Apollyon, he was the next best thing.

"You think it'll be a boy army, a girl army or a nonbinary army?" I asked, patting my stomach. It didn't seem any bigger, but every now and then, I could feel a flutter. Probably just the Flaming Hot Cheese Bombs, but still.

Maiz gave me an incredulous look. "What? It's not a baby, Levi. It's an energy cluster. We've talked about this."

"Yeah, I know, but that doesn't mean it doesn't have a spirit."

"It does, actually. You're harboring the seeds of countless demon spawn who will remain dormant until the appointed time."

"Right, countless demon spawn. Hence, spirits."

He groaned. "I suppose if you choose to look at it like that, you're not technically wrong."

"Not technically wrong is the same as technically right," I informed him. "I'm thinking of Stevie. Works well across genders. Wonder, Nicks, you can't go wrong."

"'Legion' would be more appropriate," Maiz said flatly.

I considered it. "Try finding *that* on a custom souvenir."

Maiz shook his head and turned back to his book. The knock at the door a moment later filled me with both relief and apprehension. I wasn't looking forward to another invasive exam, but if it came with my ticket to freedom, so be it.

I'd gotten to know the doctor in a Biblical sense, and as he swept through the door, looking sternly at me over those clear round glasses, I knew he didn't approve of my constant companion.

"Is that a hellhound?"

I'd taken care to hide her the last few times he'd visited, but I was almost out of house arrest, so he couldn't really do anything. "She's my pet."

"Of course she is," he said, looking pointedly at Maiz.

"The Demon Lord is well aware," Maiz sighed. "She's tame."

The doctor cast a dubious glance at my hellhound and came over to the side of the bed. "How are you feeling today, lightbearer?"

"We've been over this. Your finger's been up my ass, I think you can call me Levi."

"Sardonic as usual," he remarked, setting down his leather bag. He pulled out a stethoscope, a surprisingly normal implement for a guy who treated horned and winged beasts all day. I couldn't imagine he had too many other human patients. "Any pain?"

"Not today. My ass bounced back pretty quick, thanks to the demon jizz. You should really think about selling that."

"Is he always like this?" the doctor asked, turning to Maiz.

"Trust me, he's on good behavior around you."

The doctor shook his head, moving the stethoscope down to my stomach. The metal was cold and I flinched. "You hear a heartbeat?"

"Yours."

"Shouldn't there be, like, a thousand?"

"We've been over this," the doctor said stiffly. "It's not a physical infant. There's no heartbeat to detect, and certainly not thousands."

"You're wasting your time," Maiz sighed.

"It's healthy, right?" I asked.

"The energy is quite strong," the doctor answered. "Now, be quiet."

"What are you listening for?"

"If I told you the answer, you wouldn't sleep and that would be quite counterproductive."

I pursed my lips. That's what I got for asking questions. He continued to listen, frowning.

"What is it?" I blurted out when I couldn't take the suspense any longer. "Is it eating my insides?"

"No, it's not that," he said, far too casually. Like that was something that could happen. "It's..." He paused, looking at Maiz. "Would you do me a favor and have a listen?"

"Sure," he said, standing to walk over to us. He took the stethoscope and the doctor placed it back against my abdomen. Maiz's expression went flat as he listened intently. "What am I listening for?"

The doctor leaned in and whispered something.

"Hey!" I cried. "That's not fair."

Maiz's eyes widened and he studied me with great intrigue. "I don't... oh," he murmured, frowning. "Why yes, now that you mention it, I do."

"Do what?" I demanded. All sorts of B-horror movies were playing in my head. So many fucked up scenarios that could be coming to life.

"How is that possible?" Maiz asked the doctor, completely ignoring me. Why was I even surprised?

"We'll have to run some tests," the doctor murmured. "I'm sure it's a fluke."

"What kind of tests?" I asked, sitting up. "I'm supposed to be done with all this bullshit."

The doctor finally met my gaze, and the fear in his was anything but comforting. "There are two heartbeats, Levi."

"What?" Now that I had an answer, I wasn't sure what the hell I was supposed to do with it. "What does that mean?"

"I don't know." Three of the most unsettling words you can hear coming out of a doctor's mouth, and I had plenty of experience. "It shouldn't be possible."

There it was. There were the other four.

THIRTY-THREE

I WOUND up back in the exam room I would have been all too happy never to see again, but the doctor and Maiz were acting so flustered, I was too freaked to be annoyed. When Apollyon came in, I realized they had called in the big guns.

He took one look at me and frowned. "What did you do?"

"Me?" I cried, sitting up in the hospital bed.

"Whenever I get called from work by panicked demons, it's always because you've done *something*," he muttered, sweeping into the room. He turned to the doctor, his eyes narrowed. "Is something wrong with the seed?"

"Not *wrong* per se, sir, but..." The doctor hesitated. "Perhaps we'd better have you take a look."

"He's not an ultrasound machine," I said flatly. "Shouldn't you run some actual tests?"

"It's my energy," Apollyon answered, coming to stand beside me. At least someone wasn't acting like I was invisible. "I'm more attuned to it than any instrument."

He pulled up my shirt and pressed his palm against my

stomach. I immediately felt the dormant energy surge up to greet him, like heat spreading through my torso. It was kind of freaky, and conjured images of the Alien movies, but also kind of sweet in a horrifying monster movie way.

"Aww. It knows you're its daddy," I gushed.

Apollyon gave me a silencing look and kept feeling for whatever it was he was feeling for. He finally yanked his hand away and stared down at my stomach like it was a portal to the underworld we were already in. "That's not possible."

"What is it, sir?" Maiz asked nervously.

"There's only one spirit," Apollyon said, turning to face them.

"What happened to the rest?" Maiz cried. "He's perfectly healthy, there's no sign of miscarriage..."

"The energy is all there," Apollyon said, looking back at me in disbelief. "It's stronger than ever, if anything, it's just... coalesced into one."

"What does that mean?" I asked. "What about the Legion?"

"It's merged," he answered in a disbelieving tone, unblinking as he stared at me. I knew that look. It was the same one he'd given me before he'd thrown me to Maiz and I was *not* gonna take the fall for something else I hadn't even done.

"Don't you dare," I snapped. "Whatever's going on, I've done everything you asked. It's not my fucking fault."

His gaze softened. "Levi... I know," he said, cupping my face in his hand. "It's going to be fine."

Somehow, his attempt to comfort me had the exact opposite effect. I realized only then just how attached I'd gotten to the whatevers inside of me. Sure, having to be on bed rest for a month was a pain in the ass, but I'd gotten so used to protecting them with my every waking moment that the idea of something happening to any of them was horrifying.

"You can fix this, right?" I asked hopefully, my hand coming to rest on my stomach.

Apollyon's gaze was hesitant and he finally turned away from me without an answer. "I want you to run every test at your disposal. Find out what's wrong and report directly to me."

"Yes, sir," the doctor said, bowing to Apollyon. "We'll do whatever we can."

"I have an idea of where to start," said Maiz. He'd been silent for the last few minutes, and when he finally spoke up, he seemed far less hesitant. The rest of us waited expectantly for him to continue and he finally said, "This all started because we heard another heartbeat. As far-fetched as it sounds, we... might try an ultrasound."

The doctor and Apollyon both looked at each other the way they usually looked at me, but the doctor shrugged. "I suppose it couldn't hurt to rule out the impossible."

"Fine," Apollyon muttered. "Just get on with it."

"An ultrasound?" I asked doubtfully as the room became a flurry of activity. Apollyon remained by my side, and the fact that he seemed to force himself to smile at me was so much more unnerving than his smartassery would've been. "You said this wasn't an actual pregnancy."

"At this point, I have no more idea than you do," he admitted.

"Alright, Levi. This is going to feel a bit cold," the doctor warned me before squirting some clear lube onto my stomach.

"Really? After everything you fuckers have put me through, *that's* what you feel the need to warn me about?"

"Just try to relax," the doctor said, looking up at the screen in front of him. It was surprisingly normal looking, for Hell's ultrasound machine. A bit more advanced than what they probably had in the average OBGYN's office on Earth, but still just a screen with a weird wand attached to the monitor.

I held my breath and watched the screen as he spread the wand through the gel on my stomach. It was hard to tell the difference between Little Legion and this morning's breakfast. It all just looked like shades of gray.

"You can breathe," said the doctor. He squinted at the machine as a whooshing sound came through the speakers. It was rhythmic and steady, but there was a much quicker pattern right behind it. It sounded like tiny droplets of water splattering on the pavement in rapid fire.

"What's that?" I asked.

"A heartbeat," the doctor answered in a tone of dismay as he stared at the screen.

"His?" Apollyon asked hopefully.

"And another," the doctor responded, pointing at one of the gray blurs on the screen. "See that?"

Apollyon squinted. "What is it?"

"It's a physical abnormality. A womb, of sorts."

"A womb?" I echoed. "Look, I swallowed so much random shit as a kid, someone definitely would've picked that up on all the tests they had to run."

"It's not an organic structure," the doctor said, his eyes still glued to the screen. "The darker hue is how infernal energy shows up on these machines. It was... created."

"By what?" Apollyon asked.

"This," the doctor answered, gesturing to the small mass inside what he'd declared a womb that shouldn't have existed. It was the same dark shade of gray. "It's the origin of the heartbeat and, I believe, the coalescence of the Seed."

"It's physical?" Apollyon asked, his voice strained. I was pretty sure he'd never worn that expression in his life, but I didn't even want to know what mine looked like.

"It would seem so," said the doctor. "I don't know how to explain this, but the Seed has taken on a singular, physical vessel. It appears to be in the form of an infant."

For a few moments, the room was dead silent. Even I didn't have a remark. Maiz was the first to speak.

"Forgive the intrusion, but I may have a theory."

"Go ahead," Apollyon said, gripping the rail at the side of my bed like he needed the support.

"Levi is an architect," Maiz said carefully, studying me. "Lucifer's vessel, to be exact. His abilities of manifestation are beyond what we could possibly fathom."

"So you're saying what, he joked about this being a pregnancy so long he manifested it?" Apollyon asked.

Maiz shrugged. "I've been inside his mind. He's always harbored the desire for a family, albeit through more conventional means. It's not beyond the scope of reason, given everything else I've seen him do."

Apollyon was silent, like he was actually considering what the other demon was saying.

"That's crazy," I protested, looking back at the screen. Even though my head refused to wrap around it, there was a strange tug in my heart that at least wanted it to be true.

And then the rest of me, which was just plain horrified. It was one thing to carry Apollyon's energy, but an actual demon baby? What the fuck was I supposed to do with that?

"It makes as much sense as anything else," Apollyon

muttered, staring down at me. "And it would explain why the energy is all intact."

"You're saying our imaginary demon baby came to life and ate its siblings?" I croaked.

"'Absorbed' would be a more accurate term, if that's the case," Maiz mused.

"Not helpful!" I cried.

Apollyon sighed. "It wouldn't be the first time Legion merged into a singular vessel, but it is quite unusual."

"Unusual," I echoed. "Yeah, that's one word for it. So what does this mean?"

"It means I should congratulate you," the doctor said flatly. "You're going to be parents."

Apollyon and I stared at each other for a long while, as I struggled to process the whirlwind of emotions tearing through me. Somewhere, deep beneath the terror and confusion, was a kind of giddiness. "Holy shit," I breathed.

"Indeed," Apollyon muttered.

I gulped. "So... what now?"

"That remains to be seen," he answered. "But I'd expect we'll find out in a matter of eight months or so."

THIRTY-FOUR

I THOUGHT I was under close supervision while carrying Apollyon's seed, but it had nothing on the full lockdown mode every demon in Hell went into the second it was revealed I was carrying an actual baby.

It took awhile for the news to sink in. Sure, I'd found out more than a week ago, but knowing something didn't make it feel real.

Even Janis was walking on eggshells around me. She kept whining and nuzzling my hand, and bringing me bones from God only knows where. I could see why the demons were so scared of her, but it was hard to feel the same way when she worshipped the ground I walked on.

"There you are," Maiz said in an exasperated tone, walking into the library where I'd taken up residence. It was the only place I could get a moment's peace, and I wasn't going to pass up the opportunity to learn more about Hell.

This whole time, I realized that despite my reassurances to Apollyon that I had no plan of returning to Earth, in the back of my mind, I'd always figured I would. Someday.

Now, I was finally accepting that this place was going to be home for the foreseeable future.

God, if Sirena could see me now. I didn't know what she'd say. Hell, at the time, I didn't know what *I* thought. And then there was Mom...

Still, I couldn't help but wish I had my sister to talk to. I mean, I was gonna be a parent. Mother? Father? Something in between?

This was big news, either way, and Maiz just wasn't cutting it as far as deep, emotional conversations went.

"Was I supposed to be somewhere else?" I asked.

Maiz looked at me and sighed. "You know you're not supposed to be off by yourself."

"No, I know I'm not supposed to go outside the palace walls without supervision. Last I checked, the library wasn't off-limits. Has that changed?"

Another sigh. "Not at all," he said cheerfully. "I'm just supposed to keep an eye on you while Apollyon is out of the realm."

"Doing what, exactly?"

He refused to say anything about where my demon lover had gone off to, and Apollyon had been just as secretive before leaving. Whatever it was, I knew it had something to do with the baby.

For the moment, I was the only one actually calling them that. The others all referred to it as the seed, sometimes Legion. I was getting ever so slightly annoyed, but I was sure they just blame it on the imaginary pregnancy hormones.

Then again, maybe there *were* pregnancy hormones. I hadn't thought I had a womb before, either.

"You know I can't tell you that," said Maiz.

"And you wonder why I run off to the library. You're such a great conversationalist."

He rolled his eyes. "Be that as it may, I am in charge while Apollyon is gone. Next time you want to run off, make sure you tell me first."

"And what would the point of running off be then, exactly?"

He gave me a look. The one I'd gotten to know so well.

Much as I didn't want to admit it, I'd grown almost as attached to Maiz as I had to the thing inside of me. He wasn't that bad when he wasn't torturing me on Apollyon's order, and I had grudgingly come to accept that I couldn't exactly be mad at him for something I'd forgiven Apollyon for.

Why I had forgiven Apollyon was beyond me, but my emotions had never made that much sense and going to Hell hadn't changed that.

"Come," Maiz said, "you could use some fresh air."

I stood up from the couch to put aside the book I'd been reading. "Really?" I asked doubtfully.

"We haven't been on that walk in a while, and I've heard that it's good for pregnant humans to exercise as much as possible. Especially during these early months."

"If you've been doing research on human pregnancy, surely you also read that cisgender males don't typically end up in this situation?"

He smirked. "I'm aware. However, as unorthodox as the situation is, I have been assigned to facilitate your care in Apollyon's absence."

"So you have," I sighed.

I followed Maiz out in the garden. It was quickly becoming one of my favorite places in hell, and there were surprisingly many to choose from. Apollyon had taken me exploring a bit once the doctor had assured him that moving around wasn't going to endanger the impossible pregnancy any further. I had to admit, it was a far more expansive realm than I'd ever imagined, which only made it a greater mystery why he felt the need to do anything outside of it.

Something told me that no matter how long I was here, there was always going to be part of Apollyon's life that was a mystery to me. It shouldn't have bothered me, but it did.

The skies were the same dull gray as ever, but even that had begun to seem beautiful to me. It was strange how much depth there could be in a single shade. Sometimes I'd just look up at the sky and it would seem endless. Maybe that's all eternity was. Just staring up at the sky and losing track of time.

Funny how I contemplated it more now that I wasn't going to die than I ever had back when an early death was inevitable.

"Can I ask you something, Maiz?"

He looked down at me and motioned for me to sit on the bench by the garden path. I did, since I got tired more easily than I ever had.

"What is it?"

"This kid. Assuming it makes it to term, what's its life going to be like?"

"That is quite an assumption," he mused.

"Ouch."

He gave me a knowing smile.

"You did make me promise I wouldn't lie to you," he reminded me.

I groaned. "I don't remember that."

"Well, you did. After..." He trailed off. We tacitly agreed

not to speak of the seemingly endless torture he'd put me through at Apollyon's request.

"Right," I sighed.

"What was your question?"

"What's going to happen to the kid?" I repeated.

He sighed deeply, and stared off into space, making me think he had heard the original question.

"That's a difficult question to answer."

"Why?" I asked.

"Because nothing like it has ever existed before, nor do I imagine will ever exist again."

"You say that like it's a bad thing."

"Our worlds are not so dissimilar in how they treat things that are different."

"You're saying it won't be accepted?"

"Well, we have no idea what kind of creature it will even be. That alone means that there are many who will view it as a threat. Even within this realm."

"And you?"

"How I feel is irrelevant. I exist to serve the Lord Apollyon, and that means I serve his family."

"Family?"

He smiled slightly. "I believe the term carries the same meaning in both our worlds."

"Yeah, but..." I trailed off. "Not sure Apollyon sees it that way."

"You might be surprised," Maiz said casually. "I've known him for a very long time."

"Meaning?"

"It means I've never seen him this way." He considered it for a moment before adding, "Happy."

It took me a moment to process that. Happy? That

really wasn't something I associated with Apollyon--or myself, for that matter. But it did have a certain ring to it.

Happy. Was that really what we'd become? Both of us? At one point, I never even imagined it was possible. As much fucked up shit as had happened to me since I'd come to this place, it was the first time in my life I could remember actually feeling like I belonged somewhere. There had been a time when I wasn't even sure what that meant.

Sure, I could be happy for other people. But happiness for myself? That had never seemed like something within my reach. Not something that was ever meant to actually apply to me.

Had I really changed so much since coming into Apollyon's service that I was capable of something like that? Even more improbable, was I capable of making *him* happy?

I knew that was a dangerous road to go down. Assuming an important demon overlord felt the same way as I did could only lead to disappointment.

For now, I was just happy he wasn't trying to kill the little Legion I'd grown so attached to.

"Question," I said, since I was on a roll. Maiz listened patiently and I continued, "Since I'm technically Lucifer's vessel, does that make this kid the antichrist?"

Maiz raised an eyebrow. "I suppose that depends on your definition."

"And what's *your* definition?"

Maiz chuckled. "We don't believe in the antichrist here. That would require a religious conception that is simply not present."

"Is there ever such a thing as a straight answer with you guys?"

He grinned. "You've been here long enough to know the

answer to that."

"Right," I sighed. "I should've known better."

Maiz patted me on the shoulder. "I wouldn't worry too much. Apollyon isn't going to let anything happen to either of you."

"You mean as long as I'm pregnant."

Maiz cocked his head. "If I'd meant that, I would've said it."

Huh.

"Let's get you back inside," Maiz said. He looked up at the sky, and if it wasn't just my imagination, it seemed like a darker gray than usual. "Looks like it's going to rain."

I'd been in Hell for months and I'd yet to see actual rain. "Is that even possible?"

"Yes," he said carefully. "But it's not the kind you're use to."

Well, that sounded ominous. If the difference between Hell rain and Earth rain was anything like the difference between Hell pudding and Earth pudding, I certainly wasn't eager to find out.

I followed him back toward the palace, but when Maiz slowed down, I realized something was wrong. It didn't take me long to see what.

The palace was gone.

"What the fuck?"

Maiz shook his head, looking around the empty expanse where the palace should've been. When I turned my head, the garden we'd just come from was gone too. There was only gray, and a strange swirling void somewhere in the distance. It was difficult to tell how far away it was since there was nothing on the horizon to compare it to.

"Stay behind me," Maiz warned, drawing a knife from the holster at his side.

No chance of me going anywhere, I thought.

Something was wrong. The air felt alive. I wasn't sure what that meant, but now that I felt it, I knew that it was just about the worst feeling in the world. Felt like there were eyes in the air, the wind, the sky, and everything seemed to have a faint static glow.

At first, I thought I was hallucinating, but when Maiz looked around at the air like he was feeling the same thing, I realized the truth was much worse.

My hand instinctively flew to my stomach, and as the ground trembled, I braced myself. It felt like it would open up at any moment. Then the void in the distance grew closer all of a sudden. Darker. "What the hell is that?" I asked, realizing it was some kind of fucking *portal* before I'd even finished the question.

Maiz stared solemnly at the fast-approaching portal. His arm was still out to block me, as if I had any plans of charging toward the damn thing. "It's an angel," he said suddenly, his voice breathy with fascination. Or maybe it was fear. When he turned toward me, I knew it was the latter. "Levi... run!"

I probably would have, if I hadn't found myself frozen as the portal exploded into a burst of light. That was the last thing I remembered before something grabbed me and plunged me into darkness.

THIRTY-FIVE

"AND THEN, when I opened my eyes, I was in heaven's maximum security being interrogated by your creepy friend," I say, smiling pleasantly at the angel who's been interrogating me for the past six hours. "From there, you know what happened."

"I'm well aware of Haniel's report," Chemuel says, his arms folded as he stands before me, still as a statue. "For the sake of the official record, please recount your version of it."

"Sure," I say stiffly, glancing back at the clock. Six hours. If I can just drag it out a little bit longer...

"So, when I woke up wondering where the hell I was, your buddy Han informed me I'd been 'acquired,'" I continue. "I take it that's your fancy angel word for 'kidnapping.'"

"If by 'kidnapping,' you mean liberating you from the soul-damning fate of belonging to a Monarch, then yes," Chem says without missing a beat.

"Guess we'll just have to agree to disagree."

"You expect me to believe that you've actually formed

any kind of meaningful connection with Apollyon beyond Stockholm Syndrome?" he scoffs.

"You heard the story yourself. It's not my job to tell you what to think about it."

"And yet, you claim you love him."

I clench my jaw. It wasn't a realization I'd had before realizing there was a damn good chance I was never going to see Apollyon again, but my time in heaven has clarified quite a few aspects of my life that were previously blurry.

I have to get out of this fucking place. Not the least of all because if I don't, I know they're going to kill my kid.

"I don't claim," I say through gritted teeth. "We're not talking about thinking Bigfoot is real. I *know*."

"Fair enough," says Chemuel. "Please. Continue. What happened when you woke up in our custody?"

"You know damn well what happened," I growl. "You attacked. You destroyed everything."

"I'm not talking about the invasion of Hell," he says coldly. "I'm talking about what happened here."

I hold the angel's gaze, which I can tell is just burning him up, but eventually, it becomes too difficult to look into those blue orbs, as bottomless as the ocean, and I have to look away. "I woke up," I mutter, staring down at the floor. "And the nightmare started."

"OPEN YOUR EYES, LEVI."

The unfamiliar voice was soft yet mocking. I did as it said and found myself sitting upright, even though it took a second to realize. The room looked like the stark white backdrop of some overly lit photoshoot, and as far as I could tell, I was alone. Not that it was possible to see beyond the light.

"What the fuck?" I groaned.

"I'm sure you're confused," the voice continued. "Allow me to introduce myself. My name is Haniel, and you are in heaven."

"Funny. I thought there'd be pearly gates, or at least more models."

"It's good that you've managed to keep your sense of humor throughout your captivity, but I believe you'll find it serves you less here," he remarked in a souring tone.

"How did you even get me?" I asked, struggling to think through the ache in my head. It felt like it had been split open on concrete even though I couldn't remember falling. Just that awful portal, then... nothing. "Where's Maiz?"

"He's being held with the others. Those who didn't resist."

"Resist?" My heart was pounding, like it recognized something my injured brain wasn't processing yet.

"It was an invasion," Haniel answered. "The outer realm is under our control now."

Now it was sinking in. My chest clenched in terror I didn't fully understand. I wasn't sure when I'd grown loyal to Hell, beyond my attachment to Apollyon, but I felt like someone had just announced they'd leveled my home.

Janis... and Shera... Something told me asking about either of them would put them more in danger, so I swallowed my dread and tried to focus on seeing anything through the white light in front of me.

"And Apollyon?" I asked through gritted teeth.

"While the cat's away..." Haniel said smugly.

"Of course. So what's the game plan? Hell gets annexed into heaven? A few new donut franchises pop up?"

He chuckled. It was a stiff, unconvincing sound that made me sick deep inside. Something unnatural about it.

"It's really none of your concern, is it? You're human. I'm sure you'd prefer to return to your world."

"Something tells me that's not actually an option."

"Perceptive," he said in the condescending way I was beginning to realize only an angel was capable of.

"What do you want with me?"

"It's not what I want with you. You're being held until our informant can come pick you up. I'm told you have something that belongs to him."

"Him...?" It took me a second, but the idea forming filled me with more terror than I knew what to do with. "Lucifer?"

The angel was silent, but that told me more than I wanted to know.

"It's him, isn't it?" I pressed. "That's the only way you could've gotten into the realm. Apollyon never leaves anything to chance. You'd need the master key..."

"Very good, Mr. Curtis," Haniel said flatly. "You're not as foolish as your recent choices would make it seem."

"Don't underestimate me, I've still got plenty of bad decisions left," I snarked. "Since when do angels work with the devil?"

"The distinction is in the details," he answered. "But since you're not going anywhere, I suppose it doesn't matter if I tell you. We've struck a deal."

"Deal with the devil. What could go wrong?"

"Lucifer was an angel before he was the Prince of Hell," said Haniel.

"And now he's come full circle and sold out? Charming."

"I'm not certain if you're brainwashed or simply naive enough to believe that Apollyon actually cares about you.

Either way, you're nothing more than a tool to him. That's what being a lightbearer is."

"And you're going to hand this all-important tool over to the enemy?"

More silence.

"Wait," I muttered. "Of course. Man, I'm dense. That's the whole deal, isn't it? He traded you the keys to his biggest threat's kingdom and in return, you delivered a one-person army to him."

"Very good. You're beginning to understand how things work. I'm sure Lucifer will find you amusing."

"You can't," I said, my voice hoarse with indecision. I knew I couldn't trust Haniel, but if there was anything good in him that I could appeal to, I knew I stood a better chance with him than with Lucifer. And the second the devil found out I was carrying a baby, not an army, we were both dead.

"And why is that?" the angel asked boredly.

"Because I'm not the lightbearer. Not anymore."

"You're lying."

"Get a doctor in here and test it out," I challenged. "I'm pregnant, with an actual baby, not an army, and I can prove it."

He didn't say anything for a moment, but when he finally spoke, his voice was chilled. "If you're lying--"

"I'm not," I said firmly.

I didn't get an answer, but the glaring light eventually faded and some faceless guard came in and dragged me out of the chair I was tied to. It didn't take long for me to realize that heaven's hospital facilities weren't nearly as cushy as the ones I was used to, and after being poked and prodded by a team of assholes, I found myself thrown back in another observation room.

From there, I believe you know the rest, Chem.

THIRTY-SIX

CHEMUEL WATCHES ME DUBIOUSLY, his severe face set in a permanent frown. "And that's all?" he challenges.

"Yep," I lie.

"You've had no contact with Apollyon since coming here?"

"Nope. When did I have the chance?" I ask, hoping desperately that he isn't perceptive enough to call my bluff. "I've been sitting in this shithole for the last few days. Or hours. Kind of all blends together. No offense, but you guys are boring as fuck."

"This isn't a playroom, it's a holding cell," Chemuel says, clearly offended. "You are being interrogated."

"And you're doing a lovely job. Don't mean to criticize your skills at all," I say with a placid smile.

He keeps staring at me, like he's trying to peer into my head. For all I know, that's something he's capable of. The truth is, my time in isolation hasn't been as uneventful as I need to make them think. Apollyon has contacted me. I'm still not entirely sure it was real and not a dream, but as blurry as my memory of his promise is, it's all I have to cling onto.

I'm coming for you.

Four little words, but they're the most meaningful ones I've ever heard in my life. I've given up on trying to decide if my feelings for Apollyon are as fucked up as I fear they are. Either way, they aren't changing.

"I'll admit, in all my years at this job, yours is by far the most unique case I've come across," Chemuel muses, finally taking the seat across from me. The room is drab and the furniture looks like it's made of sticks, but at least it isn't as nauseatingly bright as the other one. I can actually hear myself think.

"It's because of the pregnancy, isn't it?" I ask flatly, running my hand over the slight curve of my stomach.

He rolls his eyes. The first sign of a personality he's shown the entire time I've had the "pleasure" of being his subject. "Do you know how you came to be a vessel, Levi?"

"Is that a trick question? Because if not, I'm gonna have to guess it's that time I played with an Ouija board at a slumber party."

"As atypical as it's turned out to be, your story actually began the way these things usually do," he continues, ignoring my sarcasm.

"These things?" I echo.

"Deals with the devil," he answers casually. "It's really a stereotype that most end up contracting with him to sell their soul for fame and fortune. The truth is, it's very often a parent promising his or her firstborn son in exchange for something far less glamorous."

His words settle in slowly, but I don't want any part of them. "You're saying my mom is the one who sold me to Lucifer?" I laugh.

"Not your mother."

His face is blank, but it says plenty in his silence.

"Bullshit," I mutter. "My dad never believed in any of this shit."

"Your sister got it from somewhere," Chemuel says casually. "Or did you think she purchased that book off eBay?"

"What?" I croak.

"It was inherited, Levi. Passed down from your father to the child I'm assuming he believed to have the most alacrity for energetic manipulation." He smiles faintly. "Amusing, really, considering what you turned out to be."

"Bullshit," I repeat.

"Your father abandoned you. Is it really so far-fetched to think that he'd trade your soul for his life?"

"Prove it," I challenge.

"If you wish." Chemiel holds out his hand and a screen slowly begins to materialize above it. At first, the picture is just a street view of a normal if swanky looking suburban home. Then, a car pulls up. Jet black and gleaming like a diamond. There is something strangely familiar about the guy who gets out, but it isn't until the picture zooms in on the woman who greets him with open arms at the door that I recognize him.

It's Dad. He looks about ten years older than he did when he left, and his hair is graying around the temples, but it's him. Very much alive. Very much the picture of health. And he is living a slice of domestic bliss.

My stomach churns. It shouldn't be possible. Even if he somehow managed to defy every odd of the condition I inherited from him, he shouldn't be walking around like nothing is wrong.

"Fuck," I growl, realizing Chemuel is still watching me. "I've seen enough. Turn it off."

The angel folds his hand and the screen disappears. He seems to get a kick out of that cruel little trick, but the gut punch tells me it's real.

"If it's any consolation, your sister didn't know the price he paid for his new lease on life," Chemuel says, still staring at me.

"But she knew he was still alive," I grit out. "She knew, and she didn't tell me."

More confirming silence. "If you can't trust your own flesh and blood, do you really think you can trust Apollyon?"

"And what's the alternative?" I challenge. "Handing over my baby to Lucifer?"

"That thing inside of you is not a baby, regardless of the illusion your power has distorted reality into," Chemuel says firmly, standing. "The sooner you realize that, the better."

"Go to hell."

He gives me an infuriating smile and walks over to the door. "Lucifer will be here to collect you soon. I suggest you check the attitude before then. He's not half as patient as I am."

THIRTY-SEVEN

IT TAKES hours before someone comes to "collect" me, but when they finally do, I don't bother to look up. All the angels are the same. Spineless assholes who never bother to address me beyond making some smartass remark.

This one drags me to my feet and down the hall before throwing me into another room. I catch myself on my hands and knees, and when I look up, I find myself staring at boots.

"Levi," a decidedly familiar voice whispers. My head snaps up so fast my neck hurts, and when I find myself staring up at my twin, I realize I have to be dreaming.

"Sirena?"

She's disguised in a long white robe with a golden hood, but how the hell that worked on the angels is beyond me. Surely they know who she is. "What the fuck are you doing here?"

"I'm here to get you out," she says, glancing at the door. "We don't have much time. The spell is going to wear off soon."

"Spell?" I ask. "The hell are you talking about?"

She looks at me impatiently, like we're teenagers again and sneaking around. "I swapped bodies with a saint," she says, as if that's just a normal thing people do. Or something I'm supposed to even understand.

"I'm sorry, is that supposed to mean something to me?"

She rolls her eyes. Definitely Sirena. "Just come on," she says, grabbing my wrist as she rushes toward a window on the other side of the room. I watch in confusion as she pushes the window up and starts to climb out.

"Wait," I hiss.

She looks impatiently at me and all I can do is stare in disbelief.

"You're not supposed to remember me," I murmur.

Her eyes narrow, filled with anger. "I'm well aware of the deal you made with Apollyon, but I'm a witch. I know when I'm being mind fucked and I reversed the spell."

"Where are we?" I ask, looking down at the steep drop off on the other side of the window.

"Heaven adjacent," Sirena answers.

"And what the fuck does *that* mean?"

She gives me a withering look. "Just jump out the window when I say to."

I stare at her. "Is that a joke? Because I'm really not in the mood."

"I have a plan," she says intently. "You're just going to have to trust me and drop."

"Is this one of those, 'if your sister said to jump off a bridge, would you do it' things? Because--"

"Levi!" she growls. "We don't have time, and trust me, if Lucifer gets his hands on you, it's gonna be a lot worse than the drop."

"Wait," I say, my self-destructive instincts taking precedence over survival. Nothing new, really. But still, I know if

I'm ever going to get a clear answer out of her, it's now. "I need you to tell me something. The truth. Did you know Dad was still alive?"

Sirena's face goes blank. "Levi, this isn't the time."

"Did you know?" I demand, pulling my hand out of her grasp.

She sighs. "Yes."

I swallow hard. Finding out she knew and hearing it directly from her are two different things. "And you didn't say anything? To me or Mom?"

"What was I supposed to say?" she cries. "By the way, our father, who should be dead by now? He's actually a witch, and he's alive because he struck a deal with the devil. Now he's living out in Boca Raton."

"And the price he paid for that fresh start?" I ask. "Did you know about that?"

She frowns. "What are you talking about?"

"Me," I answer. "His firstborn son. He traded my soul to Lucifer for a fresh start. You're telling me you didn't know about that?"

The shock on her face comes as a relief. "No," she says hoarsely, shaking her head. "I didn't. Levi, I swear, I didn't. I knew about the ritual from the book and put two and two together, but I never..."

"Good enough," I mutter. "Not that I don't appreciate you coming for me, but I'm waiting on Apollyon."

She raises an eyebrow. "Who do you think sent me?"

"Seriously?" I can't hide my irritation. "He won't come himself?"

"He's a demon," she says flatly. "He can't get into heaven without a proxy."

He's alive. And to think at one point, that would've been the opposite of a relief.

"Come on," Sirena says firmly, halfway out the window. "We don't have much time."

Now that I know Apollyon and Sirena are working together, I don't exactly have an excuse, other than the fact that I'm not eager to jump into the abyss.

"Here goes nothing," I decide out loud. I walk out onto the ledge with Sirena, alarmed by how calm she seems about traipsing inches away from certain death. Or at least an eternal freefall.

"Just trust me," she says, like someone who isn't asking me to jump off a building. She holds her hand out and I take it, trying not to pass out.

"Jump on three," she says. "One. Two. Three!"

I had plans of jumping casually, all *Mission Impossible* style, but they go out the window as soon as I do. Our screams--or maybe just mine--echo around us, loud enough to wake the dead and whatever else happens to be up here. I clutch Sirena's hand tightly as we go tumbling toward clouds that are, disconcertingly enough, below us.

Something comes into view below and I get a sickening feeling in my stomach when I realize it's an all-too-familiar portal similar to the one the angel had come through--and we're hurtling toward it at the speed of light.

Just when I think we're about to make contact, we pass through to the other side. It's a new enough experience that I feel sure I'm going to splatter against the ground on the other side, rather than stumbling and falling to my knees.

"Where are we?" I ask, looking around as I get my bearings.

"Not out of the woods yet," Sirena mutters. "We're in Purgatory."

"Purgatory?" I echo. "Are you serious?"

"I said the same thing," she sighs, brushing the dirt off her long robe. "Come on."

I follow her, looking around the seemingly endless void that's just as nondescript as the outside of the building we just jumped out of. "Where is this?"

"Between Heaven and Hell," she answers.

"No wonder they're so territorial," I remark. "Did you know angels have taken over Hell?"

"Not all of Hell," Serena clarifies. "Just Apollyon's realm."

"You know, for just once, you could let me be the one in the know."

She rolls her eyes. "Sorry," she says flatly. "When your boyfriend came to me for help, he gave me the rundown."

"I'm still not sure how you got involved in this and I can't really imagine Apollyon asking anyone for help."

Sirena shrugs. "He needed a human with magical experience to get into Heaven and reach you, and besides, he knows I've been itching for the chance to kick your ass for that stunt you pulled."

"Are you talking about the erased memories or the fact that I stole the guy you sold your soul to?" I ask dryly. "Because after you stole my favorite jacket, I think we're even."

She narrows her eyes at me, walking faster. I pick up the pace, figuring there's a damn good reason. Even though there seems to be nothing around us, I'm sure it won't take long for the angels to realize I'm gone.

"I still can't believe you," she says. "You had no right."

"*I* had no right?" I scoff. "Really want to go there? When you lied to me my entire life, and then tried to sell your freaking soul for me?"

She rolls her eyes again. Must run in the family. "Trying

to save your life. And for the record, it worked. Or at least, it would have, if you hadn't interfered."

"My deal did work," I correct. "And you still have your soul."

She groans in irritation. "I never sold my soul. And this all resulted in you ending up pregnant and kidnapped by angels, and the devil himself, so I wouldn't get too high and mighty about your plan working out better than mine."

It's a fair point. Not one I'm going to acknowledge, but fair. "So, I guess I don't get to tell you you're going to be an aunt with a banner or anything."

She raises an eyebrow. "Assuming the thing that comes out of you isn't a three-headed dragon."

"You say that like you wouldn't love it if it was."

"Just keep walking," she orders. "We have to reach the portal that leads to Earth."

"Earth? I can't go back," I say, putting on the brakes. "I made a deal with Apollyon."

Sirena gives me a disbelieving look. "You're seriously going through with this?"

"I'm carrying his baby. It's kind of more than a one-night stand at this point."

"I can't believe this," she mutters. "In any case, we *have* to go to Earth. Apollyon and the demons he has left have already fled Hell. Lucifer's got eyes everywhere."

"There are others who survived?" I ask hopefully. "What about Maiz and Shera?"

"I have no idea who either of them are, I just know Apollyon gave me explicit instructions to follow, and I'm getting you out of here."

That's good enough for me, or at least, it'll have to be. "Where is this portal?"

"I have no idea."

"How are we supposed to know when we find it?"

"If it's anything like the one we just went through, I think we'll know."

"Fair enough."

As it turns out, she's right. She usually is, but the roar of the portal is unmistakable. I've gone through three already, since the fateful ritual I undertook so foolishly, and I'm still not anywhere close to accustomed to it. Each time, it feels like my soul is being sucked out of my body.

"There," Sirena says, like there's any chance I'm gonna miss the giant gaping void eating up the gray sky in the distance.

I quicken my pace to keep up with her, feeling a strange resistance the closer we get to the energy field. I touch my stomach instinctively and the familiar warmth stirs up again.

"What's wrong?" Sirena demands.

"I don't think the kid likes the portal."

She rolls her eyes. "Get your ass over here, we don't have time."

I look back over my shoulder. I can't see anything, but she's right. It's only a matter of time before the angels find us. Reluctantly, I follow her through and this time, we end up landing on pavement.

"What the fuck?" I groan, looking around the abandoned parking lot. From the looks of the faceless building behind it, it was once a discount supermarket, and I'm pretty damn sure we aren't in Rhode Island anymore. There's the salty scent of ocean air, but the pavement is hot even through my shoes.

"The portal changes locations, to keep it protected," Sirena explains.

"Just how involved in this magic shit are you?" I demand.

"Do you really want to get into that right now?"

"No," I grunt. "Where's Apollyon?"

"Give him a second. The portal spits you out randomly, could be anywhere in the world."

"Anywhere and we ended up *here?*"

"It could be worse."

Apollyon's voice makes my heart do a little cartwheel in my chest and when I turn around, the sight of the inky black shadows creeping into the corner of the building should scare the shit out of me, but it just makes me giddy.

"Apollyon!" I cry, running toward him as he materializes from the shadows.

He takes me into his arms and we hug each other so tightly I can hardly breathe. "Did you think I wouldn't find you?" he asks softly.

"Honestly, not really," I say, looking up at him. "You did just get fucked over by Heaven *and* Hell."

He sighs. "It's good to see you again, too." He looks down, putting his hands on my waist. "How's the baby?"

"Fine, as far as I can tell," I answer. "Not like there's a book about what to do when you're expecting the antichrist."

"This is so fucking weird," Sirena mutters, grimacing at us.

"Rude."

"I'm not talking about the baby, I'm talking about you being in a relationship with a demon," she shoots back.

"You can continue your sibling rivalry later," Apollyon says, putting an arm around my shoulder. "We shouldn't linger."

"Where can you take him that's safe from Lucifer and

the angels when you can't even get back into Hell?" Sirena challenges.

"There's a place even angels fear to tread," Apollyon says wryly.

"Massachusetts?" I blurt out. Now he and Sirena are both giving me withering stares. "Sorry. Couldn't resist."

THIRTY-EIGHT

TURNS OUT, I wasn't far off with the waterfront location. The tropical island Apollyon poofed us to is about as far from Hell as it gets, and while it doesn't seem particularly angel-proof, it's definitely remote.

"Where are we?" Sirena asks, looking around the dense jungle and huge tropical flowers lining a stone path.

"It's better if you don't know the location. You won't be staying," Apollyon says.

I stare, probably slack-jawed, because I've never heard anyone talk to her like that. Not even a demon.

She glances from me to him, her eyes narrowing. "The hell I won't. I helped you for his sake, but I'm not leaving him with you."

"That's not really up to you, is it?"

"Okay," I interject. The last thing I need right now is for the two most important people in my life to go at it. "Everyone, settle. Sirena can't go back right now, they'll be looking for her as soon as they realize I'm gone."

"I'm sure they already have," says Apollyon. "Let me guess, you want me to bring your mother here, too?"

Sirena and I look at each other and blink.

"I'm sure she's fine," she insists.

"Yeah," I agree. "No need for that. You can just send a demon to watch her, right?"

"As you wish," Apollyon says, raising an eyebrow.

"And Ben," I add. Sirena looks away guiltily. I'm sure they've talked since my disappearance, but I'm not going to bring it up in front of Apollyon.

"Anyone else you want security detail on?" asks Apollyon. "The mailman, perhaps?"

"Nope. Guy's a dick. Never brings my catalogues," I answer. "Seriously, though, how long are we staying here?"

"*You* are staying as long as it takes for me to regain control of my realm," Apollyon says.

"Uh, given what Haniel and Chem told me, that could be a while," I warn him.

He frowns. "Chem?"

"Chemuel. We're on a nickname basis."

"Right. Well, the fact remains that as long as Lucifer is working with the enemy, Hell isn't safe," says Apollyon.

"How are you supposed to go up against him?" Sirena demands.

"Lucifer might be the Prince of Hell, but the title is not immutable," Apollyon says flatly. "He moved against one of his own, and when word gets out, there are going to be many willing to oppose him on those grounds alone."

"Why would he even do that?" I ask. "Things have been fine between you for what, centuries?"

"Millennia," Apollyon corrects.

"So what changed?" I ask.

"Isn't that obvious?" asks Sirena. "You."

"She's right," says Apollyon. "I took a risk by claiming

Lucifer's vessel, and he took a risk by capturing you. Only one of those risks is going to pay off."

"He wanted the army," I mutter. "Now, they know it doesn't exist."

"It exists," says Apollyon, pressing his hand to my stomach. "It's just consolidated. He was counting on doubling the size of his army and double-crossing the angels, I'm sure. Lucifer will be coming for the child."

"Well, he can go fuck himself," I snarl. "Our kid's not anyone's pawn."

"He's not going to touch you," Apollyon says firmly, pulling me to his chest. "Either of you."

I find myself relaxing in his arms, but the fact that we aren't alone keeps me from being fully at ease. "Where are the others?" I finally ask. "Where's my dog?"

"Your dog?" Sirena frowns. "Since when do you have a dog?"

"Come on," Apollyon says, motioning for me to follow him down the path. A massive one-story house comes into view with ornate pillars supporting a red tiled roof. A screened patio lush with vines surrounds the entire property. There's even a pool, and the house is surrounded by tall bushes adorned with flowers of every color. In the twilight, it looks too beautiful to be real.

"What is this place?"

"A sanctuary of sorts," Apollyon answers, opening the tall black door. Before I can take a step inside, a black shadow flies out, taking me to the ground. I'm sure it's Lucifer coming to repay me for my smartass comments until I feel the familiar swipe of a dripping wet tongue along my face.

"Janis!" I cry, wrapping my arms around the plush fur at her neck.

"What the fuck is that thing?" Sirena shrieks, clearly horrified. Not that I can really blame her. Janis is definitely a sight to behold if you aren't expecting her.

Even if you are...

"This is Janis," I say, patting her bony head. "She's a hellhound."

"Of course she is," Sirena says, unblinking as she takes in the monster before her.

"You're back."

Maiz's familiar voice is surprisingly welcome, given the fact that I never thought I'd see him again. He isn't unscathed after our mutual encounter with the angel, though. There's a long, deep scar on the left side of his face that wasn't there before.

"What the fuck happened to you?" I blurt out.

"Good to see you, too, Levi," he says with a faint smile that's slightly lopsided due to the scar.

Apollyon helps me to my feet and Janis remains pressed close to my leg as I walk over to Maiz.

"I had a bit of a run-in with Haniel before he took you," he answers, his gaze softening with guilt. "And I failed. I'm truly sorry."

"Don't apologize," I mutter. "At least... not for that." I know if I bring up our full history, Sirena will be the one who kills him, so I decide to leave it be. "What happened? I don't remember much, except waking up in Heaven. Which, by the way, sucks."

"You were blinded by the light," Maiz answers. "It's a tactic angels use to stun their subjects for easier abduction."

I blink. "Why does that sound like aliens?"

"I'm sure there's many an abduction story that could be more accurately attributed to them," Maiz muses.

File that under 'what the fuck.' "Where's Shera?" I ask, afraid to know the answer. "Please tell me she wasn't..."

"She's alive," Apollyon says flatly. "And we have reason to believe she was the one who tipped Lucifer off."

"What?" I cry. "Bullshit. She wouldn't do that."

Or maybe I just don't want to believe it. Maiz's silence speaks volumes, and I'm surprised at just how deep the sense of betrayal runs. Maybe the angels were right and it did start out as Stockholm syndrome, but fuck, that stings.

"What do we do now?"

"You're not going to do anything but stay here and rest," Apollyon answers. "This place is protected. It will be adequate shelter until the child is born."

I wince. "Yeah, about that. Uh. How exactly does that work?"

"For the sanity of all involved, I would recommend a caesarean," Maiz says in a dry tone.

"I second that," Sirena says, raising her hand.

"And the doctor?" I ask hopefully. "He's uh, one of the survivors, right?"

"He's in Hell at the moment, but I'm sure Maiz will be able to fill in if we can't get him here by then," Apollyon says casually.

I look doubtfully at the other demon. "Easy for you to say. You're not the one carrying a demon baby."

"I've been around for many thousands of years, Levi. I have far more experience than the average physician," Maiz assures me.

I can only vouch for his skills doing harm, so I'm skeptical. At least we have some time to figure it out.

THIRTY-NINE

"YOU SHOULD GET SOME REST," Apollyon says, climbing into bed. The master suite isn't quite as spacious as the one back home--and my head hurts if I think too much about the fact that I officially consider *Hell* home sweet home--but it's nice enough with a view of the beach and breezy wicker furniture.

Not exactly my taste, but it isn't bad for a vacation getaway. Looking at it that way is the only way I'm going to be able to keep my sanity.

"After that? Are you kidding? I've still got the jitters from all that interdimensional travel."

He chuckles, pulling me into his arms. "You handled yourself well. I'm very impressed."

"I didn't think I'd ever see you again," I admit.

"I told you I'd come for you."

"That was really you?"

He presses his forehead against mine and the warmth I'm so used to feeling by now runs all the way up and down my spine as I melt against him. "I told you, there's nowhere I can't reach you."

Funny how the words that were once a chilling threat make me shiver for entirely different reasons now. "I realized something while I was up there."

"And what is that?" he asks, lowering his head to kiss the side of my neck.

My eyes fall shut and I slide my fingers into his silken hair. "I don't want to be away from you. Ever again."

"You say that like it's a new development."

"It is," I admit, thinking of Sirena's reluctance over my desire to return to him. "Guess you've grown on me."

He chuckles, a husky, seductive sound as he kisses his way down my bare chest. "Glad to hear it."

"What if you hadn't been able to find Sirena?" I ask, looking up at him. "Would I have been stuck there?"

"I would've found another witch," he answers.

"Guess they're more abundant than I would've thought," I mutter. Another question occurs to me, one I'm afraid to know the answer to. "If I asked you a question, would you be honest with me?"

He tilts his head. "Doesn't your ability to believe the one answer hinge on the other?"

"I'm too tired to make any sense of that. Just answer me."

"Yes," he sighs. "What is it that you want to know?"

"Chemuel told me about my father. That he's the one who sold my soul to Lucifer."

"I warned you that was a possibility."

"Yeah, but did you know it was more than just a possibility?" I ask. "Did you know he was still alive?"

"No," he says without a bit of hesitation. Somehow, I know the part of me that believes him isn't just a result of wanting to. "I didn't know, Levi, but I'm sorry."

I nod. Somehow, it doesn't make me feel any better. Just less devastated on the one front.

Apollyon gathers me back into his arms, and this time, the kiss he places on my cheek is more comforting than seductive. "It's his loss. Whatever he gained, he missed out on knowing you, and that makes him a fool."

"Nah," I mutter, turning my head so he can't see my smile. "You're full of shit, but... thank you for saying that."

"It's true," he says, kissing my forehead as he gazes down at me. "I just lost my realm and the entire time, all I could think about was finding you."

"Bullshit."

"You think it brings me any pleasure to admit that?" he taunts. "You've changed me, Levi. I can't say whether it's for the worse or for the better, but it's irrevocable."

I don't know what to say. What *am* I supposed to say to that? I just stare at him breathlessly and the only words that come are, "Kiss me."

His lips curve into a delicious smile and he fulfills my demand, his soft lips brushing against mine. The kiss deepens as he moves on top of me, pressing his thigh between my legs. My body opens for him instinctively, and even though I know the pain that comes with his penetration, I crave it more fiercely than ever.

His cock grazes my ass as he positions himself and I hold my breath, preparing for the sweet ache as he eases into me. He's even gentler than he was the last time, somehow, and it feels like poetry as he moves inside of me, his clawed fingers lacing with mine as he presses my hands to the mattress.

"Fuck," I breathe, arching beneath him in spite of my common sense.

"I missed that dirty mouth of yours," he says in a husky voice.

"I'm sure. Not like you could find anyone else willing to suck your serrated dick."

He snorts. "I'm not sure you know what that word means."

"I know it's knife-related. Close enough," I say, kissing him. His tongue finds mine and I realize I missed the taste of him as much as everything else.

He fists my hair and pulls my head back, revealing my throat. I moan like he pushed a button to elicit the sound, and the vibrations of his chuckle against my throat tell me he finds it deeply amusing that he has such control over me.

And he can laugh all he wants, because it feels too fucking good to care. Every thrust sends him deeper into my core, and the memories of the pain mingled with pleasure come surging back as I rock beneath him.

As he fucks me, another desire I'm only just beginning to recognize bubbles to the surface. It reared its head the first time we fucked, but the newness of the experience kept me from following its trail as fully as I'd like. But hell, I just escaped Heaven and I'm in the mood to take a risk.

"Bite me," I say, meaning it as an order even though it sounds more like a request.

He looks down at me like I'm crazy, as per our usual dynamic, and says, "If you don't like what I'm doing, you can just tell me."

"No, not that," I pant. "I mean I want you to bite me."

Same look, different reason. "What, do you *enjoy* pain?"

I think about it for a second before shrugging. "Yeah. Kinda. When it comes from you."

I'm expecting another smart remark, but the way his eyes darken isn't a disappointment. "I have fangs."

"So I've noticed."

"It would hurt, and not a small bit."

I lick my lips and squirm enough to make him gasp. "Promises, promises."

"Fuck," he breathes, lowering his head. His breath comes down on my skin like the fall of silk and I hold my breath, waiting for it. The moment his fangs pierce my skin, I come in a flood of ecstasy and he bites down harder, like the blood rushing into his mouth is a brand new addiction.

His lips seal around the punctures as he comes, his massive cock barely halfway inside of me. Between being knotted and being bitten, the former was far more painful, but I wouldn't have said no to both.

Maybe next time.

When he finally pulls away, his eyes are as red as the blood on his lips and I can't resist the urge to taste it. To taste him, and my blood on his tongue. It's sex and scarlet, a flavor I want more of.

"Now who's got a dirty mouth?" I taunt.

He kisses me hard enough to shut me up and I stroke his face with equal affection. "God, I love you," he mutters.

And for the first time ever, I believe those words to be true.

FORTY

THREE MONTHS LATER

IT'S BEEN three months since Apollyon whisked me away to an island paradise, and the only thing keeping it from being a super sexy getaway vacation is the fact that we're sharing the beachfront bungalow with my sister and the world's most stoic demon.

The two of them get along well, which surprises absolutely no one. As I walk into the dining room, Maiz is at the stove frying up what smells like bacon and eggs while Sirena sits at the table, reading one of the spellbooks that populates the library.

She's fully out of the broom closet now and I'm trying to withhold judgment even though her hobby got us both sucked into Hell. If Apollyon has faith in her abilities, I figure there's something to it, but I'm still not crazy about her being this involved in the occult when I know firsthand what demons are like--the bad and the unexpected good.

"Figuring out how to summon Lucifer so we can make it a fivesome?" I ask dryly.

She flips me off without looking up from the book.

"Your sister is quite the acolyte," Maiz remarks, glancing over at me. "She was just asking me about some of the profane arts."

"I'm sure she was. She majored in those during junior college."

"Says the guy who got caught sucking the dean's cock."

"He wasn't *my* dean," I argue.

"Will Lord Apollyon be joining us?" Maiz asks in a pleasant tone. I can tell all the bickering makes him uneasy. Definitely an only child.

"No, he's off doing demon things he wouldn't tell me about," I mutter, dropping into the chair across from Sirena. I scowl at the book that's almost certainly bound in human flesh. "Do you have to put that thing on the surface where I eat?"

Sirena looks up at me, her face blank with confusion. "It's not sitting in the palm of Apollyon's hand."

"You go fuck yourself. That was great, but you go fuck yourself all the same."

She smirks, looking back down at the arcane pages of a book she probably got a first class ticket to Hell just for cracking the cover of.

"I'm afraid I will never understand you two," Maiz says, setting a plate down in front of each of us.

"Demons don't have siblings?" I ask.

"We do, but we're usually raised apart," he admits. "We don't have strong family ties."

"That's kind of depressing," says Sirena.

"At least we don't fight."

"That's the best part of having siblings," I laugh. "Half the time, you want to kill each other, but you'd kill for each other, too."

Sirena smiles. "Or sell yourself to a demon, apparently."
I snort.

"So you don't hate each other?" Maiz asks doubtfully.

"Sure we do," I answer. "That's just part of it. It's a twin thing, I guess."

"At least *that* didn't get passed on," Sirena muses.

I look down at my stomach, grimacing at the thought of being twice as big as I am now. It's already a challenge to get up quickly and given the fact that I'd never even entertained the possibility of being pregnant before, it's unnerving, to say the least. "I'm good with one and it's gonna take me the full nine months to get there."

"It might not be nine months," says Maiz. He must notice me glaring at him because he adds, "The gestation period of a typical lightbearer can vary dramatically, and this is far from a typical situation."

"Thanks for the mindfuck," I mutter.

"You do look a bit beyond four months," Sirena remarks.

Now it's my turn to flip her off.

"I'm serious. From what I've been able to gather, all this is based on your expectations," she says, tapping the page in her book. "You're still a variation of an architect, even if you are a weird one. Your perception could shift the nature of the pregnancy, since it already turned Apollyon's army into a baby."

"Don't give my brain any ideas," I groan, gripping my head. "The last thing I need is a premature demon birth. Especially when Apollyon's gone."

"He's right. We shouldn't stress him out," Maiz reasons. "Levi, you haven't touched your eggs."

"I don't have much of an appetite, what with the horror and all," I say, dropping them to the floor for Janis. They barely make it before she scarfs them down and Sirena winces. She's still having trouble adjusting to my otherworldly pet, but if I have to put up with her being the wicked witch of the northeast, she can learn to tolerate my hellhound.

Besides, if Maiz is right, things are about to get a whole lot more unsettling.

FORTY-ONE

APOLLYON DOESN'T COME BACK that night, and after being reassured by Maiz that he's perfectly fine, I make myself a promise that I'm going to demand he starts carrying a smartphone. Technically, I'm pretty sure Maiz is the demonic version of a smartphone, but still.

When I wake up, the sun is streaming through the curtains as usual. Just another day in tropical wherever the hell we are. Until my hand brushes my stomach and I realize something is...

Off.

"Fuck!" I cry, nearly falling out of bed when I look down at my stomach. It's twice as big as it was been the night before, and I quickly lose hope that I'm having a weird ass dream when I pinch myself and it hurts like a motherfucker.

Janis comes to my side, whimpering and wagging her bony tail in an attempt to console me. She doesn't seem to understand what the issue is.

"What's wrong?" Sirena shouts, throwing open the door with her hand over her eyes just in case Apollyon is back and she walks in on something neither of us wants her to see. Not that the reality is much better. She finally uncovers her eyes and goes white as a ghost. "Holy shit."

"I know!" I cry, my heart racing in my ears.

"What the fuck happened?" she shrieks.

"I don't know! I just woke up like this!"

"What's going on?" Maiz demands, coming up behind her. His eyes widen when he sees me. "Oh, dear."

"This is your fault," I hiss, pointing at Sirena.

"Me? How the fuck do you figure that?"

"You're the one who planted it in my head about this being a paint-by-numbers pregnancy!" It's admittedly a shoddy argument, but I'm panicking and deflection comes naturally.

"Is that really possible?" she asks, looking to Maiz.

"It would seem so," he says, looking at me like a science experiment gone wrong. "Levi, I believe you should lie down."

"Lie down? I'm nine months preggo and you want me to take a nap?"

"Just rest, the anxiety isn't helping," he replies, leading me over to the bed. I reluctantly sit down because I feel like I'm going to tip over if I don't.

"We're not ready," I protest. "You said you'd have to perform surgery. Don't you need time to Google it or something?"

"I've performed surgeries in the past, and you're not giving birth right this moment." He pauses. "Hopefully."

"Not comforting."

"I'll go get some hot water and towels," Sirena says, looking haunted.

"What the hell is that supposed to do?"

"I don't know! It's just what they say in movies."

"Sirena," Maiz says calmly. "Do you think you could perform the summoning ritual on page thirty-three of the book I gave you?"

She hesitates. "I don't know, I... maybe?"

"Please try, and if you have trouble, I'll take over."

"Why are you talking like this is happening now?" I ask warily. "Oh, God, is it?"

The way Maiz is looking at me is far from soothing. "Levi, all I know is that this is entirely dependent on your... imagination. So, the best thing you can do right now is to calm down and think pleasant thoughts."

"I don't know how long you've been a demon, but when manipulating human emotions, telling us *not* to worry is usually the fastest way to freak-out town," I inform him.

"I'll be right back," Sirena says, darting out of the room.

"Fuck," I mutter as I feel a strange pain begin to radiate from the right side of my stomach. The more I tell myself it's the power of suggestion, the worse it becomes, because apparently, my thoughts are capable of fucking me over in a far more literal way than I'd ever imagined.

"What's wrong?" Maiz asks, looking me over worriedly.

"I think it's a contraction."

"How do you know?"

"I don't, but if I think it's a contraction, that means it is!"

He winces. "Fair point. Just... try to breathe, alright?" He strokes my hair, but the gesture isn't exactly consoling coming from him.

I do as he says anyway, breathing in through my nose and out through my mouth until I feel lightheaded.

"Good," Maiz coaches. "That's good. Your heart rate is slowing down."

"Well, now it's going up again!"

He sighs. "Just relax. I'll be right back."

"Where are you going?"

"I'm going to need to get some equipment if we're doing this here."

"This isn't a hospital room!"

"No, and I haven't had time to prepare one properly, so we're going to have to make do. Stay put."

Like I have a damn choice. I sink back against the pillows, taking a deep breath as I try to focus on the ceiling. Anything, really, except the fact that I'm about to give birth four months ahead of schedule.

Maiz comes back carrying his black leather medical bag and I eye it nervously. "What's in there? Hopefully a fully sanitized surgery with a world-class team of doctors trained in male pregnancy?"

"Levi, listen to me," he says gently, taking my hand. I'm close enough to tumbling into the abyss in my own head that I appreciate the tether. "I'm not going to pretend like this will be easy, but you have the most unique mind I've ever encountered, and if anyone can do this, it's you. I'm going to get you through this, and you're going to have to trust me, alright?"

I nod, my throat still too tight to speak.

"Good," he says, sitting down next to me. "Now, I'm going to put you under mild sedation using mind control. You're going to be awake enough to respond to my commands, but you won't feel any pain, do you understand?"

"You're going to cut me open while I'm still awake?" I croak.

"It's akin to twilight sedation, which is quite standard for these procedures, and I'll have my consciousness linked with yours the entire time--I'll know if you're feeling any discomfort."

It occurs to me that I'm going to have to rely on the guy who'd tortured me to make sure giving birth isn't as traumatic as it has the potential to be, but what choice do I really have?

"Just keep breathing," he says calmly, rolling up my shirt to feel my stomach. Not like it fits all that well anymore. "Does that hurt?"

"No more than before," I answer.

"Good," he says, smoothing a cool gel-like substance over my abdomen. It smells like alcohol and the familiar scent makes my anxiety peak.

"Relax," he coaches. "I'm just prepping you."

"Yeah, it's what it's for that's giving me a panic attack."

He gives me a sympathetic look and touches the side of my face. "I need you to close your eyes and count down from ten. Just listen to the sound of my voice and let yourself relax."

I do as he says, both because his voice is hypnotic and because I'm desperate to take any road that diverges from stark reality. Before I get down to three, I begin to feel all swimmy, like I'm not fully in my own body anymore, which is just as well.

Pretty sure I don't want to be lucid for all this.

Maiz's voice begins to drift away and just struggling to keep up with it becomes enough of a challenge. I feel a faint pressure in my belly, but true to his word, I don't feel pain. There are pockets of lucidity where I start to panic as I realize what's actually going on around me, but he always pulls me back under before it can get out of control.

I begin to have less trouble relaxing when I hear Apollyon's voice, distant and echoing, as if he's at the other end of a tunnel. Then it's just a bit clearer, and as I stare up at the ceiling, detached from reality, I feel him here. A clawed hand takes mine.

Everything's gonna be okay.

And then, I hear it--the cry. It sounds like it was far away, too, but something about it pulls at my heart, like a voice I know even though I've never actually heard it.

I try to lift my head, but my body is frozen in place. Probably for the best. I do manage to ask, "Is the baby okay?"

"The baby is fine," Maiz says, his voice soft even though it seems to be further away than any other sound. "She's just fine."

That's the last thing I hear before I black out.

FORTY-TWO

I SLEEP for what feels like forever. When I open my eyes, I'm convinced it was all just a dream. After all, I'm still in our room, still in the bed Apollyon and I fell asleep in so many times, and there's no reason to think anything out of the ordinary happened. The sheets aren't covered in blood and I don't feel like I've just been carved open.

Then again... when I last went to bed, the sheets were blue, not white.

"Maiz?" I call, starting to panic. When I sit up, the pain in my stomach causes me to stop. I lift my shirt and see a thick white bandage wrapped around my midsection, which is almost as flat as it was before the pregnancy.

"Shit."

Before I can get up, Apollyon comes into the room, looking at me with an expression of pure fear. "Levi," he says, rushing over to my side. He leans down and kisses my forehead so quickly he nearly knocks me out with a horn. "You're awake."

"Where?" I ask, my voice hoarse with terror. "Where's the baby?"

"She's fine. She's with your sister," he assures me, stroking the damp hair away from my face. One of them must have bathed me while I was out. That explains why I'm not covered in blood. "You shouldn't be sitting up."

"I'm okay, I think. Assuming I don't get an infection from the DIY caesarean."

"You're fine. I had Maiz heal you, but you could only take so much energy at once in your condition."

"Wait--wait, she? It's a girl?" I ask, fixated on the cries I can hear from down the hall.

"Our daughter," he says softly, looking down at me. "I'm so sorry I was only here for the end, Levi."

"Probably better. From what little I remember, it was kind of gnarly."

He chuckles, shaking his head. "You did wonderfully. She's... well, she's perfect."

"I'd say I didn't have much control over that, but considering that she went from super premie to full term in like a day because of my imagination, I'm actually gonna take credit."

"As you should," he says, kissing me once again. "I'll be right back."

I wait anxiously until he returns with the small bundle wrapped in his arms and my heart melts in my chest. Not just because I'm seeing my child for the first time, the child I've wanted ever since I was little and never fathomed I'd actually get to have--even if this has been the last damn way I expected her to come into my life--but because of the way he looks holding her. The way his eyes soften as he gazes down at the tiny, fragile thing in his arms.

"Here she is," he says gently, sitting down on the bed next to me. My breath catches in my throat as I look down at the fussing infant and her blood red eyes meet mine. My heart already feels like it's going to explode with adoration, but then I take in her tiny claws, grasping the air blindly, and the tiny nubby horns peeking out from the dark curls on either side of her forehead, and I start tearing up like the joy is spilling out of my eyes.

She doesn't look real, and for a moment, I'm positive he must be playing some kind of trick on me. That she's the most lifelike doll I've ever seen, and then she cries and I recognize the sound of her voice from just before I'd lost consciousness, and I *know*.

She's real, and she's ours, and like Apollyon said, she's perfect.

"Here," Apollyon says, passing her into my arms. "Careful. You're still fragile."

She's the one who seems fragile. I stare down at her in fascination as her cries quiet and her eyes widen in recognition as she looks up at me.

"Hey, baby girl," I say hoarsely.

She cooes and it's the most beautiful sound I've ever heard. I can't help but laugh and when I look up at Apollyon, the almost goofy smile on his face says she has the same effect on him.

"Holy shit, she's real."

"Yes, she is," he agrees, putting his arm around us both. I lean against him because sitting up is harder than I want to admit. Bringing this kid into existence feels like it damn near killed me, but when I take in how impossibly perfect she is, I understand. Diamonds don't just come into existence for nothing.

"She doesn't look like an army of demons," I say, melting as she wraps her little clawed hand around mine. Her pointy fingertips feel like needles against my skin, but I don't care. We are *definitely* going to have to put mittens on her, though. If regular babies scratch their faces, her claws are a straight-up health hazard.

"You'd be surprised," he chuckles. "She's all of it wrapped up in one tiny package."

"She's still vulnerable," I murmur, looking up at him. "We have to protect her. We have to keep her away from them."

"I'll protect both of you," he promises, touching my face. "With my life."

"Don't say that," I mutter, leaning against his shoulder. "Hey... what does she eat, anyway?"

"There's formula in the kitchen, and she'll need blood as well," he answers. "But it can be mixed in."

I grimace. "That's nasty."

"She is a demon, Levi."

"Half-demon," I correct.

"A demon all the same."

I sigh. "I'll get over it. Whatever she needs... as long as I don't have to breastfeed." I pat my flat chest. "Don't think I manifested milk."

He snorts a laugh. "That won't be necessary. Nor do I think it's possible."

"Good," I yawn.

"You should rest, love. I've got her."

I hesitate before passing the baby into his arms. "Maybe for just a minute."

"As long as you need," Apollyon says, standing with the baby in his arms. "We'll be here when you wake up."

Never thought those words would be comforting coming from a demon.

FORTY-THREE

ONE WEEK LATER

IF THERE'S one career I've known was never a possibility from the time I got kicked out of junior high choir, it's being a rockstar, and yet, as I rock the baby in my arms on the porch and sing, she coos adoringly at me like I'm Freddie and Aretha wrapped up in one.

"Sabbath for a baby? Really?" Sirena asks dryly, coming out to join me.

"She's got horns. I'm sure she appreciates Ozzy more than *The Wheels on the Bus*."

"It's your kid," she says, taking the rocking chair next to me. "I still can't believe you named her Stevie."

"I wanted to name her Pat Benatar Snookie the Third, but Apollyon said no."

"You know, the fact that I'm your twin and I'm *still* not a hundred percent sure you're joking should concern you. How're you feeling?"

"Like a coconut someone duct taped back together, but I'm alright. Better every day," I admit, hesitating as I look down at the infant in my arms. "Does she look older to you?"

"She's a demon baby, Levi. I have no idea what they're supposed to look like."

"I know, but... you don't think she's growing up fast again, right?" I ask hopefully.

"Like the baby in that ridiculous movie you dragged me to the theatre to watch three times?"

"Okay one, Breaking Dawn Part One was a cinematic masterpiece," I say, jabbing a finger at her. "And two, yes. That's exactly what I'm worried about."

"I doubt it. But even if she did grow up overnight, it wouldn't be the worst thing in the world."

"Shh," I hiss, covering Stevie's pointed ears. "Don't say that."

"I'm just saying. She's not much of an army like this."

"She doesn't have to be an army if she doesn't want to," I huff. "She could be a neurosurgeon, or a sculptor, or a scuba instructor."

"A scuba instructor?" She raises an eyebrow.

"You're right, the horns would probably get in the way of the mask," I muse.

"Yeah. That was totally my point."

"What about you?" I ask.

"What about me?"

"I'm sure you want to get back to your life, now that things are settled down."

"Things aren't settled, Levi. Lucifer's still out there and I'm not leaving you alone with that prick."

"That prick is more or less your brother-in-law."

"I fail to see how that matters."

I sigh. "I'm just saying, I made my choice and I don't want you to be kept from living your life because of it."

"This is about Ben, isn't it?" she groans.

"It is not about Ben. Even if you do light up everytime someone says his name."

"That's irritation, Levi, because you bring him up at every chance," she snaps.

"I'm just saying, you should've seen the way he reacted when you went missing. He still loves you, Sir."

"I know," she says, her voice softening. "I know. That's why I had to end things."

"What kind of self-defeatist bullcrap is that?"

"It's called being a realist. You know how Ben is. Everything has a rational explanation, and he wants a normal, rational life," she mutters. "That's not something I'd be able to give him."

"After all this, is normal really so off-putting?"

She raises an eyebrow. "You of all people don't have a right to lecture me on the virtues of choosing a quiet, comfy life."

"Hey, my life is plenty comfy. My sugar daddy has a private island, in case you haven't noticed."

She rolls her eyes. "I've already made my decision, Levi. I'm not going back."

"What do you mean you're not going back?" I cry. "You have a life. And a career. And Mom." I wince. "Okay, so that last one is a bad example, but still."

"I thought acting was all I wanted to do with my life," she says, shrugging. "But this... all this has made me realize, as crazy as everything that's happened since that ritual has been, that it's also the first time I've actually felt alive. Like I'm doing what I was meant to do."

"What, sipping piña coladas and babysitting the antichrist?"

"Magic," she answers. "I'm a witch, Levi. It's in my blood, just like being an architect is in yours."

"Yeah, and in case you didn't notice, that very nearly cost me my soul, through no choice of my own."

"We're not the same," she says quietly. "You didn't choose this, but I did... and I don't regret it. What Dad did was unforgivable, but there's another side to magic. There's this whole other world that exists, and I don't think I could leave it behind knowing it does, even if you weren't here."

"You're serious," I mutter. "All this witch stuff... it's not just a means to an end for you."

"It was," she confesses. "But it became more than that. It's who I am, and I can't pretend otherwise."

"So what now?" I ask after a moment of contemplation, just to make sure the next words out of my mouth don't put more of a wedge between us. It's a skill that's taken me too long to learn, but better late than never.

She shrugs again. "Maiz says they're always in need of bloodborn witches. Especially now that Hell's been divided."

"Right now, Apollyon doesn't even have a realm to rule," I remind her.

"Then he'll need people he can trust." She smiles faintly. "People with a vested interest in making sure he succeeds."

"I'm not going to complain about you sticking around. I want that, I just don't want to want it so much you give up the life you could have on earth for me."

"It's not for you," she says, leaning over to peck my cheek. "Not *just* for you, but you did make a deal with the devil for me. I'd be lying if I said that looking after you didn't have something to do with it."

I snort. "That deal turned out to be the best thing I ever did."

"Seriously?" She wrinkles her nose. "I mean, I know

you love Stevie, but if it wasn't for her, would you really want to spend the rest of your life with Apollyon?"

I think about it for a second before answering, "Nah. The rest of my life was supposed to be a few years and change, but eternity... yeah. That sounds just about right."

She sighs. "I can't say I understand, but at least you're happy."

"So I take it you're not gonna be seducing Maiz anytime soon."

She recoils like the thought horrifies her. "He's so not my type," she scoffs, standing up from her chair. "And besides, he's stone cold gay."

"Really?"

"Like you don't know."

I'm not sure what to make of her tone. "What do you mean?"

She blinks, then quickly backtracks. "Nothing. Never mind."

"Sirena, you promised," I say firmly. "No more lies."

She kicks the loose porch board under her feet. "It's just... kind of obvious, I thought."

"What's obvious?" Usually, we can practically finish each other's sentences, but this time, I'm completely at a loss for what she's getting at.

"The way Maiz feels about you."

I cough. "Maiz? You're kidding, right?"

The look on her face isn't humorous at all. "Maybe I'm wrong," she says, which is far more concerning than if she insisted on teasing me about it like she usually would. "He's a demon, so... who knows what he's really thinking?"

"Yeah," I murmur, even though the thought lingers long after she goes back inside. "Who knows."

FORTY-FOUR

TO MY RELIEF, Stevie doesn't end up growing at the rapid-fire rate at which my pregnancy progressed, but as the months pass and she begins to take in more of the world around her, it sure seems fast enough to me.

I know a time will come when we have to leave this place--the little sanctuary Apollyon has formed around us with distance and dark magic. But I still hold onto hope that it'll last as long as possible.

The weeks become months at a normal, human pace, but the months become years so ruthlessly. Two pass before I know it and my little cherub becomes a growling imp before my eyes. I understand now that the boundaries of the island jungle and shores she explores so eagerly will eventually fail to keep her in, and they'll become the prison they have so obviously become to her father.

Apollyon stays at my side most nights, but when he's gone, I know he's plotting mutiny. A return to the Hell that's been ravaged and betrayed by its own Prince.

When the time finally comes for all the plotting and planning to turn into action, I know there's a damn good chance it'll be the last time he ever returns to our bed. The last time I see any of the people who make up the fragile pillars of my world. Maiz and Sirena have become his loyal right and left hands, and her magic develops at a rate even more dizzying than my child's growth.

It's all too much, too fast, even though I know I'm the only one of our strange little family who feels it's anything but a torturous standstill. Even so, I find myself wishing I could just freeze them all in a snapshot. A single frame to keep it like this forever. This moment they all see as a prison is my paradise, and I just wish we could stay here a little bit longer...

One particularly balmy afternoon, after I finally bargained my tiny demon into a nap, I find myself out on the porch and realize I'm not alone. Apollyon and Sirena are off in whatever adjacent realm they slipped into to rally their resistance against Lucifer, but someone always stays to keep an eye on me and Stevie. This time, it's Maiz's shift.

It's been a while since I've been alone with him. Somehow, despite the fact that we're both marooned on the same tiny island, he manages to avoid me--and after Sirena's comments that never left my thoughts, I've been too afraid of the reason to press him on it.

"Hey," I say, sitting down next to him.

He gives me a tired smile. "Afternoon, Levi. I take it the little queen is down for a rest?"

"I had to promise her she could go fishing for Leviathan later, but she's asleep," I sigh, sinking deeper into the wicker rocker. "They've been gone for a long time."

"Your mate and sister, or the Leviathan?"

I give him a look. He knows damn well what I mean. "Something's happening, is it?"

"Something is always happening, Levi. You'll have to be more specific."

"It's in the air," I mutter bitterly, grabbing a beer from the cooler on the porch. Maiz reaches over and casually flicks the top off with his claw. I grunt my thanks and take a long swig. "I don't know how to explain it, I can just feel it."

I wait for him to deny it. To do his job and reassure me that whatever's going on, I needn't worry my "pretty little head" about it. Instead, he nods thoughtfully. "You should always trust your gut. It won't lead you astray."

"How can you say that?"

"Because it hasn't so far," he answers, looking over at me with a faint smile. "If there is one thing in this world I'd stake my life on, it's your stubbornness."

I'm not sure what to say to that, or why it touches me as deeply as it does. I just know that if I'm ever going to get an answer to the question that's plagued me ever since I had that conversation with Sirena, it's now.

The same gut instinct is telling me we might not *have* later.

"I need you to be honest with me about something, Maiz. Whatever the truth is, it stays between us, but I just need to know."

"You want to know if I'm in love with you."

His candor takes me by surprise, even though it shouldn't. I know well enough what lies behind that reserved exterior, and it's not some shrinking violet. "Yeah. I guess that is what I'm asking."

Now I feel like I'm the one on the spot.

"Such hesitation," he muses. "Accelerated heartbeat. Wavering certainty. It would be so easy to convince you that you're just being a narcissist, appealing to your fragile ego the way I did to construct all those other beautiful, terrible lies."

I swallow the lump in my throat as anger and embarrassment rise up alongside each other. "So call me an idiot and get it over with."

"It would be a lie, though," he says casually, studying me. "And one I can't bring myself to tell, for the same reason that torturing you back then was so difficult."

I frown. "What are you saying?"

"Love isn't something that comes naturally for a thing like me," he says, looking out over the water. "It's all shades of gray, and it's hard to say where it became something distinguishable from all the rest of my long existence, but it did."

"Maiz..."

"I know you love Apollyon," he says before I can find a way to broach the subject myself. "You're his lightbearer. His mate. And he is my closest friend."

His reverence is obvious in the way he speaks the other demon's name. There's love there, too, much deeper and older, even if it's of a different shade. "I'm sorry," I say, because it feels like the only thing I *can* say. "I can't say I get why you feel that way about me, but I know what it's like to fall for someone you can't have and... I'm sorry."

"You have nothing to apologize for," he says, sweeping a stray strand of hair away from my face. "Serving you on his behalf has been my greatest honor. I could ask for nothing more."

I keep waiting for the snarky add-on that would render the sincerity and vulnerability he just showed moot, but it doesn't come and I really fucking wish it would. Before I can say anything, the screen door opens and I hear the familiar call of, "Daddy?"

I stand to face Stevie as she comes out onto the porch, still wearing her Godzilla footie pajamas. She rubs her red eyes as I lift her into my arms. "Hey, sweetie. You have a bad dream?"

She nods drowsily, her lips pulling down into a frown. "Fiel Man opened up the sky."

It takes me a second to run that through my toddler-to-English dictionary, but nothing comes up. "Who's Fire Man?"

"Levi..."

I turn around to find Maiz staring at the water, his stiff back to us both. At first, the only thing that seems out of the ordinary is the fact that the smattering of long, wispy clouds that were there a moment before are now gone. Then, I see it. The familiar shadow on the horizon. The way the water trembles against its natural ebb and flow, like something is vibrating just above the surface.

"A portal," I whisper.

If "opening up the sky" is Stevie's way of announcing a premonition of a portal, I have a bad feeling about the true identity of Fire Man.

"I don't understand. This place is protected," I say, holding Stevie close so she won't look. I'm trying not to panic for her sake, but as the portal grows on the horizon, that becomes a chore.

"Lucifer must have found a way to break through," Maiz says in an uncertain tone that suggests he knows about as little as I do. He turns to me, his gaze piercing. "The basement, Levi. It's the only place you'll be safe."

My heart thunders in my chest as I think of the basement wall where Apollyon's name is painted in blood, just as it was the first time. There's all but a single connecting line to make the sigil complete.

"Come with us," I plead.

I know even before he shakes his head what the answer is going to be. "Just run, Levi. Keep her safe."

My heart has broken a thousand times throughout my life, but I realize now that it's capable of fracturing once again, even for the man who's broken it more than his fair share of those times. If it weren't for the child in my arms, my response would be different, but I took a sacred oath the moment I became Apollyon's lightbearer. It morphed to a different oath when that promise became flesh and blood, but being a father is no less sacred or solemn.

"I will," I say, struggling to keep the fear out of my voice. I carry Stevie into the house and rush toward the stairs, feeling her straining to look outside. Janis leaves her spot on the rug in the living room to trot after us.

"Whe' ah we going, Daddy?"

"Papa has a special place where we'll be safe," I tell her.

"Wha' 'bot Unca Maiz?"

I swallow hard, setting her down in the relatively mundane-looking basement so I can lock the upstairs door and hopefully buy us some more time. "He'll follow us there."

I hate lying to my kid, but the older she gets, the more apparent it becomes that doing so is a matter of love. Especially when she lives in a world she can't possibly understand. I pull down the tapestry covering the incomplete writing on the wall and her eyes bug out.

"How come *I'm* no allow to daw on the wall?"

"This is a special occasion," I sigh, looking around for something with which to prick my finger. Something other than Janis' stinky teeth.

Stevie walks closer, staring up at the letters. "Wha's it say?"

"Apollyon," I answer.

"Papa?" She turns to me right as I dig a nail into my fingertip. Toddler timing, always looking at the worst moment, like when that bird had collided with our living room window a week ago.

Back then, explaining death in terms she was capable of understanding had been the most difficult parenting obstacle I'd faced, but it's about to get a whole lot more challenging.

"Why you poke you self, Daddy?" she cries.

"It's okay, sweetheart," I tell her, running my finger down the unfinished arm of the "y" in my mate's name. I scoop her up into my arms as the text lights up and becomes a blinding light. I have to squint, but her eyes widen and she stares at the opening portal like it doesn't bother her.

I cover her eyes anyway and carry her through with Janis close behind us as I feel the ground above and around us trembling.

"What's that?" she shrieks, staring up at the ceiling as chunks of paint and rust rain down.

"Just hold onto me," I order, holding her close as the portal closes behind us with an otherworldly groan and I feel the sensation of falling.

Fortunately, the fall is short, and as I look around and take in the blank gray sky, churning with unnatural clouds, I know we're home. We're back in Hell.

The portal leads to a wasteland beyond even Lucifer's close observation, and while it's only to be used by the others as an entrypoint to conduct the business of building their resistance, it's a last, *last* resort in the event that we need an escape.

"Whe' ah we?" asks Stevie.

"This is where Papa's from," I answer, walking toward

the single star visible on the horizon as quickly as I can. It's an illusion visible from any remote point in Hell, but Apollyon assured me that if I ever had to use the portal without him, I could follow its path and he would find me.

I just have to hope nothing else finds us first.

"I want Papa," Stevie whimpers, her arms wrapped tightly around my neck.

"I know, kiddo," I assure her, focusing on moving forward and trying to keep my thoughts off the waste that lies behind us. "So do I."

FORTY-FIVE

AFTER WALKING for what feels like forever, Stevie starts complaining about being thirsty. And then, I remember something. I'm a fucking architect. I can make shit with my mind.

I set Stevie down on a nearby rock and tell her to stay put for a moment. Janis sits beside her, tail wagging in the sand.

"Wha' you doin'?" she asks tiredly, watching me stare at the desert floor.

I give her a reassuring smile. "Just trying something," I say as I focus on the empty space in front of me. It's been a while since I actively materialized anything, since all my needs are accounted for on the island, but slowly but surely, the outline of an oasis begins to take shape in front of me.

"Pool!" Stevie cries, running over to the water's edge.

"Be careful, don't fall in," I warn her, tugging on the back of her shirt.

She kneels down and scoops up a handful of cool water before laughing in delight. "Magic! Do again!"

"Better use it sparingly," I say with a chuckle.

"How do?" she asks, stamping her feet excitedly, eyes glimmering with excitement and hair bouncing. I know better than to argue with her when she gets an energy spike like this. It's either appease her or deal with a tantrum.

"It's hard to explain, but I'm sure you'll be able to do all that and more, when you're older."

"Now, now!"

I sigh. Well, if it's going to keep her entertained...

"Alright, why don't you try to make something you want? Like a balloon?"

She scrunches up her nose. Clearly, balloons are not the shit as I remember them being when I was her age.

"I want a dragon," she says decisively.

"Maybe start with a dragon plushie?"

Before she can answer, her face goes blank and I follow her gaze to the looming shadow overhead. Immediately, I snatch her up into my arms and start backing away. Not like there's anywhere to take cover in the endless desert.

"Es okay," Stevie says, wrapping her arms around my neck as if to comfort me. "It's Papa!"

I look doubtfully at the shadow, still prepared to run, but as it takes on a familiar shape, I realize she's right. Janis doesn't seem bothered, either. In fact, she seems positively excited.

"Apollyon," I practically wheeze, running toward him. Stevie squirms out of my arms and gets to him first.

The sight of him lifting our daughter into his arms and swinging her around makes my fractured heart feel whole, even if I know it won't last. Not until this is over.

"There you are," he says warmly. Our eyes meet, mutual relief that will have to remain unspoken until we're alone. Stevie doesn't need to know how much danger we're truly in, or the tragedy we almost certainly left behind.

"Sky open up. We walk-ed through a wall. Daddy made pond!" she cries enthusiastically, as if this is all some elaborate game.

Apollyon looks at me knowingly, processing the sinister truth behind the innocent lens of her experience. "The sky?" he asks, clearly addressing me. His voice is calm and steady, but I know the fear in it. It's not something I often hear in his voice.

"Uncle Maiz stayed behind to take care of it," I say, my throat tightening up as I speak. "I think our old friend came for a visit."

Understanding flashes in his eyes and he nods. "Come," he says, holding his free arm out to me, keeping Stevie close to his chest. "Let's get you both inside."

I step under the protection of his cloaked arm and the shadow envelopes us all. By the time it clears, we're standing in a stone room far less expansive than the ones in Apollyon's palace, but similar in construction.

For the first time since we went through the portal, I let myself breathe. Apollyon puts our daughter down and she instantly starts running around, exploring.

"Be careful," I call after her.

"It's alright. The place is secure," Apollyon assures me.

"We thought that about the island," I remind him.

The way he flinches makes it clear he took that as blame, even though I didn't meant it that way. "I'm sorry. I never would have left you there if I thought--"

"I know," I say, taking his hand. His claws brush my palms as I weave my fingers through his. "For all we know, it's me. I was supposed to be his vessel..."

"You're not," he says firmly, gripping my hand tighter. "He's never going to touch you."

"He wants her." My voice trembles with rage. "Why now?"

Apollyon shakes his head. "I don't know. Maybe he realizes the resistance is gaining traction. We've already got the southeast realm, where his forces are neglected. This means we have to act now."

"Are you ready?" I ask doubtfully.

"We have to be." The steel in his gaze is inspiring, but I can't help but worry. All the planning and plotting... now that the time is here, will it actually be enough?

"Do you think Maiz is...?" I can't bring myself to finish the question. The look in his eyes isn't helping.

"I don't know, but I have to find out."

"You can't go back there!" I protest.

"I can't leave my most faithful soldier behind, love," he says, pressing his hand to my cheek. My heart aches at the thought of losing both of them, but I know he's right. "You'll be safe here."

"Come back," I mutter.

He leans down, smiling against my lips. "Is that an order?"

"You're damn right, it is."

He kisses me until I can't breathe and I'm still left wanting more when he pulls away. I tell myself there'll be more time, but in the back of my mind, I know it's far from a guarantee.

I watch as he disappears down the hall, and the soldiers who come in shortly after bow low to me.

"Lord Levi," the one in the middle says, clearly their leader judging from the regalia on his ornate uniform. His shoulders are saddled with horned armor that matches the antlers nested in his hair. His eyes are eerily white, but I've grown used to the strange variations among demons. "I am Carthos. I am at your disposal."

"Thanks," I say, nodding to the other two surrounding him. They're both women. Hell's army doesn't discriminate. "Have you seen my sister?"

"She's just down the hall," says Carthos. "Would you like me to fetch her?"

"No, that's okay. I'll go. Just... make sure the little imp running around doesn't sneak out. She's tricky."

"Understood, sir. The princess will be monitored."

"Princess?" I blink.

"When the conquest is complete, Lord Apollyon will be the reigning Prince of Hell and you, as his mate, the Duke," he answers. "That makes Lady Stevie a princess."

"Got it," I sigh. I'd happily trade the royal titles for a slice of life in a suburban neighborhood somewhere, but Lucifer's appearance made it clear that isn't happening.

I excuse myself and leave to explore, looking for Sirena in the process. I can see why Apollyon wasn't worried. The place is literally a fortress and the glimpse I get through a tall and narrow barred window shows the rocky cliffs below, falling into churning white waters that look ready to swallow up anything that ventures too close.

As I enter a room with papered walls and old furniture, I see the outline of a tiny shape standing out from the wallpaper. Janis is in the room, too, panting as she stares at the shape and giving Stevie away. I'd learned the hard way about Stevie's chameleon abilities, but Apollyon assured me that the best way to discourage the habit was playing along so she'd get bored of it.

"Hm," I muse, walking toward the window on the other side of the room. "I wonder where my little imp could be..."

The sound of her stifled laughter makes it hard not to

smile. I gaze out the window thoughtfully for a moment, giving her time to collect herself. "Too bad she's gone. I was getting hungry and I'm sure she'd want a snack."

"I want snack!" she cries, running out from the wall even though the damask pattern is only just beginning to fade from her skin.

"Stevie!" I gasp, feigning shock as I lean down. "Where did you come from?"

"I gots you," she announces triumphantly, throwing her arms around my neck so I'll pick her up.

"You sure did," I laugh, hugging her tight. Her antics are a much-needed distraction from the heaviness in my heart, even if it is largely due to fear of what will happen to her if Apollyon fails.

No... I can't let myself entertain that possibility. Ever since I learned I can control reality to one degree or another, I've been overcome by an obsessive fear over manifesting anything negative, even with my subconscious mind.

The door to the next room is closed, but as soon as I knock, Sirena flings it open. "Levi!" she cries, hugging us both. Behind her, there's a table with a map and a shit ton of candles, so I'm sure she's doing some form of witchy reconnaissance. "What are you doing here? Did something happen?"

"We came through the portal," I say, knowing that'll explain enough without having to say anything disturbing in front of Stevie.

"Oh," she says, her expression falling. "Well, you're both safe here."

"We were just about to go find the kitchen," I admit. "Any idea where it is?"

"Down that hall, then turn right. You can't miss it," she says, smiling at Stevie. "You two go on, I'll join you in a bit."

As I carry Stevie down the hall in search of the kitchen, I realize the hallway is getting darker. In fact, despite the torches on the wall, the only light seems to be coming from a doorway at the very end of the hall that I'm pretty damn sure wasn't there before.

I swallow hard, setting Stevie down again. Something is drawing me to that room, and it's the last place in the world I want her to be. "Go find Aunt Sirena," I tell her. "Bring Janis."

Stevie looks up at me, then at the room, and frowns. "Why? Come with," she says, tugging on my hand.

"I'll be there in a minute," I promise, stroking her hair. "Go straight to her, alright?"

She hesitates a moment before nodding. "Okay, Daddy."

I wait until I see my daughter and dog walking back in the direction of the room I left Sirena in and turn back to the door. The strip of light coming from underneath it intensifies, beckoning me.

I open the door and the light swallows me up.

FORTY-SIX

I SHIELD my eyes from the piercing rays of light, but the light seems to penetrate my bones themselves, leaving me feeling irradiated and hollow inside. By the time it finally clears enough to reveal the shape of a man on the other side of the room, my heart is racing, but I feel strangely calm. Detached somehow from the panic my body is experiencing for an entirely logical reason.

I've never seen the striking man with blond hair and pale blue eyes standing before me, but I know his identity as surely as if I'm coming face-to-face with my twin. In some bizarre way, he feels even more familiar. As if we've known each other for centuries.

The longer I stare at him, the harder it is to remember he's a separate person. It feels like he's sucking my soul into himself, pulling and making it hard to stay where I am.

"Lucifer," I breathe. The name feels heavy in my chest and once it escapes, it feels like a lion is loose in the room.

"It's such a pleasure to finally meet you," he says in a voice like silk and sand, shifting and never lingering on one tone. It's beautiful and it's terrifying, and I'm torn between the primal instinct to kneel and the lucid fraction of my mind screaming at me to run.

He takes a step forward and I'm frozen, my quaking spirit ready to tear from my bones to escape, but there's no time. He's standing right in front of me in an instant, his cool hand sweeping down my jaw, slipping into the tendrils of my hair like they're made of smoke. Everything is aloft, even the curtains on the window across the room. The window is pitch black behind them, as if someone boarded it up. Gravity seems to have broken in this singular place in time.

"How did you get here?" I ask shakily.

"The same way I got to the island," he answers, his gaze sweeping over me. In a moment, he takes in everything. My body, my mind, my soul. That intangible, unknowable thing that lingers even when my mind has gone to sleep and my spirit is empty. In that moment, he *knows* me, better than Apollyon. Better than I know myself. Better than anyone ever has or ever will.

"Through me." I don't know how I know, I just do. Like he's drawing the realization out of me.

He smiles and it's both intoxicating and terrifying. "Clever boy. We were bound from the moment your father made you mine, and there is nowhere I cannot reach you. I take it you know why I'm here?"

I swallow hard. "You want her. And I'm telling you, you'll have to kill me and Apollyon and every last member of the resistance first."

"Her?" He chuckles, as if my answer is the most amusing thing he's heard all eternity. "You think this is about some halfling brat?"

I feel a surge of rage at his flippancy, but more confusion. "Then what?"

"You. It was always you, Levi," he answers in an unnaturally gentle tone. The air around me becomes heavy, like a cocoon wrapping around me, making it even more impossible to escape.

"What the fuck do you want with *me?*" I shout. "Looks like you're plenty physical."

"This body isn't as fresh as it looks," he says wryly. The lights flicker and he goes from the image of perfection to a rotting corpse, barely holding itself together before me. The shock makes me stagger back, breaking whatever hold he has on me, but he returns to his beautiful appearance a second later.

"As you might imagine, this vessel isn't quite fit for travel on the surface."

"Let me guess. Armageddon is calling?"

He smiles. "I have unfinished business."

"If you could get to me all this time, why now?" I ask. "Why not just possess me?"

He doesn't answer, but I get the feeling the only time he ever tells the truth is in his silence. "You can't, can you? You need me to let you in…"

"Clever, indeed," he purrs.

"And why the fuck would I do that? No offense. You're definitely the most famous guy who's ever asked to go inside me, but it still seems like a losing proposition."

"Because there are people you love more than the world up there," he answers without hesitation. "People you'd tear it apart and give up your freedom just to save."

I grit my teeth. He's right, but I'm trying not to show it. Like it's possible to hide anything from those eyes. "And I'm supposed to believe you'll spare them, just because I give you what you want? That you'll keep your word?"

"You know how these deals work by now, Levi," he says casually, taking his gloves off one finger at a time. "My word is binding. I wouldn't be the devil otherwise."

I swallow hard. "And what happens to this place when you get to the surface?"

"Apollyon has been trying to wrest Hell from my grasp for quite some time, and as far as I'm concerned, he can have it," he answers. "Heaven and Earth, as they say, are mine."

"And the people on Earth?"

He gives me a knowing smile. "Does it really matter? You'd destroy them all with the push of a button if it meant saving your little girl and your precious twin. Tell you what, I'll even throw in that dog, your mother and the cop for free."

"Ben?" My voice thickens as my mind races. A better person might hesitate, but he's had me pegged from the start. I'm still hoping to buy myself as much time as possible.

"It'll be just like sleeping," he assures me. "You won't even register the passage of time. In fact, you won't have to miss them at all."

"What the hell are you talking about?"

"The difference between your dreams and reality is just a matter of frequency," he explains. "And I can give you the sweetest dreams you've ever had. Your deepest desires come true, and it'll all feel as real as this does." He stretches his arms out. "All you have to do is say yes."

"And here I thought there'd be a contract."

He sneers. "If you like, I'm sure I can have something drawn up."

He reaches into his jacket and flicks his wrist, unrolling a long scroll. There's no fine print, but then again, I'm selling my soul outright. I reach out hesitantly and take the pen he gives me, but the nib is dry.

"You must sign in blood," he explains.

"Oh. Of course I must," I mutter.

"You can wait as long as you like, but we both know what your answer is going to be," he says patiently. "You will do anything for those you love. Even if it means becoming the devil himself."

He's right, of course. I would do anything. Even this.

I close my eyes and take a deep breath, pressing the sharpened nib of the pen into the meat of my palm. A droplet of blood springs to the surface, but I stop short of touching it to the page. "Can I at least say goodbye?"

"There's no need for that. You'll be seeing them shortly. The version of them that doesn't hate you for what you're about to do."

His words leave a crushing weight on my chest.

The weight of truth.

I sign my name in blood and as soon as I finish the last letter, blinding pain grips me like a massive hand is crushing me in its grasp.

"Just relax," Lucifer says calmly. The rot and decay beneath that mask of beauty is beginning to show as his skin splinters and cracks, letting streams of radiant light burst through.

I fall to my knees, struggling for breath, and when I can fight it no more, the sensation of floating takes over. It feels like the time I almost drowned as a kid, going out too far into the choppy water off the Jamestown cliffs. Each wave kept dragging me under, but I refused to surrender.

When the vessel before me finally explodes, the light finds its new home inside my chest.

For a moment, there's only warmth and the light. No pain. No fear. No regret. Just the feeling of weightlessness and floating.

The feeling of coming home.

FORTY-SEVEN

"LEVI. OPEN YOUR EYES."

Apollyon's voice brings me out of the emptiness I've been so completely submerged in for...

Seconds? Centuries? There doesn't seem to be a difference.

It takes me a moment to gain control over my body, or to feel anything besides the salty breeze on my skin. There's wetness, too, touching the top of my head before it recedes. Blood?

No... the familiar sound of the ocean clears the fog in my head and I'm finally able to open my eyes. When I do, I find Apollyon staring down at me, except...

It isn't him. It can't be. He doesn't have horns and his eyes are a warm honey brown. Not a trace of red. Or fangs, for that matter, and he's smiling at me wide enough to show them.

"You plan on lying out here all day?"

He offers his hand and helps me sit up. I look around, taking in the familiar island landscape.

Our island.

"How did I get here?" I ask, struggling to remember anything before the emptiness. The deepest sleep of my life. A state so close to death I'm almost surprised to feel my own heartbeat.

I know something is wrong. Horribly wrong, but it's just a vague feeling without explanation or memory attached to it, and the more I try to grasp at it, the deeper it wriggles inside of me until it becomes impossibly buried.

He laughs, like the question's a joke. "I know you had a bit too much to drink last night, but you haven't blacked out in a long damn time."

"Blacked out?" It seems like a plausible explanation, but wouldn't a blackout just erase the night before and not... everything else?

Everything except him, and Sirena, and Stevie. They're still here, still the stars of my universe, even if they're free-floating, without context.

"Come on," he says, squeezing my hand tighter. He's shirtless, wearing only a pair of striped board shorts far too dadly for his impeccable tastes. They look more like something I would pick out, and I'm sure I should have a comment about them, but nothing comes to mind.

I just follow him back to the house in a daze and my heart swells with relief when I see Stevie sitting at the table in her booster seat next to Sirena, who's cutting something on her plate into toddler-sized bites. A fat Pomeranian that looks like a fluffy orange on toothpicks sits next to them, panting happily as she waits for scraps. Janis doesn't look quite right, either. Cute as fuck, though.

"Daddy!" Stevie cries happily, kicking her feet. Something about the sight of her strikes me as off, the same as the way Apollyon looks. The paper crown sitting atop her smooth black pigtails seems a shoddy replacement for something else that's supposed to be there, but for the life of me, I can't figure out what it was.

There's something about her eyes that isn't quite right, either. They're the same rich brown shade as Apollyon's, shining with light and excitement, but there's something *wrong* about them. Something missing.

"There you are," Sirena says in her usual tone of mild exasperation. At least she doesn't seem any different.

Maybe I'm just being paranoid, or maybe Apollyon is right and whatever I indulged in the night before did some brain damage.

"What's going on?" I ask, pulling my hand out of Apollyon's. I look at all three of them, but the longer I do, the more distance seems to form between reality and whatever version of it I came from.

"What do you mean, love?" Apollyon asks, reaching for me.

I step back, afraid to let him touch me for some reason. When I look over, I realize Stevie and Sirena are both watching me worriedly.

"Come on, sweetie," Sirena says, lifting the girl into her arms. "Let's go finish our crayons outside. It's a beautiful day."

Once they leave the room, Apollyon turns his unnaturally gentle gaze on me and frowns. "Levi, what's wrong? Why are you acting like this?"

"Me?" I croak. "What's wrong with you? You're not... You're not Apollyon."

"Apollyon?" His frown deepens, confusion etched deep into the lines of his face that weren't there before. I'm sure of it.

Or maybe they were... I don't know anymore.

"It's your name," I say uncertainly. The way he's looking at me makes me doubt myself all the more.

"My name is Allen," he says slowly, like he's talking to a child. A child about to jump off the roof. He reaches out carefully and this time, as he settles his hands on either side of my face, I don't pull away. "You really don't remember that?"

"I..." I trail off, struggling to sort through the jumbled thoughts. Everything is becoming dislodged and disordered, shifting into bizarre permutations like a jigsaw puzzle that never lines up, no matter how hard I try. The more I think about it, the more "Allen" sounds right.

What else could it have been?

"Of course," I mutter, shaking my head. "I'm sorry, I think I'm just confused."

"Did you hit your head?" he asks, pressing his palm against my forehead. The concern in his voice is disarming and while the world itself seems to have turned inside out, relaxing into his embrace feels like the safest thing to do. The only refuge from the darkness behind me and whatever it's trying to cover up.

If I just focus on him, everything stays in focus even if the rest drifts even further away.

"No," I say, wrapping my arms tightly around him. "I'm sorry. I think I really did just have too much to drink last night."

His gaze softens with understanding. "Well, you'd better go sleep it off before your parents get here. I'll take care of dinner."

"My parents?" Another discordant note in this nonsensical symphony, but the longer I listen, the more soothing its melody becomes.

"You don't remember?" He frowns. "Your mother and

father come over every Friday night for dinner. Ben and Sirena, too."

"Of course," I choke. "Yeah. Maybe a nap would be good."

I'm not tired, but I need a moment alone. A second to think, without observation.

Allen kisses me gently, his eyes still worried as he pulls away. "I'll come check on you in a bit," he promises, his hand brushing against mine. For the first time, I notice the gold band on his left ring finger and find a matching one on mine.

I look down at the ring, fiddling with its perfect fit, and my anxiety begins to ebb away. Whatever's going on, it can't be all that bad if I still have him. All of them.

This is the way it's supposed to be. Even though I can't remember much of anything clearly, I know this is the life I've always wanted.

So why does it feel so wrong?

FORTY-EIGHT

AS I SIT at the dinner table, surrounded by laughing family members, I try my best to impersonate a normal person. A man in his thirties who isn't consumed by the irrational sense that the world around him is a lie and the people he loves are wearing someone else's skin.

Admitting any of that shit is a one-way ticket to a 72-hour stay at whatever psychiatric ward they have on the island. Nonetheless, I find myself staring at my father. He hasn't touched the drink in front of him all night, and that alone seems odd to me, even though I can't quite figure out why.

My childhood memories are obscured by an even thicker fog than the kind that hovers around more recent experiences, but the odd recollection that pops up clearly is perfectly pleasant. Quaint, even. Him coming home at six on the dot to sit down at the table with the rest of us, eating whatever overcooked meal Mom had prepared that night. Helping us with our science projects. Sitting in the front row at our high school graduation ceremony. Even the wedding that seems so distant, despite the certificate on the wall promising it only happened five years ago.

"Something wrong, son?" Dad asks, looking at me from across the table.

"No. Nothing," I lie. Just the inexplicable drive to shove my salad fork into his jugular.

"He hasn't been getting enough sleep lately," Allen says, taking my hand under the table. He smiles at me, and I try to return it, but even the fact that he's covering for me feels weird.

"I'll be right back," I say, standing from the table.

"Where are you going?" Sirena asks.

"Just need some fresh air," I mutter, walking out onto the balcony overlooking the water. The night is as perfect as everything else--not a single cloud in the dark blue sky obscures the stars that sparkle like cheap rhinestones.

So. Fucking. Perfect.

I grip the railing and my heart surges when I feel it go wobbly, like it's made of foam rather than solid oak. The hallucination fades as soon as I jerk back, but it leaves its mark.

"What the fuck...?"

"Beginning to crumble the illusion already," says a familiar voice from somewhere deep within the jungle. It echoes through the trees like wind. "I'd expect nothing less from you."

I can't tell where the voice is coming from any more than I can pick out who it belongs to, but there's something about it that feels refreshingly real. "Who the hell are you?"

"An old friend," the voice answers. "But I doubt you'll remember me. Lucifer isn't aware that we know each other, so that wouldn't be part of the setup."

"The setup?" I echo. "Lucifer?"

So the voice coming from the darkness is crazy.

"Deep down, you've already figured out that something about this place is very wrong," he says calmly. "Wrong because it's too right. Because the people around you are poor impersonations of the ones you sacrificed everything to protect."

"What are you talking about?"

"Why don't you come down and find out?"

I hesitate, looking at the stairs leading down off the balcony. I swear those weren't there a moment ago, but when I try to think too hard about it, something pushes back. I tentatively reach out to touch the railing and it feels solid enough, so I walk down until I find myself on the edge of the jungle. I can still hear the water hidden behind the winding path through the thick, knotty trees, but I can't see the stranger any clearer down here than I could on the balcony.

"Where are you?"

Finally, he steps out of the jungle and the sight of him arrests me. Not just because he's wearing a three-piece suit that's utterly ridiculous in such a humid environment, but because he has fucking horns sticking out of his head and blood-red eyes and a scar on one side of his face that looks like a shark bite.

And to make it all so much more confusing, *those* eyes are far less unsettling to look into than those of the people I love. Of my own husband and daughter.

"It's good to see you again, Levi," he says in a rich, warm tone that hums with nostalgia. It warms me in places that have grown cold without my realizing it, but the thawing process allows me to feel pain deep within my core that can't have formed overnight. Like a part of me has been split into millions of tiny pieces and glued back together with lies to fill the cracks.

The crushing pain sends me to my knees and I clutch my chest, struggling to breathe. "What did you do?" I accuse.

"I'm afraid I can't take most of the credit. After all, I'm no more real than anything else in this prison Lucifer built to keep you quiet."

"Why do you keep saying that?" I choke out. "Lucifer..."

"Because he's the one who put you here," he says, crouching down in front of me. His red gaze is so intense that I can't look away from it, but there's something incredibly alluring about the pain it brings and the clarity that comes with it. For the first time in so long, I feel like I'm talking to someone real, despite the fact that he claims not to be.

"But his vice always was pride, and like you, it'll be his downfall. He underestimated you," he says, cupping my cheek in his palm with a gentleness that feels like intimacy. My heart lurches in protest, but not because it feels like a betrayal of the man inside that house. Someone else... somewhere else...

"That's it," he coaches in an urgent whisper. "Feel the pain and the guilt. It'll guide you. Life is pain and guilt and all the ugly things we try to push away to make room for what makes it worth living."

"Who are you?" I demand, my voice raspy with strain from... I don't know what. Breathing, maybe. Holding on or letting go. None of it makes any sense anymore.

"I'm an echo," he answers, his gaze softening. "A fragment of someone who lives on only inside of you, but all it takes is a fragment--a shard--to break a diamond."

"Maiz," I whisper. I'm not sure where the name comes from, but it resonates so deeply within me that I know it's right even before I see the confirmation on his face. My rational mind knows it shouldn't be possible, that there's no way he could've survived an event I can't force myself to remember, but I know this man.

"You have to leave this place, Levi," he says, taking my hands to pull me to my feet. We're no longer standing behind the house. Without my realizing it, we've somehow been transported to the shoreline and I can feel the water lapping at my ankles, soaking into my socks. The salty chill makes me shiver, but the discomfort makes me feel a bit more lucid, just like looking into his eyes.

"This world isn't real, is it?" I finally ask. "I'm...trapped here."

"That's right," he says, nodding his approval. "You're here and they're out there."

"Who?" I demand. "You?"

The sad smile on his lips makes me ache even more. "No. Not me, but everyone else. Your husband. Your daughter. Your sister. It's been such a very long time, but they've all waited for you. They never forgot you, Levi, and contrary to what you tell yourself, the world out there is not better without you. Quite the contrary."

"What happened?" I ask, afraid to know the answer. The same sixth sense that told me his name tells me that whatever this is, I have at least a role to play in it.

"You made a deal with the devil," he says in a wry tone, but something in his eyes keeps me from taking it as a joke. "The price always comes due eventually."

I gulp. "How do I get back?"

"You have to fight," he answers. "He's more powerful with a vessel, but he's vulnerable as well. You can overpower him, but you'll have to fight. Harder than you've ever fought before."

"Vessel?" I repeat. "He's... inside of me? Right now?"

"This world is a creation of your mind," he says, looking around the canopy of trees. "And an incredible mind, it is. Twenty years and it's only just begun to crumble enough for me to break through."

"Twenty years?" I echo. "Please tell me you're joking."

"I'm afraid not. He resets it every time you begin to doubt. Every time the illusion grows worn, but it was only a matter of time. He chose you as his vessel because of your abilities, but even he underestimated just what you're capable of. It's time to prove him wrong."

"But that means they'll disappear," I say, looking back at the path that leads toward the house. "And so will you."

"I died a long time ago, Levi," he says softly. "I only live on because of you, but I'm not in your mind." He brushes his fingertips across my forehead.

My heart surges with the agonizing realization of what I have to do. Of the fact that I'm speaking to a memory, not a person, and even though I barely remember his name, I know I love him. Maybe not the way I love my husband, or Sirena and Stevie, but it's as deep and intimate of a connection nonetheless.

"What if I can't do it?" I ask. "What if I can't stop him?"

"Oh, Levi," he murmurs, pressing his forehead to mine. "If there is one thing I'd stake my life on, it's your stubbornness."

The words cut through the confusion and for a moment, just an instant, I'm myself again. Not all the pieces are in place, but I know what I have to do as surely as I know that the man in front of me isn't real, no matter how badly I want him to be.

Before I can answer, I hear the one voice that has the power to pull me back of the edge I'm about to dive off of, even if reality is waiting at the bottom.

"Daddy?" Stevie calls nervously.

I look back to find her standing hand-in-hand with my husband and Sirena, Janis at her side and my parents and Ben not far behind them. They're all just standing there, staring at me with looks of concern and betrayal on their faces, as if they know what I'm about to do.

That I'm about to destroy them.

"I'm sorry," I say, somehow managing to speak through the lump in my throat. "But you're not real."

"How can you say that?" Allen asks, his voice rough with pain. He lets go of the small girl's hand and she runs toward me, stopping just far enough away that I can see the tears in her big, brown eyes. "We're your family. We love you."

"No," I say through gritted teeth. The longer I look at them, the more obvious it becomes. The more *wrong* it all seems. "You're not."

"Daddy!" Stevie's strangled sob breaks my heart, but as she holds her arms up and toddles toward me, I stagger back.

"You're not real," I say with greater resolve. Just speaking the words seems to draw power to me, and out of the corner of my eye, I see the edges of this fantasy world begin to recede into the darkness it truly is. "None of you are real."

The real Stevie is out there somewhere in the real world with the man I love and all the other people I left behind. The world I turned over to a monster.

The responsibility is soul crushing, but as heavy as that

weight is, I feel freer than I ever have here in this place where nothing ever goes wrong.

The imitation of my husband lifts the poor rendition of our daughter into his arms and glares daggers at me, an expression that makes him far more believable than the loving clone I've fallen asleep next to for years. Twenty goddamn years, apparently.

"You're wrong," he accuses. "You'll regret this."

"I already regret so much. I've missed so much," I say, my chest tightening with every word spoken. "But not this. It's time for me to wake up."

As soon as the words leave my mouth, their images begin to fade along with the rewritten history plastered over the gritty reality of my past. Mom and Dad and the happy marriage they'd never shared. Sirena and Ben with their plastic smiles. Allen and Stevie, my world in two halves, fading more with each moment that passes.

I force myself to turn away and find Maiz standing in the water, as solid as before. He holds out his hand and I take it, stepping deeper into the abating tide.

"You know what you have to do now," he says, looking down at the near-black water. It looks like the surface of a mirror. A portal to a world unknown, filled with monsters ready to devour anything that dares to dwell in its depths.

But at least they're real.

"I'm never going to see you again, am I?" I ask, looking back at him.

He smiles, pressing his hand against my chest. The warmth of his touch makes me aware of my own heartbeat. "Your mind is a powerful thing, Levi, but it's not where your power lies. Until you give Lucifer dominion over your heart, I wouldn't say anything is impossible."

I take a deep, trembling breath as his hand falls away.

The water calls to me the same way that door did so long ago. The sliver of light I'm only just beginning to remember, along with all the other inconvenient pieces of the truth Lucifer suppressed to keep me docile. The further I creep into the water, the heavier the weight of what I'm doing becomes until it takes me under like a block of cement wrapped around my ankles.

Maiz's image ripples on the water until I sink so deep I can no longer see the light, but the darkness...

The darkness feels like home.

FORTY-NINE

I OPEN my eyes and I'm not alone in my own head. It feels like grabbing the wheel of a car hurtling down the highway at a hundred miles an hour, and the view that greets me is a ruined cityscape from the top of what seems to be the tallest skyscraper. The fact that there are two giant golden gates up ahead that stretch up so high they disappear into the clouds is my first clue that wherever the fuck Lucifer has steered my body, we aren't on Earth.

Not anymore.

And then, I see him. Apollyon, lying on the rooftop across from me in a pool of his own blood. The horns on his head and the serpentine tail peeking out from his tattered cloak are what tell me it's *my* Apollyon, not the illusion I believed for so long.

"Apollyon!" I shout, rushing toward him. Before I get halfway there, his blood red eyes open and narrow sharply in disgust. He leaps to his feet, a glowing red blade in his hand.

"I don't know why you didn't kill me," he spits in voice

that seems to come from the bowels of Hell itself. "But it's the last mistake you'll ever make."

I freeze as he runs toward me, his blade raised with a murderous roar. My reflexes seem to be the echo of the angel who'd possessed me, but even still, I fail to dodge in time to avoid the full stroke of his blade. The leather armor stretched across my chest splits open and blood sprays the stone rooftop, but I manage to slide to a halt further back on the roof, my palm scraping against the rock until the skin grounds down to tattered flesh.

"Apollyon! No!" I cry, throwing up my hands as he takes another swing, his blade coming just shy of my throat. I meet his confused and furious gaze and see a flash of the way he used to look at me.

"Levi?" He says my name like a skeptical child standing in front of a mirror, trying to summon Bloody Mary.

"It's me," I choke out, reaching for him. When my fingers brush the stubble on his jaw, my heart aches and for once, it isn't with agony. "Apollyon, I--"

Before I can finish that thought, something tightens around my throat until I can hardly breathe, let alone speak. I feel it. The noxious light, burning deep inside of me, threatening to take over again.

"No," I groan, gripping my throat as I struggle to stay upright. "He's coming back."

The bewilderment on Apollyon's face becomes horror as I feel the light break through and my consciousness is thrown back behind the veil of my invader. I remain aware of what's going on around me, if only because I destroyed the cage he'd toss me back into if he could get the chance, but I'm incapable of controlling my movements or the words coming out of my mouth.

"Sorry about that." The sardonic words are spoken in

my voice, but it isn't me. I can feel him in me, crowding me out and sinking his roots in deeper like a weed, crushing out everything that's me. "Where were we?"

"He's alive," Apollyon says in a tone of disbelief, staring at me.

No. Through me.

I strain to regain control--to reach out, to scream for him to kill me now that I know the truth--before it's too late. Before Lucifer takes him away from me forever, just like he took Maiz and all those wasted years...

But I can't. All I can do is remain paralyzed and silent, forced to watch as Lucifer reaches for the blade on the ground. To feel the icy cold grip of the handle in his grasp and be powerless to release it.

"I'm sorry. Does that put a damper on your plans to kill me?" Lucifer taunts in *my* fucking voice. "And here you'd finally worked up the nerve."

"Twenty years," Apollyon snarls. "Twenty fucking years and you've held him all this time, but you couldn't make him disappear, could you?" His voice hitches and for the first time, his eyes meet mine. "He's too strong."

"It would seem we both underestimated him," Lucifer sneers. "But don't worry. Neither of us will be making that mistake again, if only because you won't be alive to do it."

"Let him go," he roars, throwing the blade aside. I try to scream at him for being a fucking idiot, but the sound gets swallowed up in the looming silence within. "If you want a vessel, take me. I'm anchored to the Earth, and you'd have access to all my power."

Lucifer's piercing laugh dashes my fear that it would be a tempting offer. "How fascinating. I always wondered if you'd trade your daughter for him, and now I finally have my answer."

Guilt and horror have me firmly in their grip, but Apollyon's gaze is firm and his stance unyielding. "She's stronger than me. Than either of us," he says, his voice deepening with certainty. "She will destroy you, of that I'm sure."

"How touching," Lucifer purrs. "And yet, I must decline your generous offer. Heaven has already fallen to demonic control, and your gifts are meant for leveling empires, not building them. Besides. Wearing your mortal lover is the most fun I've had in ages."

Rage and possessiveness flash across Apollyon's face, and I know he would have attacked if not for one crucial detail he's too damn stubborn to overlook.

I'm still here, and in revealing that fact, I have sealed his fate.

Lucifer raises his sword and the moment he breaks into a sprint, terror surges through me. I don't know how I gained control the first time, let alone how to recreate it, but it soon becomes clear that the prelude of grief is one way.

Apollyon closes his eyes, ready to meet his fate with dignity. I manage to regain control with the blade just shy of his throat and by the time his eyes open to see why he isn't gone yet, I've gathered enough strength to toss the sword hard enough to send it flying off the rooftop.

Sorry to any unfortunate angels who happen to be lingering below. Then again, all the ones I've met so far are assholes, so chances are they deserved it.

"You fucking idiot," I seethe, throwing my arms around his neck. I catch him off-guard enough that he sinks to his knees. "I never gave you permission to die."

His arms wrap around me, stiff and tentative, like he's not sure if this is another trick. I pull away enough to meet his eyes, and his gaze softens with recognition.

"It really is you," he breathes, cupping my cheek in his

palm. "They told me it was impossible. For you to still be in there after so many years…"

"Told you I was sturdy," I say with a smile that doesn't hold up long. I can feel the light burning inside of me, demanding control, and I know that love isn't enough to keep it at bay forever, but God, I want just a little while longer.

"How did you get out?" he asks, searching my face in disbelief.

"Maiz." The name sticks in my throat and I see the confusion in his eyes, so I realize I need to explain. "My version of him, at least."

Understanding echoes within those crimson depths and his lips brush mine. "I missed you so much, Levi. I know why you did what you did, and I know I would have done the same thing, but--"

"Don't," I plead, caressing his cheek and pushing up against him, just to feel as much of him as I can for as long as it lasts. "I know, just… don't. Just let me look at you."

He lets out a shaky breath and for the first time ever, I see moisture in his eyes. "World's gone to hell without you," he says wryly.

A strangled laugh escapes me. Or maybe it's a sob. "So I've heard. What's Hell gone to?"

"It's under our domain," he murmurs. "Lucifer ceded it as soon as he took your body."

"So he kept that part of the deal, at least."

The disapproval in his eyes is a lecture in a glance. "We regained control of Earth, with the angels who survived the invasion of heaven and those who didn't switch sides, but it's still…" He trailed off, but my imagination was perfectly capable of filling in the blanks. "I'm sorry, Levi. I held out as long as I could, but someone had to stop him and I thought you were..."

"Shh," I plead, sweeping my thumb across his full lips. "You have nothing to apologize for." I swallow hard. "How is she?"

Pride swells in his gaze, but also sadness. A grief I understand all too well, for all the years that have come and gone. All the joys and trials I missed. "She's perfect," he says, his voice breaking as his brows knit together. "She's stubborn and fearless and so fucking strong. Just like you. God, I wish you could..."

"I see her," I assure him, smiling painfully. "In your eyes. She's everything I ever thought she would be."

"Guess we managed not to fuck one thing up," he says, putting his hand over mine. I've never seen him tremble, but this beautiful, awful, impossible world has taught me that there's a first time for everything.

And a last.

"The most important thing," I correct, wincing as I feel another stab of light shoot through me. I recall the cracks and rot of Lucifer's first vessel, or at least the first one I saw, and realize that he's turning on me from the inside out in a desperate effort to regain control.

"I can't hold him off for much longer," I warn him.

Apollyon nods stiffly. Wherever he touches, my skin feels like my own. It gives me the strength to hold on just a little bit longer.

"You know what you have to do," I tell him.

He shakes his head. "No. No, I can't do that," he says, backing away from me with fear in his eyes that he hadn't shown even when Lucifer was a hair's breadth away from ending his life.

"You have to," I say firmly, grabbing the blade he

discarded and shoving it into his hands. Even now, I feel Lucifer trying to take the reins, and he makes it difficult to release the sword. "I can't die as the guy who sold the world for the people he loves if I can't even keep you safe."

"I'm not killing you, Levi," he snarls, looking down at the blade in dismay. "There has to be another way."

"You know there isn't."

He does. I can see it in his eyes. And I can also see that it doesn't matter.

"I can't." His voice sticks in his throat and tears of blood slip down his cheeks. He tosses the blade aside and it hits the opposite ledge of the roof with a clatter. "I'm sorry. I just can't. Not for this world, not for anything."

The crushing pain is at its greatest, rendering all Lucifer's attempts to torment me from within moot. "It's alright," I murmur, walking over to stand in front of him once more. I press my lips to his and out of all the tender moments we've shared, out of all the passion unspeakable in "decent" company, this is by far the most intimate. "I shouldn't have asked you to do something I couldn't do myself."

He looks up, confused. I smile and whisper, "Close your eyes."

"What? Levi--"

"Just do it," I plead. "Just trust me."

Trust isn't something that comes naturally to demons. Especially not mine. The fact that he finally closes his eyes means more than "I love you" ever has, but it also makes the blow I'm about to deal him feel all the more like betrayal.

It's also the only way I can ever make things right.

As I walk over to the ledge, I form the shape of my doppelganger in the spot where I was standing a second ago.

It's a perfect replica, certainly good enough for these limited purposes.

"Alright," it says in my voice as I stand on the ledge, fighting off the guardian angel within me who rails against the promise of our mutual demise. "You can open your eyes."

Apollyon obeys, and I watch his confusion fade to horror as his gaze travels from the replica to me. "No!" he cries.

Too late. Too far. Not enough time for him to reach me, but just enough to say the words I need him to hear. "I love you," I say before I fall back over the ledge.

Heaven's gates stretch up above me as if to send me off and Lucifer finally wrests control from my gasp, but it doesn't matter. There's nothing even he can do now.

"You fool!" he rages, thrashing against the air while I release control fully and close my mind's eye. The darkness is there, and so is Maiz. They speak in one soothing voice.

Welcome home.

FIFTY

DEATH IS STRANGE.

It turns out, when Heaven and Hell are both closed for business, it's not so much something that happens to you as a state you linger in. Like the lobby of a bus station or an airport terminal, somewhere between the gate and the Cinnabon stand.

Death is the arms of a mother welcoming you home off the bus, wrapped around you so tight you forget all the painful words and broken promises. It's the voice of a lover swimming into your ears and burrowing so deep it settles within your veins. It's the feeling that lasts as long as it takes to shiver, the paper-thin separation between your soul and body that becomes a seam capable of splitting them both, if it could only last long enough.

It's a beachfront house full of the ghosts of memories and lies told sweetly. The face of an old friend sitting across the table and sipping tea, neither of you asking whether the other is real, because you don't want to know.

Because this is all there is. Forever.

And that's okay, because being here in this not-place

forever means they'll keep on living in the real world, and that's all that matters. Because the only way to truly live forever is to live on through the people you love.

All in all, it wasn't a bad run for a guy who was never supposed to live past forty.

Turns out, the doctors were right about that, but I did more living in those last few years than I had in the first thirty-three, and I wouldn't trade a second of it. Not for anything.

Well... maybe for another second with him, but that's all long gone. Now, there's just the memory and the table and the card game I lost track of ages ago.

"You know, you're as shitty at this now as you were fifty years ago," Maiz informs me, placing down a royal flush on the table. "I win," he announces, scraping all the chips toward his side of the table.

"Fifty years, huh?" I sigh, leaning back in my chair. "That's a long damn time. Don't suppose you've got any other card games we could play?"

"Poker is really the only one demons play. Go Fish is more of an angel thing."

"Figures."

There's a knock at the door, which hasn't happened in a long fucking time. So long I barely remember the last. "Who do you think that is?"

"Chemuel, I'm sure," Maiz says unhappily. He props his elbow on the table and leans. "You should probably get it."

The fact that he disappears whenever the angel comes in to check up on me is probably a sign that he is, indeed, a figment of my dead imagination, but I like not knowing for sure, so I never ask. Easier to delude myself that way.

I open the door and to my surprise, it isn't Chemuel, the

angel they usually send to take the census for the occupants of Purgatory or whatever the fuck this place really is. It isn't an angel at all, not if the twin horns curling back over her long, raven locks are any indication.

"Who the hell are you?" I ask, blocking the doorway. If I'm going to be stuck in the same hundred-by-hundred storage room for all of eternity, I don't want some demon coming in and fucking shit up.

"Ease up, grandpa," she says, folding her arms. "I came to spring you."

"Grandpa? Excuse me? I haven't aged one bit."

Judging from that armor, she's pretty damn high up in the demonic hierarchy and my heart skips at the thought that she might have some connection to Apollyon.

Then again, I don't want to believe that it's possible for a demon to access me here. That might mean he hasn't tried.

Unless he's still angry at me for jumping off that rooftop, which is a very real possibility I try not to think too much about, because that train of thought always turns Purgatory into Hell.

Actual Hell. The kind my mind is far better at creating than any demon.

"Spring me?" I frown. "What are you talking about? This is Purgatory, the only people who can get in or out are angels."

Which makes her presence all the more confusing.

"Purgatory is for dead souls," she answers. "You're being evicted."

"Evicted? Look, kid, I don't know if you're new at this or just lost, but I'm as dead as a doornail." I hesitate. "Actually, that phrase makes no sense. How is a doornail dead if it's never even been alive?"

She raises an eyebrow at me and there's something eerily familiar about that gesture. "God, you're just like they said you were," she mutters, shaking her head. "Follow me."

"What?" I demand, staring as she walks down the same dark hallway Chemuel always comes from. I spent the first few check-ins trying to rush past him and the one time he'd let me succeed, I wound up throwing open the first door at the end of the hall to find myself right back where I'd started.

As hesitant as I am to try that again, I follow her and feel a mixture of relief and confusion when I realize that door is no longer there. Instead, she turns a corner that wasn't there before and opens another door, revealing nothing but pure white light for as far as I can see.

"Oh, no," I say, stepping back. "I know how this movie goes. You go into the light when you want to disappear, or when you wanna become one with all the universe, and I'm not down for either scenario."

The demon rolls her eyes. "That door leads home. You're not dead anymore."

"Excuse me?"

"You've been resurrected," she says in an impatient tone, as if it should be obvious. "Do you want to go back or not?"

My heart pounds in my ears. Every day for the last fifty years, assuming it's even possible to count the passage of time in a place like this, has blended in with all the others. Nothing new ever happens. Nothing to break up the monotony save for Chemuel's visits and those are hardly a pleasant change. This is definitely new, and while I still don't believe her about what's on the other side of that door, if it's at all possible, I want to go.

I have to.

But first...

"Wait here," I tell her before I book it back for the room.

"Hey!" she cries in an exasperated tone. "That was a rhetorical question!"

I ignore her, throwing open the door to the room that has been my prison for so long. Or my sanctuary, compared to the prospect of nothingness. "Maiz!" I cry, looking around. The cards and chips are still on the table, but the room is empty and my heart sinks with the realization that I really have been alone all this time.

Guess I've been holding out a little hope, after all.

"What are you looking for?" the demon demands from the doorway. "There's nothing in here."

"No," I murmur, finally turning around to face her. "I guess there's not." I take a deep breath. "I'm ready."

"Come on," she says, keeping an eye on me like I might try to make a run for it again. This time, when she opens the door, I step through it without hesitation. Whatever's waiting on the other side, it has to be better than this.

The light fades and I stagger out onto a stone path winding through a forest that seems to stretch on forever. There are flowers of every color and variety dotting the tall grasses and the light that streams through the trees is a soft, glowing blue. I have no fucking clue where I am, but if I had to imagine wherever it is that fairies live, this is it.

And there have to be fairies, right? There are demons and angels, so it stands to reason that there's other shit, too.

While I'm still contemplating the likelihood of fairies, a door closes behind me and the demon is still there, giving me an, "I told you so," look.

And then, she says it. "Told you this was your way back home."

"Home?" I frown. "I've never seen this place before in my life."

"It's Hell," she says flatly. "Duh."

I look around, convinced I've missed something, but the ethereal realm seems as foreign as before.

"Maybe this will jog your memory."

Apollyon's voice.

My heart aches the way it always does before it breaks, but I won't let myself turn around. It can't be real. This is just another trick.

And then he touches my shoulder, and I give in. I turn around and he's *here*, looking the same as he did that day I left him so long ago.

"No," I breathe, staggering back. "Please don't do this to me. I can't..."

His gaze softens. Whatever fuckery Lucifer is up to, he's definitely taken the whole "revenge is a dish best served cold" adage to heart.

"It's me, Levi," he says gently. "It's not a dream or a hallucination. This is real."

"This isn't Hell," I insist.

He looks around the dreamy expanse thoughtfully. "I made a few changes once I took over. Unlike my predecessor, I'm not interested in being the most beautiful thing in the underworld."

He's wrong as shit about that. He's the most beautiful sight I've ever seen and now that I'm finally letting myself entertain the possibility that this is real, I approach him as carefully and fearfully as a hare walking up to a wolf.

"How?" My voice is strained and harsh, but when he takes me into his arms, the pain eases away.

"It took a long time," he says quietly. I can hear the pain in his voice. The same loss I've felt ever since our separation. "An eternity, it felt like, but she did it. She found a way to bring you back."

"She?" I echo, looking back at the snarky demon.

"Not me," she says, gesturing to the woman coming up behind her. "Her."

Time freezes. I've never seen either of them before, but she's even more familiar than the demon who set me free. They share the same long, dark hair and Cupid's bow. The same red eyes, of course, but most demons have those. Still, there's something different about hers. One look and I know. My heart screams the answer even as her name sticks in my throat.

"Stevie?"

"Hi, Daddy," she says with a fond smile that softens her beautifully sharp features. "Long time, no see."

I run to her and throw my arms around her, and unlike so many hallucinations, she doesn't disappear. The tears flow freely down my face, and while that isn't the first impression I want to make on my adult daughter, I can't find the will to fight them back. She returns my embrace and I finally pull back, just to look at her.

"It's you," I breathe, cupping her face in my hands. She's taller than I am, though not nearly as tall as Apollyon. "It's really you."

"I'm sorry it took so long," she says, pulling a small, blue plush dragon out of her cloak. "I had to work my way up, but I finally got the hang of it."

I stare at the toy in disbelief, remembering the last time I saw her, and my heart breaks all over again. Seeing her now, as strong and perfect as Apollyon told me she would be, begins to piece it back together. "You did this," I murmur. "You brought me back."

"She is an architect," Apollyon says knowingly, coming

up behind me. "And a demon. And Legion. She helped rebuild most of what you see around you."

I turn back to him, and all the words I want to say get choked out.

"I know," he says, pressing a kiss to my forehead. "There'll be time for all of it later."

I let out a breath of relief and sag into his arms. He hasn't aged, and as far as I can tell, neither have I, but that's by far the least impossible aspect of all of this. "How long?" I ask.

"Long enough," Stevie answers, watching us with her arms folded in a mirror of the woman beside her. I look between them, a thought forming in the back of my mind.

"Who are you?" I finally ask.

"This is Lilian," Stevie answers with a gentle smile. "She's my daughter."

"Daughter?" I cry, looking over at Lilian in disbelief. "Then that makes me your..."

"Grandpa," she says, raising an eyebrow. "Obviously. What part of that did I not make clear?"

Stevie gives her a stern look. "Watch your mouth, young lady."

"Sorry, Mom," she mumbles.

Stevie sighs, shaking her head. "Teenagers."

"I wouldn't know," I murmur.

Stevie's gaze softens. "I know why you did what you did, Dad. Took me a long time to understand, but now..." she trails off, gazing at her daughter. "I'd be lying if I said I wouldn't have done the same thing."

Her words soothe wounds that have festered in my soul for such a long time, buried too deep for any other words to touch. Fears that she would hate me forever. That she'd grow up and think I abandoned her the way my father did.

"So I'm not dead anymore?" I ask, looking down at my hands. The backs are still smooth with youth and I feel better than I ever had when I was walking around on Earth. "How does that work, exactly?"

"You're the second person I've brought back, so I'm still working on the thesis, but you're not exactly *alive*," Stevie said carefully. "More like a spirit. But as long as you're here, or within proximity of me on the surface, it's the same difference."

"So I'm not going to age, or die again?" I ask in disbelief, looking up at Apollyon. "I can stay with you all, forever?"

"You'd damn well better," he mutters, taking my wrist in his grasp. "I'm never letting you out of my sight again."

I let out a strangled laugh and when he kisses me, I lose all track of myself. It feels good, considering that myself is apparently all the company I've had for the last fifty years.

"Wait... if it's been fifty years on Earth, what about the others?" I ask, afraid of the answer. "Where's Sirena?"

Stevie and Apollyon exchange a troubled glance. She has his mannerisms. I know them well enough to be afraid.

"It's been a little longer than fifty years, Dad," Stevie says gently. She looks up at Apollyon, pursing her lips. "There's something I need to show him."

He nods, reluctantly releasing my hand.

Stevie walks back over to the door Lilian brought me through. "Come on."

I hesitate, staring at the light. "Not that I don't trust you, but..."

"It's not Purgatory," she says with a knowing laugh. "It's just a portal. It goes anywhere between Hell, Heaven and everything in-between, including Earth."

"It's fine," Apollyon assures me. "I'll be right here when you get back."

"Okay," I say, taking another deep breath before I follow her through. This time, we step out on a quiet street under an overcast sky I know too well. I close my eyes, feeling the sea breeze against my skin.

"Rhode Island?"

I've always joked that I would jump at the chance to leave my tiny home state, but the truth is, there's nowhere in this world or the next that has air like this. Nowhere.

"There's something you need to see," Stevie says, crossing the street to an iron gate waiting on the other side. I see the plaque along the stone wall and my heart sinks, but rather than the cemetery sign I'm expecting, it reads, "Curtis College of Magical Arts."

"What the fuck is this?" I ask, looking up at the huge stone building. The sleepy colonial landscape is interrupted by a flash of some heavily branded advertisement that seems to be projected onto the clouds themselves. "And what the hell is that?"

Stevie chuckles. She got that from Apollyon, too. "This is the future," she reminds me gently. "We eventually returned control of the surface to the humans. More interesting that way, but there are positives and negatives to everything."

"And this?" I ask, gesturing up at the college.

"Aunt Sirena founded it," she says proudly, walking down the path. A cluster of teenagers walk across the lawn, talking animatedly. One raises his hand and the image of a spinning globe comes up in his palm, as if to illustrate whatever point he's making to his friends.

I watch in disbelief as others dart in and out of the various large stone buildings dotted around campus. "Holy shit."

"We needed talented magicians to rebuild the world

after the war," she remarks. "This is the premier training school in the nation."

"War..." My chest tightens up again. "I did this?"

"Lucifer took over Hell and he would have done the same with or without your vessel," she answers, putting a hand on my shoulder. "If it hadn't been for you, he would have killed me and the remainder of the resistance. We never would've gotten a stronghold and between him and the angels who turned, this world wouldn't have stood a chance. None of them would have."

I let her words sink in, but it doesn't fully resolve the weight on my shoulders even if it eases the guilt somewhat.

"Come on," she urges, following the path to the tall hedges surrounding a garden. I find myself staring up at a stone replica of Sirena with a familiar book in one hand, staring boldly into the distance. It's the kind of over-the-top rendering I'm sure she would never have a direct hand in commissioning, and the fact that it exists can only mean one thing.

"She's gone, isn't she?"

"She was old, Dad. She lived a long life, and thanks to magic, it was a lot longer and healthier than most," she says softly.

"She was a witch. And you brought me back. Surely there was something that could've been done to--"

"To make her live forever?" she offers. "Trust me, I tried. So did Papa, but she refused."

"Why?" I ask hoarsely. It still hasn't sunk in that my twin is gone. Dying was so much easier than accepting that she's gone. It's like my head has the knowledge but my heart won't let it sink in any deeper.

"She told me once. Before she died," Stevie answers,

holding my gaze. "She wanted me to remember, so I could tell them to you one day."

"But I died," I protest. "How did she know I'd come back?"

She smiles. "She said she knew you'd find a way. And she also said she knew you'd try to find a way to bring *her* back and her exact words were, 'Tell that stubborn son of a bitch that I led my life exactly the way I wanted it for exactly as long as I wanted to, and I have every intention of coming back as a singlet next time, so don't fuck that up for me.'"

She's good at mimicking Sirena's tone. I can tell they spent a lot of time together and knowing they had each other, all of them, makes the weight a little lighter.

"She also said that she loved you," she continues, her tone softening. "And because of you, she did everything she'd always wanted to do, and things she'd never dreamed she could. She got to change the world, and she did it with the man she loved."

"Ben?" I ask hopefully.

"They had three children together, all of whom are just dying to meet you. Once you've settled in."

I take a deep breath and nod. As hard as it is to accept, if this is what Sirena wanted, and she led a good life, then who am I to question it?

"All that shit about coming back," I murmur. "Is there any truth to it?"

"There are debates over who gets to reincarnate and who ends up in the afterlife you experienced," she admits. "But most of those debates are based on literature Sirena wrote herself, so yeah. I'd say she figured it out. There's a kid up in Tulsa, Oklahoma who's a dead ringer for her and a magical prodigy, to boot, so I'm guessing she didn't start with a blank slate." She smiles again. "And I'm sure she'll reach out eventually. Twins are kind of like soulmates. No matter how long you're separated for, you always find a way back together."

"What about you?" I ask. "Who's Lilian's father? Or do I need to go on a manhunt?"

She laughs, walking back toward the gates. "He's a great guy. Even Papa approves. You'll meet him soon."

"I'd better," I mutter. The door is waiting across the street and this time, I'm all too eager to walk through it. "Is this here for anyone to go through?"

"Only a few of us can see it," she answers. "There are certain passages even I can't make, which is why I had to send Lilian after you."

"Why is Lilian capable of something you're not?"

She hesitates. "About that guy... He's kind of an angel."

"Kind of?" I echo. "And your father knows about this?"

"He introduced us, actually," she answers. "Taruel is one of the angels who helped us restore the Earth after Lucifer's death."

"So he's really gone?" I ask hopefully.

"He was trapped in your vessel when you jumped," she says, a hint of sadness in her voice. "There's no trace left of him."

The news comes as a relief, even if my survival seems all the more unlikely in contrast. All of a sudden, I feel drained. I might be a spirit, for all intents and purposes, but I still feel physical enough to be exhausted.

"I'll take you home," Stevie says, smiling at me as she leads me toward a familiar stone castle. This really is the same place.

"I'm shocked this is still standing."

"We rebuilt it over time," she admits. "Papa wouldn't let it go."

The knowledge is bittersweet, but as I stare up at those huge doors, all I can think about is falling into his arms and sleeping forever.

"You're not coming in?" I ask once the front gates open and Stevie remains on the other side.

"I'll visit soon, but I'm sure he wants some time with you," she says with a knowing look. "And no offense, but a *thousand* years isn't enough to make me want to stick around for that."

I laugh, hugging her tight. "I'm proud of you. I hope you know that."

"I always have," she assures me, finally pulling away. I turn toward the familiar castle and walk up the stairs I know so well. Even the grain of the railing feels the same.

The hallway is silent, even though in the past, there would usually be servants and soldiers darting to and fro. The only sign of life I see is Janis, a gloriously frightening hellhound again instead of the little puffball she was in my false reality, slumbering in the sunlight shining in through a window. I make a kissing sound, but she keeps snoring, dead to the world.

When I make it to the room I haven't seen in forever, the familiar scent of sandalwood envelopes me.

The room is empty, and I jump when the doors fall shut behind me. I turn around and find Apollyon waiting there, giving me a smile that burns straight through me.

Good to see that hasn't changed.

Without a word, he takes me into his arms and throws me up against the wall. I kiss him breathlessly, because who needs to breathe?

His body presses up against mine, his huge cock jutting into me like he can't wait until we're undressed.

"Hello to you, too," I drawl.

He nips my bottom lip as his claws tear my shirt to shreds. I drag my fingers through his hair and wrap myself around him as much as gravity will allow. He pulls me up the rest of the way and the next thing I know, I'm on my back in bed, where I've fantasized about being so many times.

I took every night I ever spent here for granted, but never again.

He disrobes me easily and I make far more clumsy work of his pants, but when it's just flesh on flesh, the process of getting there doesn't matter.

Nothing else does, either.

"I love you," I say against his lips, grinding my hips against him.

"I love you, too, but it's been a long time," he warns.

"Why the fuck do you think I'm so horny?" I ask, my hands hungrily exploring the hard ridges of his abs.

He snorts a laugh, running his claws through my hair. I missed that, too. I missed everything about his touch. Starved for it. "I could hurt you. You're not as young as you used to be," he teases.

"Fuck you, old man, I don't look a day over thirty."

He laughs, pinning my wrists down as he gets into position. "As you wish, human."

Lust surges down my spine like a lightning bolt as he presses against me, his demon cock hard and textured the way I remember. I remembered the pleasure but forgot all the little details that make sex mind-blowing, like the friction and the heat and the ridges.

So, that last part might be specific to getting fucked by a demon, but still.

"Son of a bitch," I mutter in a single gust of breath as the crown of his massive cock pushes past my entrance, biting down hard on my bottom lip.

"I told you we should've prepped first."

"Not patient enough for that," I growl, gripping his hair tighter. "Just fuck me."

Pain doesn't seem so bad after an eternity of nothing ever changing. Nothing ever bringing pain or joy or anything else that makes life both exhausting and worth fighting for until the bitter end.

"I missed your obscenities," he says, his hands roving down my chest, exploring every muscle like he's comparing my body to his memories. The lust in his gaze reassures me that he's still as inexplicably infatuated with me as he was before.

Not that I'm complaining. "I missed your everything."

I expect a quip, but instead, he kisses me and drives deep. I moan in bliss. Even the ache is beautiful, when I never thought I'd feel it again. I hiss as his cock presses into my spot, my head falling back.

"Did I hurt you?"

"Yeah, but keep going," I plead, pulling him back down onto me. This isn't the time for holding back. I need all of him, everything he has, and I want it forever. It still doesn't seem possible that this is anything other than a dream, but fuck, if it is, I don't want to wake up.

Not this time.

That's how I know it's real.

I only realize there are tears streaming down the sides of my face when Apollyon sweeps one up with his thumb. "Levi..."

"I don't know what that's about," I say with a breathless laugh, running my hands down his chest. His heartbeat is the most comforting rhythm I've ever felt, pulsing steadily beneath my fingertips. "I just..."

"I know," he says, kissing me. His fingers lace through mine, squeezing tight. "Me, too."

His tongue explores my mouth, cool and searching, and when his lips travel down to my throat, my back arches. "Please," I murmur, fisting his long hair even harder, my other hand scratching lines down his back just to feel him. Just to know he's here and that this is real.

His fangs pierce me in answer to my breathy request and I come in a rush of blood and ecstasy. His pleasure explodes in a torrent within me, searing heat bringing back familiar waves and aftershocks of orgasmic bliss.

The tears keep streaming as my breath falters, but I can't stop kissing him. He's inside of me, not all the way, but enough. There'll be time for the rest later. For the knotting, the reminder of just how close we can be. But tonight, fuck, he's inside me and that's all that matters.

He's mine, and as I lie there tangled in his hair and muscular limbs, I breathe in the scent of him, sweeter than any incense. The demon is mine, and I'm his, and it's the sweetest deal I've ever made.

One I'd make all over again.

EPILOGUE

I WAKE UP EARLY, too afraid of discovering my resurrection was a particularly torturous dream to risk any more shuteye. I actually manage to beat Apollyon, who's still sleeping soundly, looking like a shirtless god with the sheets draped enticingly over his lower body.

The sight of him has me eager for an encore, but I'm also starving. I didn't feel hunger the entire time I was in Purgatory, but now I feel a century's worth. I decide to head downstairs to see if the kitchen is remotely like I remember. There are a few new gadgets, but to my relief, he's largely kept it the same. The whole palace, really.

It's a surprisingly touching realization. Guess even demons get sentimental.

I turn on the stove and grab a package of eggs from the refrigerator, relieved that it's still reasonably well-stocked despite the fact that there don't seem to be any servants around.

Not that I mind. I'll get used to it just being him and me. Now, getting used to the fact that Stevie isn't going to come toddling into the room, rubbing her eyes and asking for pancakes...

One day at a time, I tell myself.

There's always Janis, who sits beside me the whole time I cook, just like the good old days, begging for the scraps I'm more than happy to give her. Hell, I make her a couple of eggs of her own, even though she's acting like I was never gone. Then again, she's never had a good grasp of time. I could be gone five minutes and she'd act like it was an eternity, then ignore me when I was gone for hours.

Apollyon still isn't downstairs by the time I finish the toast and eggs, so I pile it all onto a tray, having sampled plenty throughout the cooking process. I carry the tray up the stairs, and even the way the seventh one up creaks fills me with nostalgia.

Home. Nothing like it.

I set the tray on the floor outside the bedroom door so I can open it, but stop short when I see a sight that's familiar in an entirely unwelcome way.

"No," I mutter under my breath, staring at the growing sliver of light underneath a door across the hall that *definitely* wasn't there before.

Except, it isn't like the door that led me to Lucifer. In fact, it looks exactly like the one Stevie and Lilian took me through. What did Stevie say before, about it being a portal to other worlds that moves around wherever it pleases?

My heart pounds as I take a step forward. I'm halfway down the hall before I realize what I'm doing, and when I finally reach it, I've come up with a thousand reasons to turn around.

But I don't. The doorknob is cool against my fingertips, buzzing with energy. The light underneath the door is warm and inviting. Nothing like the searing glare that took over me during possession.

There's something familiar about it, too. Something hopeful.

I close my eyes and take a deep breath. If I could come back... maybe *he* can, too.

No, he's not mortal. The separation between demons and their spirits seems to be far more tenuous than it is with humans, but still...

What was it he told me once?

I only live on because of you, but I'm not in your mind.

The world my mind created might've been long gone the moment I walked through that door, but there's nothing that can erase Maiz from my heart.

It's probably impossible, but I've seen stranger things happen. I've made them happen. If this gift I have is half of what Lucifer and all the other demons and angels make it out to be, then surely it has to be good for *something*.

"Please be there," I mutter, turning the knob and yanking open the door before I can lose the courage. Or regain my sanity.

At first, all I see is light. Light so blinding I have to raise my arm just to shield my eyes, but then... A shadow takes shape. A shadow with two familiar horns, and he steps out, looking just the way he did. I stop breathing because I'm sure he's going to dissolve like a wisp of smoke.

And then, he doesn't. "Hello again, Levi," he says warmly.

"Maiz," I whisper, walking up to him. At first, all I can stand is touching his shoulder. When he feels solid enough, I wrap my arms around him and hold him so tight a mortal would probably choke. He hugs me back with a soft laugh.

"It hasn't been *that* long."

I pull away, glowering at him. "Is that supposed to be a joke? It's been over a fucking century since you..." I trail off, unable to put his sacrifice into words that won't have me reliving that awful day. The day everything changed, for all of us.

He cocks his head. "I didn't endure a snippet of eternity with your shitty poker playing skills for you to pretend like that didn't even happen."

I blink. "You remember that? But... it wasn't real. *You* weren't real."

He shrugs. "Real is relative, but I'd say I'm about as real as you are right now."

"How did you get out? When I went back to that room, you were gone."

"You called me," he answers. "Time is a bit glitchy on this side of the door."

I grab his wrist and pull him through all the way, just in case the room decides to reclaim him. "I still don't get how this is possible. You died."

"So did you," he smiles knowingly. "I told you. I'll always bet on you, Levi."

"All that time, I wasn't alone. You were..." The words catch in my throat and I just stand there staring at him like an idiot until I hear a door shut behind me. I jump, turning around to find Apollyon staring at us in the same confusion I haven't been able to shake.

"Maiz...?"

"My Lord," he says, bowing gallantly to my mate with a gleam of amusement in his eyes. It really is him. I can feel it, the same way I'd felt how wrong the others were in the illusion Lucifer created to be my prison.

"How the fuck--?" Apollyon breaks off that thought and

he looks at me, his red eyes widening with understanding. "You brought him back."

"I guess I did," I say, turning back to the door. Or rather, the spot on the wall where the door was nestled a moment earlier. "It's gone."

"Good riddance," Maiz mutters, glancing at the tray further down the hall. "Is that toast? I'm starving."

"Help yourself," I mumble in a tone of disbelief, gawking at him until Apollyon places a hand on my shoulder.

"Are you alright?" he asks gently.

I look up at him, smiling. "Yeah," I say hoarsely. "I'd say I'm pretty fuckin' great."

"Still shit at cooking eggs," Maiz remarks, sitting cross-legged on the floor as he eats the breakfast I made for Apollyon. "It's a good thing you brought me back. You're both useless without a butler."

"There it is," I sigh, looking up at Apollyon. He stares down at me in confusion.

"There's what?"

"The most important part of the story," I answer, leaning up to kiss him. "The happily ever after."

"Story, huh?" Apollyon snorts, slipping his arms around my waist. "A horror, perhaps?"

"Nah," I say, smiling. "Definitely a romance. You've got the long, flowing hair and cape and everything."

"Good to know," he says, lifting me into his arms and carrying me past Maiz. "Not that I'm not happy to see you, old friend, but there's one more scene I'd like to write and three's a crowd."

"Don't worry, your lovemaking is not to my literary taste," Maiz says wryly, standing to leave with the tray in his hands. "I believe I have some catching up to do, anyway."

The door falls shut and Apollyon's lips claim mine. He takes me into his arms.

"Wait," I gasp as his hands slip underneath my shirt to peel it off. "There's something I need to say."

He looks at me, his eyes dancing with need and curiosity. "What is it?"

"I want another baby," I blurt out.

He blinks a few times, like he isn't sure he heard me right. "You want to go through all that *again*."

"Hell, yeah," I mutter, tearing open his shirt. "This time, I'm not gonna miss a second of it."

"You're serious," he scoffs.

"Deadly," I answer, holding his gaze. "So, are you gonna fuck me or not?"

His answer is clear enough when he pulls me back into his arms and kisses me breathless.

Technically, it's the end of our story--but that's the thing about a romance, the thing that makes it different from every other kind of story. The end is just the beginning, and as for the most important part?

Yeah. They lived happily fucking ever after.

The End.

ALSO BY L.C. DAVIS

Wolf Conan & L.C. Davis Books

Undercover Alphas

Gray

Jayce

Lionel

L.C. Davis Books

The Mountain Shifters Series

His Unclaimed Omega

His Reluctant Omega

His Unexpected Omega

His Runaway Omega

His Second Chance Omega

Their Omega

His Reformed Omega

His Verum Omega

His Reclaimed Omega

Alpha, Beta, Omega

His Taken Omega

His Reclassified Omega

The Great Plains Shifters Series

A Cowboy for Caleb

Darren's Second Chance

A Mate for the Alphas

The Vampire's Omega Series

The Vampire's Omega

The Vampire's Wolf

The Vampire's Mates (Coming soon!)

ABOUT THE AUTHOR

L.C. Davis is a queer trans man who enjoys writing mpreg romance and sharing tales from his "imaginary friends." He also writes MM romance under the pen name, Joel Abernathy. He lives with his partner and their furry companions in beautiful coastal New England, and loves hearing from readers!

Twitter: twitter.com/lcdavisbooks
Email: author@lcdavisbooks.com
Facebook: www.facebook.com/LCDavisAuthor/
Reader Group:
https://www.facebook.com/groups/319671585179123

Made in United States
Troutdale, OR
11/23/2024